Praise for the novels of Danielle Steel

"One of the things that keeps Danielle Steel fresh is her bent for timely storylines. . . . The combination of Steel's comprehensive research and her skill at creating credible characters makes for a gripping read." —*Newark Star-Ledger*

"Danielle Steel has again uplifted her readers while skillfully communicating some of life's bittersweet verities. Who could ask for a finer gift than that?" —*The Philadelphia Inquirer*

"A literary phenomenon . . . and not to be pigeon-holed as one who produces a predictable kind of book." —*The Detroit News*

"Steel knows how to wring the emotion out of the briefest scene." —*People*

"The world's most popular author tells a good, well-paced story and explores some important issues. . . . Steel affirm[s] life while admitting its turbulence, melodramas, and misfiring passions." —*Booklist*

"Steel is one of the best!" —*Los Angeles Times*

"Steel pulls out all the emotional stops. . . . She delivers." —*Publishers Weekly*

"Magical." —*Library Journal*

"Steel's plots are first-rate." —*Newark Star-Ledger*

"Steel yourself." —*Library Journal*

"Ms. Steel excels at pacing her narrative, which races forward, mirroring the frenetic lives chronicled; men and women swept up in bewildering change, seeking solutions to problems never before faced."
—*Nashville Banner*

"Steel has a knack for writing about real-life issues and invoking an emotional bond with her characters." —*My Reading Rainbow*

"Steel is a skilled storyteller." —*Booklist*

"One counts on Danielle Steel for a story that entertains and informs." —*The Chattanooga Times*

"Steel writes convincingly about universal human emotions." —*Publishers Weekly*

"The plots of Danielle Steel's novels twist and weave as incredible stories unfold to the glee and delight of her enormous reading public."
—United Press International

"Few modern writers convey the pathos of family and material life with such heartfelt empathy."
—*The Philadelphia Inquirer*

"Ms. Steel can be counted on to please her faithful readers." —*Richmond Times-Dispatch*

By Danielle Steel

INVISIBLE • FLYING ANGELS • THE BUTLER • COMPLICATIONS
NINE LIVES • FINDING ASHLEY • THE AFFAIR • NEIGHBORS
ALL THAT GLITTERS • ROYAL • DADDY'S GIRLS
THE WEDDING DRESS • THE NUMBERS GAME • MORAL COMPASS
SPY • CHILD'S PLAY • THE DARK SIDE • LOST AND FOUND
BLESSING IN DISGUISE • SILENT NIGHT • TURNING POINT
BEAUCHAMP HALL • IN HIS FATHER'S FOOTSTEPS • THE GOOD FIGHT
THE CAST • ACCIDENTAL HEROES • FALL FROM GRACE • PAST PERFECT
FAIRYTALE • THE RIGHT TIME • THE DUCHESS
AGAINST ALL ODDS • DANGEROUS GAMES • THE MISTRESS • THE AWARD
RUSHING WATERS • MAGIC • THE APARTMENT
PROPERTY OF A NOBLEWOMAN • BLUE • PRECIOUS GIFTS
UNDERCOVER • COUNTRY • PRODIGAL SON • PEGASUS
A PERFECT LIFE • POWER PLAY • WINNERS • FIRST SIGHT
UNTIL THE END OF TIME • THE SINS OF THE MOTHER
FRIENDS FOREVER • BETRAYAL • HOTEL VENDÔME • HAPPY BIRTHDAY
44 CHARLES STREET • LEGACY • FAMILY TIES • BIG GIRL
SOUTHERN LIGHTS • MATTERS OF THE HEART • ONE DAY AT A TIME
A GOOD WOMAN • ROGUE • HONOR THYSELF • AMAZING GRACE
BUNGALOW 2 • SISTERS • H.R.H. • COMING OUT • THE HOUSE
TOXIC BACHELORS • MIRACLE • IMPOSSIBLE • ECHOES
SECOND CHANCE • RANSOM • SAFE HARBOUR • JOHNNY ANGEL
DATING GAME • ANSWERED PRAYERS • SUNSET IN ST. TROPEZ
THE COTTAGE • THE KISS • LEAP OF FAITH • LONE EAGLE • JOURNEY
THE HOUSE ON HOPE STREET • THE WEDDING • IRRESISTIBLE FORCES
GRANNY DAN • BITTERSWEET • MIRROR IMAGE • THE KLONE AND I
THE LONG ROAD HOME • THE GHOST • SPECIAL DELIVERY • THE RANCH
SILENT HONOR • MALICE • FIVE DAYS IN PARIS • LIGHTNING • WINGS
THE GIFT • ACCIDENT • VANISHED • MIXED BLESSINGS • JEWELS
NO GREATER LOVE • HEARTBEAT • MESSAGE FROM NAM • DADDY • STAR
ZOYA • KALEIDOSCOPE • FINE THINGS • WANDERLUST • SECRETS
FAMILY ALBUM • FULL CIRCLE • CHANGES • THURSTON HOUSE
CROSSINGS • ONCE IN A LIFETIME • A PERFECT STRANGER
REMEMBRANCE • PALOMINO • LOVE: *POEMS* • THE RING • LOVING
TO LOVE AGAIN • SUMMER'S END • SEASON OF PASSION • THE PROMISE
NOW AND FOREVER • PASSION'S PROMISE • GOING HOME

Nonfiction

EXPECT A MIRACLE: *Quotations to Live and Love By*
PURE JOY: *The Dogs We Love*
A GIFT OF HOPE: *Helping the Homeless*
HIS BRIGHT LIGHT: *The Story of Nick Traina*

For Children

PRETTY MINNIE IN PARIS
PRETTY MINNIE IN HOLLYWOOD

DANIELLE STEEL

Finding Ashley

A Novel

Dell
New York

2022 Dell Mass Market Edition

Published in the United States by Dell,
an imprint of Random House, a division of
Penguin Random House LLC, New York.

DELL and the HOUSE colophon are registered trademarks of
Penguin Random House LLC.

Originally published in hardcover in the United States by
Delacorte Press, an imprint of Random House, a division of
Penguin Random House LLC, in 2021.

This book contains an excerpt from the forthcoming book
High Stakes by Danielle Steel. This excerpt has been set
for this edition only and may not reflect
the final content of the forthcoming edition.

ISBN 978-1-984-82148-5
Ebook ISBN 978-1-984-82147-8

Cover design: Scott Biel
Cover image: © Krasimira Shishkova/Trevillion Images

Printed in the United States of America

randomhousebooks.com

2 4 6 8 9 7 5 3 1

Dell mass market edition: February 2022

To my Wonderful Children,
Beatie, Trevor, Todd, Nick,
Sam, Victoria, Vanessa,
Maxx, and Zara,

You are the greatest gift in my life!
I thank God for you every minute
of every day
in my life.
The greatest blessing,
the greatest joy!

I love you
with all my heart forever,

Mom / ds.

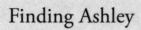

Finding Ashley

Chapter 1

The sun beamed down on Melissa Henderson's shining dark hair, pinned up on her head in a loose knot, as sweat ran down her face, and the muscles in her long, lithe arms were taut with effort as she worked. She was lost in concentration, sanding a door of the house in the Berkshire mountains in Massachusetts that had been her salvation. She had bought it four years before. It had been weather-beaten, shabby, and in serious need of repair when she found it. No one had lived there for over forty years, and the house creaked so badly when she walked through it, she thought the floorboards might give way. She'd only been in the house for twenty minutes when she turned to the realtor and the rep from the bank who were showing it to her, and said in a low, sure voice, "I'll take it." She knew she was home the minute she walked into the once beautiful, hundred-year-old Victorian home. It had ten acres around it, with orchards, enormous old trees, and a stream running through the property in the foothills of the Berkshires. The deal closed in sixty days, and she'd been hard at work ever since. It had almost become an obsession as she brought the house back to life, and came alive herself. It was her great love and the focus of every day.

She'd learned carpentry, and made plenty of mistakes in the beginning, taken a basic plumbing class, hired a local contractor to replace the roof, and used workmen and artisans when she had to. But whenever possible, Melissa did the work herself. Manual labor had saved her after the worst four years of her life.

As soon as the house was officially hers, she'd put her New York apartment on the market, which her ex-husband, Carson Henderson, said was foolish until she knew if she liked living in Massachusetts. But Melissa was hardheaded and determined. She never backed down on her decisions, and rarely admitted her mistakes. She knew this hadn't been one. She had wanted to buy a house and give up New York for good, which was exactly what she did, and had never regretted it for a minute. Everything about her life there suited her, and was what she needed now. She loved this house with a passion, and since moving there, her whole life had changed dramatically.

The four years before she'd bought it were the

darkest days of her life. Melissa sat on the porch and thought about it sometimes. It was hard to imagine now what she and Carson had been through when their eight-year-old son, Robbie, had been diagnosed with an inoperable malignant brain tumor, a glioblastoma. They had tried everything, and taken him to see specialists all over the country and one in England. The prognosis was always the same, one to two years. He lived for two years after the diagnosis, and they made them the best years they could for him. He died at ten in his mother's arms. Melissa had been relentless trying to find a cure for him, and someone who would operate, but they were battling the inevitable from the beginning. Melissa had refused to accept Robbie's death sentence until it happened. And then her whole world caved in. He was her only child, and suddenly she was no longer a mother.

The two years after his death were still a blur, she was half numb and half crazy. She had stopped writing a year after he got sick, and she never went back to work as a writer after that. Once a bestselling author, with five smash hits to her credit, she hadn't written a word in seven years, and swore she never would again. Previously a driving force in her life, she had no desire to write now. All she cared about was her house and she wanted to make it the most beautiful Victorian home in the world. It had replaced everything else in her life, even people. It was the outlet for her to soothe all her sorrows, and vent the unbearable rage and grief she had felt. The agony was a little gentler now. Working on the house was the only way she could ease the pain she was in, using her hands, shifting heavy beams, rebuilding the fireplaces, helping the men to carry the equipment, and doing most of the carpentry herself.

The house gleamed now, and was exquisite. The grounds were lush and perfectly maintained, the historic home restored until it shone. It was something to be proud of, and a symbol of her survival. Everything about it was a tribute to Robbie, who would have been sixteen now, and had died six years before.

Her marriage to Carson died with her son. For two years they had fought to keep him alive, and lost. After Robbie died, she no longer cared about anyone except the little boy who was gone. It still took her breath away at times, but less often now. She had learned to live with it, like chronic pain or a weak heart. Carson had been paralyzed with grief as well. They were both drowning, too lost in their own miseries to help each other. The second year after Robbie died was worse than the first. As the numbness wore off, they were even more acutely aware of their pain. And then she discovered that Carson was involved with another woman, a client of the literary agency where he worked. She didn't blame him for the affair. She wouldn't have had the energy to spend on another man, but she readily acknowledged that she had shut Carson out for two years by then, and it was too late to reverse it. She made no attempt to win him back, or save the marriage. It was already dead, and she felt dead inside herself.

Carson had been her literary agent for her five successful books. She'd found him after she'd written the first one, and took the manuscript to him at the recommendation of a friend. She was thirty-one then. He was bowled over by her talent, and the purity and strength of her writing, and signed her on immediately as a client. She had worked for a magazine after college, and had been writing freelance articles for several years before she wrote her first book. She attributed her success to the brilliant first book deal Carson made for her. After several glasses of champagne, they wound up in bed to celebrate, and a year later they were married. Robbie was born ten months after their wedding, and life had been blissful until Robbie got sick. It was a respectable run, they'd had eleven happy years since they met.

Carson was a respected and powerful agent, but he modestly claimed no credit for Melissa's dazzling success. He said she was the most talented writer he'd ever worked with. When she stopped writing to take care of Robbie, neither of them thought it would be the end of her career. Afterward, she said simply that she had no words left, and no desire to write. The profound visceral need to write that she'd had for all of her youth and adult life had simply left her. "Robbie took it with him," was all she said. No amount of urging by Carson, or her publishers, convinced her to start again. She abandoned her marriage, her career, New York, and everyone she knew there. She wanted a clean slate. She spent her energy and passion on the house after that. There was no man in her life, and she didn't want one. She was forty-three when Robbie died, forty-five when she and Carson finally separated, and forty-nine as she stood in the summer sunshine, sanding the door with all her strength, using old-fashioned fine-grained sandpaper.

The quiet affair that Carson had engaged in with a mystery writer in the final months of their marriage turned into a solid relationship after Melissa left. Jane was a few years older than Melissa and had two daughters whom Carson had become close to. They fulfilled some of his need for fatherhood after Robbie died. He and Jane married after his divorce. Melissa wanted no contact with him, but she wished him well and sent him an email every year on the anniversary of Robbie's death. With their son gone, suddenly they had nothing in common anymore, and had too many heartbreaking memories of the hard battle they had fought for his life, and lost. It was a failure that tainted everything between them. To escape it, Melissa had isolated herself and preferred it that way. She had run away.

She had done the same with her younger sister, Harriet, Hattie, and hadn't seen her in six years since Robbie's funeral. She had nothing to say to her either, and no energy left for their battles. As far as Melissa was concerned, her sister had suddenly gone off the deep end eighteen years before, for no apparent reason. Despite a budding and promising career as an actress, Hattie had joined a religious order at twenty-five. Melissa insisted it was some kind of psychotic break. But if so, she had never recovered, and seemed content in the life she'd chosen, which Melissa could never accept. Melissa had a profound aversion to nuns, and considered Hattie's decision not only an abandonment, but a personal betrayal, after everything they'd been through together growing up.

Their mother had died when Hattie was eleven and Melissa was seventeen. She had been a cold, rigid, deeply religious woman from a Spartan, austere background, and had always been hard on her oldest daughter. Melissa had fallen short of her expectations and disappointed her, and once her mother died, there was nowhere for Melissa to go with her past resentments of how her mother treated her and no way to resolve them. She began writing seriously to vent her feelings in the only way she knew how. It made for brilliant books, which her readers devoured. But the memories of her mother remained painful. It was too late to forgive her, so she never had. In her own way, without realizing it, Melissa was like her mother at times now, with her harsh opinions, criticism of others, and black-and-white view of life after Robbie's death. Hattie was gentler and more like their father, who hid from life with the bottle. He had been a kind man, but not a strong one, and had let his domineering wife run the show, and ride roughshod over him. She made the decisions about their daughters, which Melissa had been furious about. She wanted her father to temper her mother's verdicts, but he never had. He'd abdicated his role and relinquished all power to his wife. Melissa resented him for it, while Hattie easily forgave him everything. But she had never suffered at their mother's hands as Melissa had. She had taken the brunt of her mother's harsh decisions, while Hattie was treated as the baby.

Once their mother died, when Hattie was eleven, Melissa became her stand-in mother. For fourteen years they couldn't have been closer. Their father died a year after their mother, and Melissa was all Hattie had to parent her and it had been enough. Melissa was always there for her, to protect and encourage her. And then suddenly at twenty-five, Hattie had thrown it all away, and on what seemed like a mad impulse, had decided to become a nun, which Melissa told her was her way of avoiding life, like their father, and was the coward's way out. All Hattie wanted was to hide in the convent, protected and removed from the world. She said acting was too hard.

She had had dreams of becoming an actress, and studied drama at the Tisch School at NYU, and gave it all up after her first trip to Hollywood and a single screen test. Melissa saw it as pure cowardice, but Hattie didn't listen to what her sister had to say. She claimed that the religious vocation she had discovered was stronger than her previous desire to be an actress.

Once their parents died, there were no other adult influences in their lives, other than Melissa and a trustee at the bank who barely knew them. Both their parents were only children, and history had repeated itself. Their respective parents had died young too. Melissa and Hattie's mother had been left nearly penniless, and had to drop out of Vassar College and get a job as a secretary. She'd been bitter ever since.

Their father had been left with a sizable inheritance, which dwindled over the years, after long bouts of unemployment, working at various banks, and mismanaging his money. It was the cause of endless fights between Melissa and Hattie's parents, and their mother was terrified of being poor again. Their father was ill equipped to take care of himself once he was orphaned as a young man and began drinking heavily, which cost him many jobs. They often lived on what was left of his inheritance, with no other income. Despite that, there was enough of his money left when both their parents died for Hattie and Melissa to pay for their education and live in a small apartment, after they sold their parents' Park Avenue co-op. Their father had had the foresight to pay for a large life insurance policy which would carry both girls for a long time securely, not in luxury, but in comfortable circumstances, as long as they worked at solid jobs after they'd graduated from college.

At eighteen, when their father died, Melissa shouldered their responsibilities and handled them well, better than their parents had. She was bright, determined, and capable. She saw to it that they both attended good colleges, and made sure Hattie kept her grades up. She was serious beyond her years, less stern than their mother would have been, and far more responsible than their alcoholic father. She moved them to a decent, less expensive neighborhood in New York on the West Side, and stuck to a rigorous budget so what they had inherited would last as long as possible. And she took good care of Hattie. Everything seemed to be going well, and then Hattie had run away to the convent. It shattered Melissa's world yet again. After caring for her sister for fourteen years, she suddenly found herself alone, and began writing more seriously then to fill the void and try to process why Hattie had abandoned her dreams.

Melissa vented her anger at their mother in her first, very dark book, which was an instant success.

She could better understand her mother's bitterness at finding herself a pauper when her parents died than she could fathom Hattie's flight from life. It made no sense to her. She'd had such a bright future ahead.

Losing Hattie to the convent came as a severe blow. Melissa wrote incessantly after that to exorcise her demons, with excellent results, once she met Carson, he became her agent, and sold her books for real money. But, she had never forgiven Hattie for retreating to the convent, nor could Melissa understand what Hattie had done, or why. Hattie had real talent, and Melissa had encouraged her. Hattie had had a few small parts on daytime TV, and a walk-on in a Broadway show. She got a chance to audition for a movie then, and went to L.A. for a screen test. Faced with a real opportunity, she had panicked, come back from L.A. in less than a week, and told Melissa about her impulsive plan to join a religious order. She said it had been a lifelong desire she had hidden from her sister, knowing how Melissa hated nuns. Eighteen years later she had never forgiven Hattie and the two sisters were still estranged. Melissa had barely spoken to Hattie at Robbie's funeral. She didn't want to hear what her sister had to say, the platitudes that Robbie was in a better place and his suffering was over. They hadn't seen each other since.

Melissa wrote to her once a year, as she did to

Carson, mostly out of a sense of duty in her sister's case. And Hattie dropped her a note from time to time, determined to stay in touch with the sister she still loved and always had. She was convinced that one day Melissa would come around and accept the decision she'd made, but there was no sign of it yet. Melissa preferred to be alone now. She didn't want anyone's sympathy, which rubbed salt in the wounds left by her losses. All she wanted was her house and the satisfaction it provided her. She didn't need people around, and certainly not her cowardly sister who had run away from the world, or her ex-husband who had cheated on her and was married to someone else. And she didn't need an agent anymore, since she had stopped writing. She didn't "need" or want anyone.

The convent had sent Hattie to nursing school when she joined the order. She was a registered nurse now at a hospital in the Bronx. Melissa went to her graduation when she got her R.N., but had refused to attend the ceremony when Hattie became a novice, and later took her final vows. Melissa didn't want to be there. It was too painful to see Hattie in the habit she wore.

After her vows, Hattie had spent two years working at an orphanage in Kenya, and had loved it. Her life had taken a completely different turn from Melissa's, and she was content. Melissa said she was happy too, married, with a child and a successful writing career, but her sharp edges hadn't softened with time. They had gotten harsher. And once Robbie died, the walls around her were insurmountable.

After she bought the house in the Berkshires, the men who worked for her considered her an honest and fair employer. She paid them well and worked as hard as they did on the projects at hand. But she wasn't friendly or talkative. Melissa said very little when they worked side by side, and they were impressed by how strong and capable she was. She didn't balk at any task, no matter how difficult, and accepted every challenge. She was a courageous woman, but not a warm one.

The men she hired often commented to one another about how taciturn she was. She was a woman of few words. Norm Swenson, the contractor she used, always defended her. He liked her, and sensed that there was a reason for how hard she was on herself and others. Now and then he saw a spark in her eye and guessed that there was more to her than she let anyone see now.

"There's usually a reason for people like her," he said to her critics, in his quiet New England way. He liked her, and enjoyed his occasional conversations with her, when she allowed that to happen. They talked about the house, or the history of the area, nothing personal. He felt certain there was a good person in there somewhere, despite her cold demeanor and sharp tongue. He always wondered what had caused it. One of his workmen called her a porcupine. It was an apt description. Her quills were sharp. The locals left her alone, which was what she wanted. None of them knew about Robbie. They had no reason to, and it was a part of her life, and a time, she didn't wish to share with anyone. No one in the Berkshires knew anything about her history or personal life.

The fact that Melissa had written under her maiden name of Stevens made her anonymous life in the Berkshires possible. She had kept Carson's last name when they divorced, in part because it had been Robbie's name too and was a link to him, and in part because the name Melissa Henderson rang no familiar bells for anyone. But "Melissa Stevens" would have woken everyone up to the fact that there was a famous author in the neighborhood. This way, as "Henderson," no one knew.

To their old friends in New York, who hadn't seen Melissa in years, Carson always said that some people just never recovered from the death of a child, and Melissa was apparently one of them. It seemed a shame to everyone and many people said they missed her. Carson had his own struggles after Robbie's death, but he had strengthened close personal ties, which had supported him. Melissa had severed hers and set herself adrift. Carson's marriage to Jane suited his quiet nature better than his marriage to Melissa. There was a dark, angry side of her that ran deep, from the scars left by her parents. She had been happy with him but didn't have her sister's innocent, sunny nature. And Jane, Carson's current wife, was a solid, stable woman. She didn't have Melissa's brilliant mind, enormous talent, or tortured soul, which was easier for him.

Carson had talked to Hattie about it a few times in the early days after Robbie's death. Hattie had thought it would soften her sister, but it had the opposite effect, and hardened her.

Carson had always liked his sister-in-law, but lost touch with her when she went to Africa. He still had warm feelings for her. He had also sensed that Hattie didn't want Melissa to think that she was disloyal, staying in touch with him once he had remarried, so Hattie no longer contacted him. She had written once to congratulate him when he remarried, and said that she was happy for him, and would keep him and his new family in her prayers. He never heard from Hattie again after that. All ties with Melissa were severed except for her yearly emails.

Melissa's literary career had taken off around the time that Hattie entered the convent, so Hattie hadn't been present much during their marriage, but she had come to the hospital regularly when Robbie was sick, and had offered to stay with him so Melissa could get some rest. No matter how angry Melissa was at her for becoming a nun, Hattie's feelings for her older sister had never wavered, and she was there until the end of Robbie's life.

Melissa had never invited her to Massachusetts once she left New York, and Hattie had never seen the house that Melissa loved so much. It had replaced people in her life, and the writing she had loved and been so good at. To Melissa, the house was enough, it was all she needed and wanted now. She didn't want anyone in her life, and no contact with the people who knew her when she was married, and were aware of the fact that she had a son who died. She didn't want to be the object of anyone's pity.

When Melissa finished sanding the door, she lifted it and carried it back into the house. She had grown stronger from all the work she'd done. She examined it closely when she set it back on its hinges, and studied the intricate molding she'd been sanding. She was satisfied with her work. She had removed all the old coats of paint, and had decided to varnish it instead. The original carvings and moldings were delicate and beautiful. You could see them better now. All she cared about was improving the house. It was a living being to her, her only friend.

After her morning's labors, she made herself a cup of coffee and stood drinking it, looking out past the lawn and the trees, and the gardens she had created, to the orchards in the distance. They harvested the apples and sold them at a local farmer's market. She had the time and the money to do what she wanted and what she enjoyed. After five astoundingly successful bestselling books, she had enough money saved to live as she chose. She led a simple, uncomplicated life, and had more than enough in the bank. Two of her books had been sold as movies.

For a while, she'd been one of the country's most successful writers, and then she disappeared from public life, to the dismay of her publishers. Carson hated to see her waste her talent. But now, working on her house and property interested her more.

She hadn't been back to New York since she bought the house, and said she had no reason to. She had let friends fall by the wayside after Robbie's death, and purposely avoided them. She didn't want to hear about their children, or see them, most of whom were teenagers now, as Robbie would have been. At forty-nine, she knew there would be no more children in her life. Robbie had been the center of her universe, just as Carson had been, but that was all over now.

Once in a while, she contemplated how odd it was never to experience human touch anymore. There were none of the adoring hugs as Robbie wrapped his arms around her neck and nearly choked her in his exuberance, or the gentle, sensual passion she and Carson had shared. She wasn't close enough to anyone now to have them hug her, or embrace them in return. Now and then someone working for her would touch her shoulder or her arm, or her contractor, Norm, who was a friendly guy, put a hand on her back. It always startled her. It wasn't a familiar sensation anymore, nor a welcome one. She didn't want to remember what that felt like. Physical contact with other humans was no longer part of her life, even though it had been important to her before. In their early years, Carson considered her a warm person. And Robbie would respond to her saying "I want to give you a hug" by leaping into her arms, and nearly knocking her down to hug her. He had been a sturdy, happy boy, until he became too weak to walk or even raise his head, and she would sit beside him holding his hand until he fell asleep. In the end, he slept most of the time, as she watched him, making sure he was still breathing, and savoring every instant he was alive.

"You can't cut yourself off from everyone!" Carson had warned her after Robbie died, but she had. She had survived the worst that life could dole out to her, losing her only child. She wasn't the same person anymore, but she was still standing and functioning. She used to love to laugh. Hattie had been livelier and more mischievous as a child, but Melissa had a good sense of humor. There had been no sign of it since Robbie got sick. The immensity of the loss had changed her.

She rose early every morning and watched the

sun come up, and then got busy with her day, doing whatever work was at hand, and she often went to bed soon after dark. She read at times, and liked to sit by the fire relaxing and lost in thought, but the memories snuck up on her then. She didn't like giving herself time to think and drift back to the past, and avoided it. She was living in the present, and her present was the house she had restored, mostly by the work of her own hands. She was proud of the results and what she had achieved. The house was living proof of how far she had come since she had bought it, and a symbol of her survival. No one in the area knew how hard she had fought to cling to life and not give up when she'd lost the person she loved most. Working on the house had brought part of her back to life, and kept her busy, happy, and fulfilled for four years. It was her therapy and had become one of the handsomest homes in the Berkshire mountains, with exquisite handcrafted workmanship. In its own way, it was a work of art. To Melissa, the house was alive, a living being to be cherished and embellished, and had become her reason for staying alive.

She let herself think of her sister, Hattie, sometimes, with her fiery red hair and huge green eyes, like a pixie when she was a child. Her copper hair was hidden under her nun's veil now. She had been a tomboy, and then blossomed into a beautiful young woman with a natural, striking beauty men were drawn to. Boys pursued her even when she was a teenager. Melissa, with dark hair and blue eyes, had a cooler beauty and seemed less approachable. When Melissa went to Columbia, she was more concerned with taking care of her sister than meeting men. She never dated until her junior year.

When Melissa graduated from college and got a job, Hattie was sixteen and a beautiful, voluptuous young woman by then. All the boys at the school she went to in New York were crazy about her, which made it all seem even more absurd when Hattie decided to become a nun. She had always been the boy-magnet of the two of them and loved to flirt. Melissa was more reserved. Hattie was fun-loving, gregarious, and at ease with everyone. The idea of her being sequestered from the world seemed a criminal waste to Melissa. She was sure her sister would fly back out of the convent in six months, it was all a whim, but she hadn't. She had stayed for eighteen years, faithful to a vocation Melissa couldn't understand, and had never accepted, although she knew their mother would have loved it.

They had shared an apartment until Hattie joined the order. Melissa met Carson around that time, before she published her first book, right after she wrote it. He sold it, and a year later they were married and she gave up their old apartment. She hated being there once Hattie was gone. It was silent and lonely, but she didn't feel that way about her house in Massachusetts now. She was never lonely there, and had made peace with the solitude she'd chosen. It was a relief to be alone when she and Carson had separated in New York. They'd lived in Tribeca, and their marriage felt so dead to her by then that it was painful being with him, and she was grateful for her freedom when he left.

She'd started looking for a house immediately, and had found the right one quickly. It was a merciful release when she left New York and started fresh. She didn't have to look at Robbie's empty room anymore. It was the end of the happiest time in her life, when Robbie was alive, which was nothing but a memory by the time she moved to Massachusetts.

When Melissa went upstairs that night, after sanding the door all morning, she glanced at a photograph of Hattie in a frame on the desk in the small den off her bedroom. The photo was of Hattie dressed for her senior prom at her high school in New York. She was wearing a pale blue dress, with her bright red hair pulled back and swept up in a mass of curls. She looked sexy and gorgeous and was beaming in the picture. Melissa perfectly remembered the moment when she took the snapshot. She had helped her sister pick the dress. There were no photographs anywhere in the house of her dressed as a nun, only a few from their childhood and youth, which was how Melissa still thought of her. Her sister's habit was a costume that made no sense to her.

Melissa smiled briefly at the photograph of Hattie

as she sat down at her desk and signed some checks, and then she went to bed to read for a while, before falling asleep. She always slept with the light on, to keep the memories at bay. She had gotten good at it over the years, and had learned to live with the loss. It was part of her now, like everything else that had happened to her, her marriage to Carson and the divorce, the career that was an unexpected, startling success that she walked away from, the people she no longer saw, the sister who betrayed her by becoming a nun and was a stranger now, the father who had died of alcoholism, and the mother who changed Melissa's life forever and then died with none of their issues resolved, especially the most serious ones. As Melissa slipped into her comfortable bed, she had so much to forget. The ghosts of the past would haunt her if she let them, but she had become an expert at avoiding them. She looked around the bedroom and smiled. All that mattered to her was in the present. The past was buried and almost forgotten, a dim memory now. She was at peace in the silent house. She reminded herself that the past was gone, and she was happy now. She almost believed it, as she got under the covers and fell asleep, exhausted from the hard work she'd done all day. She had learned that pushing herself to her limits physically was the only way to escape the ghosts that still waited for her in the silent room at night.

Chapter 2

The day after Melissa had sanded the first door, she carefully took another one off its hinges. She carried it outside, put it on sawhorses, examined the work to be done in the bright sunlight, and got to it. Within half an hour, there was sweat pouring down her neck and back. The summer sun was blazing, and it was even hotter than the day before.

An hour after she began, she picked up the door, leaned it against a tree, and moved the sawhorses. It was too hot to work beyond the shade. The air was still and she could hear crickets all around her. The sanding was painstaking work, but she enjoyed it. She ran out of sandpaper at noon, and pulled a T-shirt over the bikini top she'd been working in. There was no one around. It was a Saturday. There were grounds-keepers working at the edge of the property, clearing away brush on the perimeter, and boys picking apples in the orchard to take to the farmer's market. It was the hottest summer she'd experienced since she'd lived there. It had been hot and dry since April.

Melissa drank a tall glass of water in the kitchen, and then went to get her bag and car keys. She had a list of things she needed at the hardware store, and it was only a ten-minute drive to the village. It was a small, quaint town, and at this time of year, the area was full of summer renters, families who came to spend the summer there with their children, as well as residents who lived there year-round like Melissa. She usually stayed out of the village as much as possible in the summer. She preferred the area in the off months when it was less populated.

She had a car with four-wheel drive, but drove her truck into town, to bring back what she needed. She had a new wheelbarrow on her list, and a lawn mower part the head gardener wanted, the sandpaper, and weed killer. There was a time when she would have gone to Bergdorf's to buy shoes in New York on a Saturday, or taken Robbie to buy a new windbreaker for school, or taken him to Central Park to play with him. They had rented a house on Long Island in the summer, and gone to Sag Harbor, where other couples and writers they knew spent their summers. But those days were long gone. The hardware store in the village was the main event for her now. She hadn't bought new clothes since she'd lived there. She wore what was left of the wardrobe she'd kept. She'd given most of it away when she moved.

She had no need for fancy clothes. She had no social life, and only wore jeans and her rough work clothes. The bikini top she'd worn was one she'd bought in the South of France, on a trip there with Carson and Robbie. She looked better in it now than she had then. Her body was toned and strengthened by four years of hard labor. She swam once in a while in a nearby lake in the off-season, or took a dip in the stream that ran through her property. No one saw her in the bikini or cared about how she looked. The T-shirt stuck to her as she drove to the village, her long, dark hair piled helter-skelter on her head again.

Phil Pocker, who owned the hardware store, nodded at her as she walked in. The T-shirt she wore was an old faded one from her days at Columbia nearly thirty years before. He usually smiled at his customers, and was more effusive, but he knew better with Melissa. She rarely smiled, and was loath to engage in conversation, except to comment on the weather, or ask his advice about a product she had read about and wanted to try.

"Hot enough for you?" he asked her with a serious look. He was in his seventies and had a son, Pete, who was about her age and worked in the business with him. His son had never liked Melissa, and thought she was stuck up and unpleasant. Phil thought she was a beautiful woman, even though she didn't talk much. She was tall and graceful, with a pretty face and a slim figure.

"She's not stuck up," Phil had defended her. "She's just quiet. She's a woman of few words. She's always polite to me. I'd rather deal with her than the summer folk around here. She knows what she's doing, and her contractor, Norm Swenson, says she works harder than any of the men on her property. She hires from around here, and pays a good wage. She pays her bills on time. She's a good woman. She's just not friendly."

"That's an understatement," his son, Pete, had said. "She nearly took my head off and treated me like an idiot when I didn't have the size wrench she wanted."

"It's just her way. She doesn't mean any harm by it." He always gave her a pass. Phil and Norm agreed that there had to be a reason for how reclusive she was. She was still young enough, and striking looking, and there had been no sign of a man, or visitors of any kind, since she'd owned the property. Norm said that there were pictures of a boy around the house, but she had never said who he was, or if he was any relation to her. They both sensed something tragic in her background. It was in her eyes, and her stiff demeanor, as though she might break if you pushed her too hard.

"I worry about fire this time of year," Phil said to her, as he piled the objects on her list on the counter. She was going to pick up the wheelbarrow outside, and he said he'd have someone put it in the truck for her.

"I worry about that too," she said quietly. "I have my boys clearing away the brush down by the stream. I think it's going to be a long, hot summer." It was still only July.

"What are you working on now?" he asked her in his Massachusetts twang.

"I'm taking all the doors down to the original wood, and getting a hundred years of paint off them. I just started." She smiled at him.

"That's hard work." He smiled back at her. She was a pretty woman, although she never played up her looks and didn't seem to care. She had a great body, which he never admitted to noticing, but even at his age, he enjoyed seeing a good-looking woman as much as the next man. Pete didn't agree with him, but his own wife was a knockout, and had been a cheerleader in high school. They had been married for twenty-seven years, and had five children. Phil had been widowed for fifteen years, lost his wife to cancer. His hardware store, Pocker and Son, was the best one around for miles and did a booming business. Phil kept their product line up to date with high-quality goods, and he knew every trick in the business for doing complicated repairs, particularly plumbing and electrical work. Melissa often asked his advice and found it useful. And Norm had a deep respect and affection for him too. Norm and Phil had dinner together once in a while. Norm was closer to Phil's son's age, but liked Phil better. He was a no-frills person, with a sharp mind, and had helped Norm many times with good advice when he started his contracting business.

Melissa carried her own bags out to the truck, as she always did, after she said goodbye to Phil, and the boy they hired in the summer put the wheelbarrow in the back for her. Less than an hour after she'd left, she was home again, with everything she needed.

Norm stopped by Melissa's place that afternoon. He dropped in occasionally when he had something to do on a construction site nearby. She was sanding again, and didn't hear him until he was standing in front of her. He was a tall, burly man, with a full head of dark blond hair, bright blue eyes, and powerful arms and shoulders. He had a kind face. He had gone to Yale, and dropped out after a year, and decided to do what he loved instead, working with his hands and building houses. He said college life wasn't for him, but he read voraciously, was knowledgeable on a wide variety of subjects, and they'd had some interesting discussions in the past four years. He was divorced and had no kids, which appeared to be her situation too. He was fifty years old. He referred to a girlfriend from time to time, but it never sounded serious, and they never discussed their personal lives or her past history with each other. She never volunteered it, and he asked no questions, although he had wondered who the little boy was in the photographs. He didn't want to pry. There were no photographs in the house of any man, and there had never been any evidence of one for the four years he had known her. She chose to remain a mystery, and he respected that. All he knew about her was that she had moved up from New York. And since her books had been written in her maiden name, he didn't know about her life as a bestselling author either.

"Phil said you're stripping all the doors," he said, smiling at her. She nodded, and put down the sandpaper. "That'll keep you busy for a while."

"Yeah, like a year or two." She grinned at him. "It suddenly occurred to me that they'd look a lot better if I take them down to the wood."

"I can help you if you want," he offered, but already knew what the answer would be. She liked doing everything herself.

"I'll let you know if I run out of steam," she said, and offered him a glass of iced tea, which he accepted gratefully and followed her into the kitchen he had rebuilt for her. It was a relief to get out of the heat, although it didn't seem to faze her. She was perspiring from the work but didn't care. She was comfortable with him. He had never done or said anything inappropriate, and wouldn't have. It was obvious that she wasn't open to male attention, and was content as she was, and he didn't want to spoil or jeopardize the successful working relationship he had with her. He had installed air-conditioning for her throughout the house three years before, and it made a huge difference in the summer. The house was cool and pleasant, as they both drank the iced tea she poured them, with thin slices of lemon in it. She kept a pitcher in the fridge, and one of lemonade.

"There was a fire fifty miles from here last week," he informed her. "We're lucky there hasn't been any wind. Something like that can take off in a hurry. It started in a campground, but they caught it quickly." She nodded. Fire was a concern to all of them in a summer as hot and dry as this one. "Some of the campers don't know what they're doing." Melissa was careful to keep the dry brush on her property cleared in the summer months. Norm had taught her that in the beginning. He was impressed by how much she had learned, and how avidly she followed his advice. She was a responsible property owner, and an asset to the area, although few people knew her.

He left after he'd finished his iced tea, and Melissa went back to work on the door she was sanding. It was dusk when she stopped, and went inside to take a shower and wash the dust off. She made a salad for dinner. She wasn't hungry, and didn't like to cook. In the summer months, she ate the fruit and vegetables they grew on the property with a meal of chicken or fish now and then. She didn't enjoy cooking, and never had, and did as little as possible. She knew that Norm was a gourmet cook, and made a hobby of it. Sometimes he brought her the vinegar or jam he made, or some delicious treat he had concocted in the state-of-the-art kitchen that he had built for himself. Hers was much more basic, although it was adequate for her needs as a single person who never had visitors or entertained.

She had made that clear to him when she hired him to remodel the house. But she enjoyed the things he brought her once in a while. Melissa didn't have hobbies, she put all her attention and energy into the house, just as she had put it into her writing, marriage, and son before. She was a highly focused person. She had been a powerful tennis player before, but had no one to play with now.

He was adept at dodging her occasional acerbic comments about the world, or life in general. She never turned her sharp tongue on him, and he recognized her moods easily. He was good with people, and didn't take her taciturn nature personally. He accepted that it was just the way she was, and like Phil at the hardware store, he still thought that underneath the bristles, she was a good person. She wasn't rude to his workers, but she wasn't warm and friendly either. She was kinder to Norm than to his employees, because he was so unfailingly nice to her. Even Melissa recognized that she wasn't an easy person, and admitted it to him often, though she made no effort to change. He accepted her as she was, and liked her anyway. In his opinion, despite the lack of frills, he recognized that she was an honest, honorable woman, with good values, and many qualities.

She watched the news that night, and heard a report about another fire that had started in a campground, closer than the last one. She wondered if she should hose down the house. But she decided the fire wasn't close enough or serious enough to worry about. That night, in bed, she woke to the sound of a windstorm and saw the trees swaying outside her windows. She got up and went out. A fierce wind had suddenly sprung up out of nowhere.

She went back to bed, turned the news on in the morning, and saw that the nearby fire had grown to alarming proportions, and the wind hadn't died down yet. If it continued, it could push the fire in her direction. She decided to hose down the house. Norm came by and found her doing it an hour later. Her entire home was a wooden structure, as were all the outbuildings, and she was watering down the roof when he got out of his truck and walked over to her.

"I was going to offer to do that for you." She had already done most of it, and hosed down the trees nearest the house. She wasn't sure how much it would help if the fire came straight for them, but did it anyway.

"It sounds like a bad one," he commented. "I've been listening to the news since five o'clock this morning. I hosed down my place too."

"It's another campground fire," she commented, holding the hose steady in her strong hands.

He hesitated for a moment before he answered. "They suspect arson this time," he said in a serious tone, and Melissa looked angry. She had a short fuse, and was worried about the fire, and her house.

"If it is arson, they should hang whoever started it." Fire was their worst fear in the summer, and the most dangerous.

"If it's arson, whoever set it will go to prison," Norm said calmly.

"How could anyone do something like that?"

"Do you want me to start on the sheds around the property?" he asked her and she nodded, frowning.

"I'll come with you. I've done everything I can here at the main house."

She got in his truck, and together they drove to each of the outbuildings, and stopped to hose them down. She had installed water sources throughout the property and an extensive irrigation system. When they finished, Norm left to check on one of his other clients who lived closer to the fire, which was now raging, according to radio reports. They had continued listening in the truck, and the situation sounded serious. News channels in Boston reported that night on the news that a major fire was now burning in the Berkshires, spurred on by unusually high winds that hadn't died down yet. Melissa continued listening to weather reports late into the night, and checked the fire map on her computer that was tracking the fast-moving blaze.

By midnight, she was seriously worried as she saw the fire zone growing and getting closer. There was a river and a county road between her house and the fire, and if it jumped either one of them, her property would be in immediate danger. She dozed off while looking at her computer, and at two A.M., she was awakened by a loud pounding on her front door.

She woke up with a start, and raced downstairs, still dressed, and came rapidly awake. The wind was still blowing when she opened the door and saw two deputy sheriffs she didn't know, with an official car with flashing lights behind them.

"We're evacuating the area," one of the deputies said. "You need to be out as quickly as possible. The fire is heading this way." She stood staring at them, and made a quick decision.

"Thanks for letting me know," she said politely.

"Do you need help? Are there children in the house, animals in the barn? You can let the livestock loose, and you'll have to let them fend for themselves." Several people in the area were panicking about their horses, but the fire was moving too fast now to get them into trailers and drive them out. Some homeowners were refusing to leave until their horses were safe.

"I don't have kids or animals," she answered. "Just me."

"Well, get out fast. Do you want us to drive you anywhere? The main road is still open, but the smaller ones are closed." As she looked over their heads, she could see the bright orange glow of the fire in the night sky.

"I'll be fine," she assured them, and they left as she closed the door.

The decision she had made on the spur of the moment was that she wasn't leaving. She didn't want to evacuate. She was staying, to do whatever she could to save her house. She didn't care if she died trying. She had nothing that she cared about to lose now, except her home. It was all she had, and the only thing she loved. And she hadn't worked that hard for four years in order to abandon it now. She wasn't afraid of the fire itself, or getting hurt, only of the damage it would do. It would have been different if Robbie had been there with her. But he wasn't. She only had the house to worry about, and was responsible only for herself.

The fire seemed to grow minute by minute as she watched from her windows, and the air was filled with smoke and ash, which made it hard to breathe.

Her truck was covered with a thin film of ash. She went out to hose down the roof again, coughing in the acrid air, and was intent on dousing the whole roof when Norm drove up a short time later. He looked unhappy to see her there, and shouted over the sound of the hose as he walked toward her.

"Haven't they evacuated you yet? They evacuated me an hour ago." She nodded but didn't say more, and concentrated on what she was doing as he picked up another hose. "You've got to get out, Melissa. There's nothing else you can do here. It's headed your way. There's no time to lose."

"I'm not going," she said firmly, her eyes fixed on her roof to make sure she wet every inch down.

"Don't be crazy. You can't risk your life for a house. If the worst happens, you can rebuild." She just shook her head, and he could see that she meant it and wasn't going anywhere. He had been on his way to volunteer to help the firefighters who, so far, had been unable to control the blaze. But he didn't want to leave her. There was something terrifyingly determined about the way she looked. He knew how much she loved her home, but this was insane. He grabbed her arm, and the water from the hose sprayed them both. Her shirt was wet as she looked at him.

"I'm staying, Norm. You can go."

"I'm not leaving here without you." He tightened his grip on her arm and she shook him off with a look that said she would fight him if he tried to take her away. "Come on, Mel, be sensible. It's too dangerous for you to stay. If the fire gets here, you could be trapped, or hit by a falling tree or part of the house." An old Victorian, wooden structure like her home would go up in flames within minutes.

"I don't care. This is all I have now. And if I die in the fire, no one will miss me." As she said the words, she knew it wasn't true. Her sister, Hattie, would miss her, she knew that her sister still cared, even if their lives were far apart now. Hattie was faithful about reaching out to her a few times a year. She initiated contact, Melissa never did. "All I have is a sister who's a nun, and she believes all that crap that if I die, I'll be in a better place. I haven't seen her in six years." Norm could tell there was a lot more to the story there, but this wasn't the time to ask, and Melissa probably wouldn't have told him anyway. She had never mentioned her sister before.

"I believe in that crap too, and I have no desire to wind up in that better place with you. I'm not leaving until you come with me, so you'll be responsible for killing me too, if we stay." They were both coughing in the smoke by then, which was being carried for miles by the wind.

"Leave me, Norm. I'll be fine." And if she wasn't, it didn't matter to her. He could see that now, for the first time. He had never realized before how determined she was to be alone, and how little she cared about her own life. Whatever had happened to her before had made her indifferent to whether she lived or died. It made him sad for her.

"You're a stubborn woman," he said, and she didn't deny it. They walked into the house then to get away from the smoke, and saw on a news bulletin that the fire was two miles from her house and advancing at a furious pace.

"I'm going to lose the house," she said in a grim voice, pulled a pillowcase out of a closet, and then rushed into the living room and started throwing the photographs of the little boy into the pillowcase, as he watched her with a question in his eyes he didn't put words to. She glanced at him, and continued what she was doing.

"He's my son. He died of a brain tumor when he was ten, six years ago. It destroyed my marriage, that's why I'm here," she said matter-of-factly in a flat voice. She had never said that to anyone before. The pillowcase was heavy and full when she finished, with all the silver frames with photographs of Robbie in them. Norm looked sad for her as they walked back into the kitchen to check the TV again, but the image had changed dramatically when they saw the weather map again. The wind had turned at a ninety-degree angle and was heading north, taking the fire with it, which was bad news for the people who lived in its path, but it meant that Melissa's home had been miraculously spared. She looked at Norm in disbelief. His home would be safe now too, unless the wind changed direction again. "If I still believed in God, I would think it was the answer to prayer, but the people in its path are in big trouble now. I feel sorry for them."

"I still believe in miracles," Norm said quietly, and finally found what he wanted to say to her after what he'd seen her do in her living room and the look on her face. "I'm sorry about your boy, Mel. I never knew who the child was." He had seen the photos many times while working on her house. He was a beautiful little boy with dark hair and big eyes like hers.

They sat down in the kitchen for a minute. Her legs were shaking with relief that the wind had turned and her home was safe. She didn't even care that Norm knew about Robbie now. It had been a naked moment when he had seen more of her than he ever had before.

"It changed everything when he died," she said in a soft voice. "It almost killed me, and actually, it did kill a lot of me. I've been half dead ever since. I gave up my work, my life, my marriage. None of it made sense anymore without him. The only thing that has made any sense and kept me alive since then is this house. And if it burned down, I'd go with it. It's all I have to live for now."

"That's not enough," he said gently.

"It is for me," she said with a tired smile. It had been a long night.

"What about your sister, the nun? Why don't you see her?"

"I can't stand nuns. We were very close until she took the cowardly way out, eighteen years ago. We haven't been close ever since. The last time I saw her was at my son's funeral. I don't miss her," she said sharply. "She's not the same person she used to be. Neither am I. I took care of her after our parents died. She was twelve, I was eighteen. I became her only parent then. It made me grow up very quickly. I spent all my college years taking care of her. She went nuts at twenty-five and joined a religious order. I was furious with her. We drifted apart after that. I got married a year later, and had Robbie. And our lives were too different from then on."

"Why do you hate nuns?" There was a hardness in her that he had guessed at, and glimpsed, but never seen full on before.

"That's a long story you don't need to know. I just do. My mother was a religious fanatic and would have loved it if we'd both become nuns. She got her wish with my sister, although my mother was long dead by then. There was no risk of it with me. I gave up on religion a long time ago, at sixteen." To Norm, it sounded like she had given up on everything, people, life, her family, God. All she had left was this house. It made him realize more than ever what it meant to her, and it explained why she never let anyone get close to her. She was locked behind her walls, alone. "Do you want something to eat?" she offered. The sun was coming up by then, and she made it clear that the subject of her past was closed. He nodded, and she made scrambled eggs for both of them. They ate, talking about the fire, and then he left. He still wanted to see what he could do to help with the fire as a volunteer. He knew that Melissa was safe now, and could manage on her own. She would have done so anyway, even without him, but he was glad he'd been there with her. He admired her more than ever now, but also felt sorry for her as never before. Now he knew what she was running from, or what had driven her into seclusion in the mountains. It was a glimpse into who she was, which he had never fully understood before.

Melissa put the dishes in the dishwasher after Norm left, a little sorry that she had told him about Robbie. He didn't need to know. They were on friendly terms, but they weren't close. The photos of Robbie were still in the pillowcase on a kitchen chair. The phone rang shortly after seven, and she was startled when she heard a familiar voice she hadn't heard in years.

"I've been watching the news in New York. Are you okay, Mellie?" It was Hattie. They always communicated by letter or email. She hadn't heard her voice in six years. At forty-three, Hattie still sounded like a kid. "I've been praying for you all night."

"I don't believe in that," Melissa reminded her, "but it must have worked. The wind suddenly turned two hours ago, and my house was spared. A lot of other people lost their homes, though. The fire is still out of control, but it's not heading here for now." But that could change in an instant if the wind shifted again.

"I'm so relieved. We were praying for them too. Did you have any damage?"

"We might have some singed trees at the edge of the property, but it never got to the house. It was heading straight for us last night. They tried to evacuate me, but I stayed."

"You shouldn't have. Are you okay, Mel? I mean other than the fire."

"Of course. I'm fine. How are you? Still the angel of mercy, nursing gunshot wounds in the Bronx?" The hospital where she worked was in one of the worst neighborhoods in New York.

"Yes, I am. I miss you. I think about you a lot." There was a long silence between them then, and neither of them knew what to say. The chasm between them was vast, and had been for so many years. It was hard to bridge that now, except with brief emails wishing each other a merry Christmas, or a happy birthday. The wound between them suddenly seemed raw again. "Would you ever let me come to visit you?" Hattie asked her, and Melissa didn't answer for a minute.

"I don't know. Maybe. Why would you want to?"

"Because we're still sisters. Our order doesn't wear the habit anymore, except on important religious occasions. You could ignore the fact that I'm a nun." She knew how Melissa hated seeing her in her habit.

"How could I forget that? You're the better person, Hattie. There's nothing left of who I was. Robbie took that person with him. I'm beginning to sound more like Mom," she said matter-of-factly.

"You'll always be my sister, and I'll always love you. You did so much for me when we were growing up."

"That was a long time ago. It was nice of you to call," Melissa said with emotion in her voice. "I guess you could come up sometime, and see what I've been working on for four years."

"Are you happy there?"

"It keeps me busy, and I'm at peace. That's enough for me. I'm glad it didn't burn down last night."

"So am I," her younger sister said with feeling. "I'd love to see you, Mellie."

"I'll think about it," was all Melissa would commit to. "Take care, Hattie," and then, at the very last second before they both hung up, she whispered, "I love you too," and ended the call. It was the most emotional thing that had happened all night, as intense as almost losing the house. It reminded her that she still had a sister, whether she saw her or not, and no matter how far apart they had grown.

She put Robbie's pictures back on the bookshelf then, went upstairs to lie on her bed, and thought of both of them, Robbie and Hattie. She wondered what it would be like to see her sister again. It had been a long frightening night, but thank God, the house she loved was safe. It would have broken what was left of her heart if it had burned to the ground. She had lost enough. She couldn't lose the house too. Her mind was flooded with her memories of Hattie, all that they had been through and meant to each other so long ago. It frightened her to open the door to those feelings again. It brought so much with it that she wanted to forget.

Chapter 3

The fire was still raging out of control the next day, but it was well north of Melissa's house, and the wind hadn't shifted again. Firefighters were pouring in from Boston, other parts of Massachusetts, Connecticut, and New Hampshire, trying to get it under control. According to news reports, it was only ten percent contained.

Norm had spent the night on the fringes of it, with a group of volunteers. It was exhausting, frightening work.

Melissa had had an email from Carson, wanting to know if she was all right, and she had answered briefly, thanked him, and said she was. She was grateful for his concern. The fire was bringing back the people and memories of the past.

On the third day of the fire, Rochester and Buffalo sent them additional firefighters, and they finally managed to get the fire sixty percent contained.

There was no question by then that it had been arson. The fire chief had confirmed it. Three hundred homes had been lost, and nearly two thousand people were crowding in shelters that had been set up in local schools.

The day after the fire had been mostly contained, they showed the arsonist on TV. He had been apprehended at his mother's home. He was seventeen years old, and he looked like a frightened little boy when they arrested him. They said that he and his mother had been homeless for a while, and people who were interviewed said he had shown signs of psychiatric problems, after being bullied by his classmates in school. They had recently moved again. Given the severity of the crime, and his age, he was going to be tried as an adult. Melissa sat watching him on TV with hatred in her eyes. He had nearly robbed her of her home.

She and Norm spoke about it when he came by to see how she was. It struck her as she looked at the arsonist that he was only a year older than Robbie would have been. She couldn't imagine anyone disturbed and vicious enough to start a fire the way he had. The report said that he had started small fires before. He seemed terrified in the brief footage they saw of him.

"I hope they send him to prison for a long time," Melissa said angrily when she and Norm talked about it during his visit.

"He's just a kid," he said, feeling sorry for him.

"How can you say that after what he did? Think of all the homes that burned."

"He belongs in a psychiatric hospital, not jail," Norm said compassionately. Melissa had no pity for him, with so many homes lost. They had said on TV that his mother was in a rehab facility, and couldn't be reached for comment. And he had been living alone at her home, which looked like barely more than a shack.

"Someone should have picked up on how sick he was a long time ago. It's a failure in our system," Norm said quietly. "It sounds like he's had a terrible life." There had been no mention of his father, and the boy's life sounded tragic.

"Other people are victims of the system, they don't go around setting fires." There was no mercy in her voice.

"Have you heard from your sister again?" he asked, to change the subject, and Melissa shook her head.

"She wants to come and visit. I haven't decided what I want to do about that yet."

"Maybe the two of you could make peace with each other," he suggested gently, as Melissa looked off into the distance, thinking about it. It seemed too late for that, after so many years. And too painful to try.

"We have nothing in common anymore. Maybe we never did. We were always different. She was much more outgoing than I was, which made it seem even crazier when she decided to become a nun. She always wanted to be an actress, and just when she started to get the right breaks, she ran away."

"Isn't that what you did when your son died?" he asked her, and she looked shocked for a minute, and shook her head.

"That was different. Our whole world fell apart. Hattie was just beginning. She was young, good things were happening for her. She had no reason to run away. It was sheer cowardice, to seek refuge in the convent, instead of dealing with life."

"Not everyone is as brave as you are, Melissa."

"I'm not brave, and you're right, I ran away too."

"What kind of work did you do before?" It was the first he had heard of her career when she said she had given up her work.

"I used to write. Articles, books. I ran out of words after my son died. Everything seemed so irrelevant after that, so small compared to him."

"Do you miss writing?" He was curious about her now. She had shown him pieces of the puzzle, but not the whole, which had whetted his appetite to know more.

"Not anymore," she said. "It was part of another life. My husband was my agent, that's how we met. He's still active in New York. His wife is a moderately successful mystery writer. He keeps busy with her. He tried to get me to start writing again, but I couldn't.

I'd rather work with my hands now. I have no desire to write again. My books were pretty dark. It was another time." He had a suspicion that she had talent. She was well read and very bright. There was a look of determination in her eyes when she spoke of not writing again. She had chosen a different path.

"Would I have read any of your work?" he asked, curious. "Did you write under your name? Fiction?"

"I wrote under my maiden name, Melissa Stevens. It was the truth thinly veiled as fiction."

He looked shocked. "That's you? I read a few of your books. They were very upsetting and haunting. We've all felt like that at times, enraged by the injustices done to us, and helpless to avenge the past, or forget it. You spoke for all of us, but were brave enough to say it. I read two of them twice. They were beautifully written. You're a big deal, Melissa," he said, impressed.

"It felt important to me to say it. But what's the point? The people I was angry at are all dead. My mother was a bitter, angry, mean woman. My father was weak and a drunk who wasted his life. There's nothing left to say."

"It's a shame to bury a talent like that," he said kindly, and she shrugged.

"I have other things that I want to do. It's painful, stripping yourself naked like that."

"But it must be healing too, a kind of catharsis." She didn't answer. She just nodded. It was obvious that she didn't want to discuss it. He left a little while later.

He thought of their conversation on his way home. There was a mysterious side of her that fascinated him. She wasn't just an interesting woman who had opted for a quiet country life. She had run away from a husband, a life, a career, fame, success, a city, even her own family ties by avoiding her sister. He could tell that she was a woman who had been deeply wounded, maybe by more than just the loss of her son. And as the author of the books he'd read, he knew that her youth and childhood had been a nightmare of emotional abuse by a cruel mother.

Her fury at the young arsonist seemed extreme to him. Her reaction was visceral, pure rage. It seemed out of character for her. She was so distant and cool and uncommunicative, but she had never seemed that angry to him before. The boy's youth and obvious problems didn't mitigate the crime for her. He had jeopardized the home she loved, and she hated him for it.

Like a moth drawn to flame, when Melissa read in the paper of the arraignment, which was open to the public, she drove to the county courthouse the morning that it was to occur. She wanted to see what would happen, and to see his face in person. She was fueled by anger and indignation as she drove to the courthouse on the appointed day. She was shocked when she saw the boy, led into the courtroom by sheriff's deputies, in handcuffs, and shackles on his legs. He looked about fourteen years old, and there were tears streaming down his face.

His name was Luke Willoughby, and he was represented by the public defender. Other locals had come to see the proceedings as well, and how he would be dealt with. Melissa suspected that many of the people who filled the courtroom had lost their homes. She had less reason to be there, but curiosity about him and raw anger had impelled her to come.

The public defender requested that the judge remand him into the custody of the juvenile court system, which was denied, given the severity of the crime. He hadn't graduated from high school, had dropped out of school that spring, and was turning eighteen in September, so technically he was not yet an adult. He pled not guilty, and the judge sent him to an adult psychiatric facility to determine if he was able to stand trial. The only words he spoke during the entire proceeding were "Not guilty, Your Honor." He sounded respectful and looked broken, and the public defender confirmed that his parents were not in the courtroom. He explained that his father had disappeared when Luke was seven, and his mother had been sent to rehab by the court, and had been unable to come. He said that they had been homeless for several years, and he was living alone in a shack in his mother's absence. The judge nodded and his face registered no emotion.

The deputies walked him past Melissa when they took him back to jail, and the anger she had felt for him suddenly ebbed away like sand through her fingers. He looked so tragic and so forlorn that it was hard to imagine him committing so heinous a crime that had cost several lives and caused so many people pain. She wanted to reach out and touch him, and as Norm had said, the idea of sending him to prison with adult men seemed suddenly wrong. He didn't appear insane either, just desperately lost. She wanted to ask him why he had done it, but she didn't know him, and there was no chance to talk.

His terrified face haunted her all the way home, and she was ashamed to have gone there at all. He was in a hell all his own, and no good would come of it, whatever they decided to do with him. He was precisely what Norm had guessed, a lost soul who had slipped through the system at an early age, and needed help. She might have felt differently if she'd lost her home as a result of his crime, but she hadn't, and the steam had gone out of everything she had thought about him before. She couldn't imagine a life like the one he had led as a child, and the punishment he had ahead of him now, either confined to a mental hospital or in prison. Either way, he had hard times ahead, little or no future, and had led a hard life until then. Seeing him had opened her heart to forgiveness.

It struck her again that the arsonist was only a year older than Robbie would have been, and the same age she was when her mother died and she became her sister's surrogate mother and was fully responsible for her within a year. What if her own anger at her mother had expressed itself in a life of crime? Instead she had written about it and transformed it into a lucrative career. But this was a helpless, sick boy, unable to surmount his own pain except by starting fires, damaging property and causing people's deaths. Her heart ached for the tragedy of his life, and it made her own anger at her mother's coldness seem so small. The young arsonist's life was sure to get worse now instead of better. It was truly tragic, and she felt only grief and compassion for him.

It made her think of her sister when she got home. Her worst crime, in Melissa's eyes, had been joining a religious order, which Melissa had been deeply critical of at the time. But apparently it suited her, if she was still there eighteen years later. Her two years in Africa nursing orphans and life as a nurse in a hospital were admirable. Suddenly Melissa wanted to see her again. Even if they had nothing in common now, they had a shared history, and still loved each other, even though things had gone so wrong.

She sent her an email, and invited her to come up.

Hattie's response came through on Melissa's computer in less than an hour. She accepted the invitation gratefully, said she wouldn't spend the night, but would make the round trip the same day. It was a four-hour drive from New York, which meant they wouldn't have too many hours together, which might be for the best for a first visit after so long. They were almost strangers to each other now.

Hattie wrote again later in the day, and said she could come up on a Saturday in ten days. She was working every day until then. Melissa responded that the date was fine with her. She sat thinking about it for a long time after she had sent Hattie her response. She was half excited to see her, and half afraid. Being with her would open so many doors of memory again, some of them so painful, but she suddenly longed to see her and Hattie had said the same.

She promised to arrive as early as she could. They were going to let her use one of the convent cars. Melissa thought about her almost constantly for the next ten days, and dreamed of her at night. In her dreams, they were both still children in New York, Hattie six or seven, and Melissa twelve and thirteen, always feeling responsible for her. And then, she thought about taking care of her when their mother was sick and after she died, and feeling so maternal toward her once they were alone after their father's death. They had been so close, and then suddenly it was all broken when Hattie disappeared from her life, and gave up the world. Melissa had her own life then, with Carson, and then Robbie. And now so much time had passed. There was no one left of the people they had loved, just the two of them.

Melissa slept fitfully the night before Hattie came to see her. She woke up several times during the night, and lay wide awake for a long time before she fell asleep again. She got up early in the morning, went downstairs, and made coffee. It was a hot, beautiful July day, but not as warm as it had been before the fire. A slight breeze rippled through the trees. She had gone to the grocery store the day before to buy some things she thought Hattie might like to eat. She didn't even know what she liked anymore.

Hattie had visited them a few times when Robbie was small, but Melissa had still been angry with her then. They didn't let her leave the convent often in the first few years. They liked the younger nuns to stay within the community, and kept them busy with projects and chores. Melissa refused to visit her in the convent. She couldn't bear the thought of it. So Hattie got permission to visit her, but it happened less and less frequently as they continued to drift apart. Her two years in Africa had created a real break in time, and Hattie seemed more certain than ever of her vocation when she got back. Melissa had seen more of her once Robbie got sick, and she came to sit with him to give

Melissa and Carson a break. After he died, Melissa left New York, and cut all her ties with her previous life. Then Melissa was living in the Berkshires, she and Carson were divorced, and Melissa didn't want to see anyone. The last time they had seen each other was at Robbie's funeral, and Melissa had barely spoken to Hattie. She was in a daze. Melissa was afraid that seeing her would bring it all back.

The station wagon she had borrowed from the convent came up the driveway at ten A.M. Melissa knew she must have left New York before six to get there by then. She squinted in the sunlight to see her sister and was surprised when she got out of the car in jeans, a white T-shirt, and sneakers. She looked like any other woman in her early forties, going to pick up or drop off her kids. The bright copper hair was cut short, and had faded somewhat to a duller red, but was still surprisingly bright. Her red hair had been the bane of Hattie's existence when she was younger, but she had the personality to go with it. It lit her up like a neon sign the moment she entered a room, and every teacher she'd ever had remembered her for her mischief, her constant laughter, and her red hair. Melissa always had an easier time staying below the radar, and Hattie envied her for that.

Melissa saw that she had put on a little weight, but she was still pretty, and had the same smiling face. Hattie looked cautious, but was smiling broadly as she approached and gave her older sister a hug.

"You look terrific, Mellie," she said admiringly. "How do you stay in such good shape?"

"I work my ass off here." Melissa smiled at her, as they sat down on the porch, and then Melissa went inside to get her something to eat. She had bought the cinnamon buns Hattie had loved as a child, and Hattie's face lit up when she saw them.

"I haven't had a cinnamon bun in twenty years. We have oatmeal for breakfast, and potatoes with every meal. It's way too easy to gain weight. This is a beautiful place," she said, looking around. She noticed all the details and impeccable touches, and guessed that Melissa had added them herself. She knew her sister and how thorough and attentive to detail she was. Melissa's apartment in New York had been elegantly done too, especially once her books were at the top of every bestseller list and she was raking in the money, but Carson did well too. Their combined incomes had provided them a very agreeable life. Melissa had invested enough of it to continue to live well now too. Hattie was happy to see it, and relieved for her. She had no idea how her sister had come out of the divorce, but the house was testimony to the fact that she had enough money to live well, even though she hadn't worked in seven years. She had stopped writing when Robbie was sick. She never left Robbie's side in the final year. "This place would make a very nice convent retreat," Hattie said, as she helped herself to a cinnamon bun.

"Not on your life," Melissa responded immediately, and Hattie laughed, with the sticky sugar all over her mouth, just the way she'd looked as a kid, which made Melissa smile.

"I just thought I'd mention it, in case you get lonely up here," Hattie said innocently.

"I don't," Melissa said firmly. "I like my own company. And I've worked on the house every day for four years."

"It looks it. You've done a fantastic job."

"Thank you." She smiled at her younger sister. "It was a mess when I bought it, and needed a lot of work. It was just what I needed to keep busy. I have a great contractor who helped me do everything I wanted to." She gave Hattie a tour of the house, and then they came back to the porch with a pitcher of lemonade. Melissa poured out two glasses, and observed her sister quietly. "You haven't changed, Hattie." She was as pretty and warm as ever.

"I doubt that, but I love what I do. That helps. And I know you hated the idea, and it was sudden, but the convent was the right choice for me. I realized when I went in that I wasn't cut out to fight the battles I'd have to as an actress. It wasn't meant for me."

"You could have picked a different line of work," Melissa said sadly.

"I feel safe where I am. And I knew you couldn't protect me forever. You needed your own life." The fact that Melissa had married a year after Hattie had gone into the convent had confirmed that to her. She had felt that she'd been a burden to her sister for fourteen years and kept her from leading a normal life for a young woman her age. It didn't seem fair.

"It sounds crazy, but I feel like Mom sometimes. I've gotten so damn critical since I've been alone, and since Robbie died. Sometimes I hear myself, and I sound just like her," Melissa admitted. "I hate that. She was so hard on everyone, or on me at least."

"You two had a bad run for her last two years," Hattie said, and Melissa nodded, thinking about it.

"I never forgave her for what she did, and then she was gone. I don't think she forgave me either. They made a terrible mistake sending me away." Melissa's voice was raw as she said it. It felt as though it had happened yesterday.

Hattie hadn't expected to get into the subject, but she waded into the deep waters with her. "She didn't know what else to do. At least that's what I thought later on. At the time I was just a kid, and didn't understand all the ramifications of their decision. I didn't get any of it until you explained it to me later."

"It wasn't 'their' decision, it was hers," Melissa corrected her, still angry at the memory. It had changed her life forever. "Dad never spoke up for me. I think he was just relieved to have Mom make the decision for him. We never talked about it before he died. The subject was taboo. But the price I paid was real."

"I know," Hattie said sadly, looking at her sympathetically. "I understand that now. But there was no other option in their minds. She was too Catholic to let you have an abortion. And people didn't keep babies born out of wedlock then. It was 1987. You were sixteen years old, and couldn't have taken care of a child yourself, and they would have been too ashamed to let you keep it." In a way it was a relief to both sisters to talk about it. Melissa hadn't intended to, but seeing Hattie brought it all back again, just as she had feared.

"So they sent me to that dungeon in Ireland, and forced me to give the baby up. Mom said I couldn't come home again unless I did. What else could I do at sixteen?"

"It would have ruined your life if you'd kept the baby. And you couldn't have stayed in a Catholic school in New York with a child born out of wedlock." They had gone to private Catholic schools all their lives.

"Instead it ruined my life giving her up. I've never been the same. And two years later, I was taking care of you. And I didn't mind it. You were my baby from the moment you were born. I was six then." Melissa smiled at Hattie. But there was always an underlying anger and bitterness just under the surface, which colored everything, when she thought about the baby her mother forced her to give up, especially now, when she had nothing else. It was why her books had been so dark, as she tried to exorcise the demons that tormented her, and never could. Her mother banishing her and making her give up the baby had traumatized her for life.

"Did Carson know?" Hattie asked her, curious. She had always wondered and never dared ask. Their mother hadn't told Hattie at the time that Melissa left home for seven months because she was pregnant, but Melissa had told her herself when Hattie was sixteen. Melissa had warned her sternly not to let the same thing happen to her. Hattie still remembered how shocked she had been when Melissa told her the whole story when she was old enough to understand.

"Of course he knew," Melissa answered her. "I told Carson after he proposed. I would never have married him with a secret like that. And I guess I only had two good eggs in me. We tried but I never got pregnant again after Robbie. Carson was very nice about it when I told him. She would have been sixteen when Carson and I got married, and he asked me if I wanted to try to contact her. He said she'd be welcome to visit. I tried, I called Saint Blaise's, and spoke to the mother superior, and she said there was no way to find her. All the records had been destroyed in a fire a few years after I'd been there. She said she had no idea where the baby went, or the name of the people who adopted her. I've heard that from other women since, and I even read a book about it. It was an exposé of those convents and mother and baby homes in Ireland and England, written by a reporter who was a fallen Catholic. There were many convents like it in Ireland then. They were baby mills. It had been going on since the late forties. Mine was probably among the last of them. Nice Catholic girls from respectable families who got in trouble, and the Church offered a perfect solution. We went to Ireland for the pregnancy, disappeared from our schools at home, and left the babies with them, which made everything nice and simple for our parents, and the nuns had the babies adopted by wealthy American couples, and even a number of movie stars. The adoptive parents gave very large donations to the Church, and everyone was happy, except the girls who gave up their babies when they were too young to know better or have a voice in it. The adoptive parents got what people call today 'designer babies,' no drugs or girls from bad homes, all white middle and upper class Catholic girls. The pregnant girls' parents who could afford to paid a hefty sum to the convent for keeping us, and then the adoptive parents paid a fortune for healthy white babies from decent families.

"The youngest girl when I was there was thirteen. She told me she'd been raped by her uncle, her mother's brother. Her parents said she was in boarding school for a year, which was what Mom told her friends too. She told them my grades were slipping because I was boy crazy, so they sent me to a good school in Ireland for a year, and I was an angel when I came home. There was only ever one boy. I loved him. And I only had sex with him once. We were too scared to do it again, and I got pregnant the first time. His parents sent him to military school in Mississippi, and Annapolis for college. I never heard from him again. I never had sex again until I was a junior in college at Columbia five years later. I was too traumatized to even date. The baby's father and I were just children. He was even more afraid of his parents than I was of ours. They sent him away two days after he told them. He snuck out to tell me. The school he was going to sounded like a military prison. His father was a retired naval officer. They treated us like criminals. We thought we were in love, but who knows what that means at sixteen? Mom and Dad shipped me off pretty fast too."

"I remember," Hattie said with tears in her eyes for her sister.

"Saint Blaise's was a nightmare, worse than I feared. And the nuns had the adoption all set up before I gave birth. They wouldn't tell me anything about the family, just that they were 'lovely people,' and they were going to name her Ashley. They were at the convent, waiting, when I had her. The moment the midwife delivered her, they rushed her out of the room to them. They said it would be a sin to let me hold her and rejoice in what I'd done. I never got to hold her and I only got a glimpse of her wrapped in a blanket as one of the nuns took her away." Melissa had had dreams of it for years. "I was never allowed to meet the adoptive parents, and they took her away to the States when she was a week old. They stayed with her at a hotel in Dublin, until she was old enough to fly back to the States with them. I never even knew what city they lived in. I knew nothing about them, except that they were American.

"There were seventy or eighty girls at the school, from all over the United States, and one girl from Paris who cried all the time. They had two nuns who were midwives right on the premises, so we never left the convent, even to give birth, unless a girl was having twins, or something went seriously wrong during the delivery, and then they'd take them to a hospital. They treated us like criminals, bad girls who needed to be punished, and worked us like slaves. There was no counseling, no therapy. We just stayed for the duration of the pregnancy, went to classes in the morning so we could go back to our schools when we went home, and worked for the rest of the day. After the baby was born, they shipped us home again two weeks later, our hearts broken forever.

"I read somewhere that the Church started getting nervous about it. Forty or fifty years of high-priced adoptions, which must have brought in a fortune, given the donations they accepted in exchange for healthy newborns to be adopted. The nuns covered their tracks by burning all the records, so no one could find the babies that were adopted later on. All trace of them was erased, including the names of the wealthy people who adopted them.

"Saint Blaise's still exists, I checked. It's a home for elderly, retired nuns now. They don't do adoptions anymore. No one in the Church likes to talk about it, but you hear about it from time to time. Most of the girls who went there were too ashamed to talk about it, even now, years later. And probably the men they married later didn't know."

Melissa looked devastated while she told Hattie the details she hadn't told her before. Hattie was deeply moved by what she said. It was an awful story if what she said was true. And Hattie thought that it was. It made her feel almost guilty for being a nun herself, but things happened sometimes even in the Church that were hard to explain, or justify. And she believed what Melissa said, that they had covered it up. She'd heard about some of those convents and mother and baby homes herself. They had served a purpose at one time, but no longer made sense in today's more liberal world.

"I never forgave Mom for it, I don't think I ever would have, even if she were alive today," Melissa said in a broken voice. Talking about it tore her heart out all over again.

"The nuns probably meant well, and it met a need in the early days. What seems wrong is their making money from it, even if it all went to the Church. And destroying the records. But in those days, people weren't looking for the babies they'd given up, or their birth parents. That's new, even in adoptions by the state. Those records used to be sealed, and no one could get that information, until the laws were changed," Hattie said quietly.

"Burning the records was a very efficient way to seal the records forever," Melissa said bitterly. "I've hated even the sight of nuns ever since. I stopped believing in God, and never went to church again when I came home. Mom didn't dare press that point. Dad acted like he knew nothing, and Mom got sick a few months after I got back, so we never talked about it. You and Carson are the only ones who know."

"Do you think it would make a difference if you went to Ireland yourself? Some old nun might remember something. It's a long shot, but it might be worth it," Hattie suggested.

"When I called them, the mother superior said there were none of the old nuns left. It was thirty-three years ago, and they're all dead, retired, or had been reassigned years ago. There have been four mother superiors since. And no one wants to talk about it or remember. They sounded sympathetic, but were very skittish when I called. I don't think going back there now would make a difference. I've tried to make my peace with it for thirty-three years. I almost have, but not quite. I still haven't forgiven

Mom, but what good does that do? With Robbie gone, it would be nice to know where my daughter is, just to meet her and make sure she is having a good life. I'm no use to her as a mother now, she's an adult, and she probably hasn't forgiven me either for giving her up, but I've lost two children. Robbie, who I loved so much, and a little girl called Ashley I never knew. I'm sorry, and it probably doesn't make sense to you, but I just couldn't stomach it when you became a nun. All I could think of every time I saw you were the nuns at Saint Blaise's. It made you one of them. It's nice not seeing you in your habit now. You look like you again. I could never understand why you'd want to be part of all that. I still feel traumatized when I see a nun. Fortunately, I don't see them much anymore."

"Most orders don't wear the habit now. I'm sorry you went through all that, and I made it worse for you." Hattie said it with deep feeling.

"Why did you do it?" Melissa looked baffled. "You were such a happy kid. Why would you want that life? We were never that religious, except for Mom."

"Things happened that made it seem like the right choice, the only choice, at the time. It's hard to explain."

"You were a good little actress. You had talent. One minute you were starting to get good breaks, and the next minute you were gone."

"Sometimes the careers we choose when we're

young aren't the right ones for us. You gave up writing, and you had a lot more talent than I did. When I went to L.A., I realized acting and Hollywood weren't for me."

"That's different. I couldn't do it anymore after Robbie died. Feeling anything was just too painful. I wanted to be numb. You have to feel everything in order to be a decent writer. You can't run away from the truth. And after Robbie, the truth just hurt too much, that he was gone and I'd never hold him in my arms again. I stopped feeling anything for Carson, or for anyone. It's why I never blamed him for having an affair. I needed to stop anything I was feeling, for a long time."

"And now?" Hattie asked, worried about her.

"I love my house, and I'm happy to see you again," she said. She hadn't opened the door wide to her, but it had opened a crack, and for now it was enough. "And sitting here like this, you don't seem like a nun, just the sister I grew up with."

"Thank you for letting me come," Hattie said, deeply moved by Melissa's openness with her.

"I think I needed to see you. It was very strange. The fire that almost took my house was started by an arsonist. When I found out, I hated him. I wanted him to rot in prison for what he'd done. I went to see the arraignment, like going to a public hanging, and all I saw was this terrified seventeen-year-old kid who's had a terrible life, and is probably very sick. He wasn't the monster I expected him to be, and as I drove away from the courthouse, I realized that I had forgiven him. He has bigger problems than my hating him, and he'll probably never have a decent life in a mental hospital or in jail. Hating him was too heavy a burden to carry, and I realized then that I wanted to see you, and I couldn't blame you forever for becoming a nun. You weren't part of what happened at Saint Blaise's. I can't blame you for that. And if you're happy with the life you've chosen, I don't understand it, but I'm happy for you, and I'm okay with it." A tender look passed between them, as Hattie reached out and touched her hand.

"I'm a nurse too, don't forget that. I love the hospital work I do. My best years were at the orphanage in Kenya. Maybe it was a little bit like this house is for you. Being there healed a lot of my old wounds. I'd like to go back again one day, if they'd send me. But for now I'm satisfied with what I'm doing. And maybe we can see each other from time to time." Hattie really hoped so. She had missed her so much.

"Do you want to spend the night?" Melissa asked her gently, and Hattie answered with regret.

"I can't. I promised I'd be back tonight, and I'm on duty at the hospital tomorrow. They're short-staffed and I can't let them down." Melissa nodded, and understood. She was grateful for the time they'd had.

"Next time. I want you to come up again," Melissa said. "But I'm never going to turn this into a convent retreat," she said, and they both laughed. It had been an important day for both of them, and explained some things that Hattie had never fully understood before. She was horrified by Melissa's story about the convent in Ireland where she had given birth to her first baby and given her up. Hattie suspected that it would haunt Melissa until her dying day. She wished that she could do something about it, but it was too late. Melissa had lost both her children, and she had to find a way to live with it. She seemed as though she had, but it had marked her deeply, just as events in Hattie's life had marked her. Life was like that, and they both knew it. The old wounds healed eventually, but the scars remained. And Melissa was deeply scarred by the baby she had given up at sixteen. There was no guilt involved in Robbie's death, they had done everything they could for him and it had been a cruel turn of fate. But she would feel forever guilty for giving up a baby girl named Ashley, and allowing the nuns to take her away and sell her to strangers. Her mother had made it happen so she wouldn't be embarrassed with her friends. There were some things Melissa could never forgive, and Hattie had paid a price for it too. Melissa's profound hatred of nuns as a result had separated them for years.

They spent the rest of the day walking around the property, and sat at the edge of the stream, with their feet dangling in the cool water. Melissa served her a hearty lunch, and packed some fruit and snacks for her, and a sandwich for the drive back.

They hugged each other and meant it for the first time in years. They had cleared the air, as much as it was possible, and no longer blamed each other for the choices they had made and things they hadn't done. Some of it just couldn't be helped. In different ways, their mother's zealous Catholicism had marked both of them. But in spite of all of it, they still loved each other.

Melissa stood in the driveway and waved as Hattie drove away. It had been a perfect day for both of them, and some old mysteries had been explained and ghosts laid to rest.

Hattie saw her in the rearview mirror as she headed toward the road and waved. Melissa was standing there, still strong and tall and beautiful, as she always had been, no matter how badly she had been injured, or how scarred she was as a result. In all the important ways, she hadn't changed. They were still sisters. There was only one thing Hattie wished that she could do for her now. It seemed impossible, but maybe it was feasible. As she drove back to New York, thinking of the sister who had done so much for her when they were young, she knew she had to try, no matter how impossible it seemed.

Chapter 4

Hattie had been called Sister Mary Joseph for the last eighteen years, which her sister, Melissa, had continued to ignore. Her friends in the convent called her Mary Joe, and those closest to her simply "Joe," but her convent life didn't exist to Melissa. Hattie thought about her older sister constantly for the week after their visit, and sent her an email, telling her what a lovely time she'd had and how much it meant to her. Melissa responded warmly for the first time in years.

Her confessions had brought them closer, and had given Hattie new insights into Melissa. She had known about the baby she had given up for adoption, but had never realized the hell she'd been through while she was away, or that she still mourned the baby girl thirty-three years later, and how deeply she regretted giving her up. She had no idea that Melissa had reached out to the convent, and that finding her now was beyond hope, with all the records destroyed in the cover-up. Hattie didn't like the sound of it, and hoped that it wasn't as mercenary and sinister as Melissa thought. It didn't sound like a proud moment for the Church.

Fearing she would lose her beloved home in the recent fire had humbled Melissa somehow and made her feel vulnerable again, something she hadn't felt in a long time. She was more open as a result, and grateful to see the sister she had shunned for nearly two decades. Hattie had seemed as sweet and kind and innocent during their visit as she always had been, and Melissa thought about her a lot in the ensuing days.

Hattie was tormented by what she had learned, and finally went to see the mother superior about it. She knew what she wanted to do, but had no idea if they would allow it. It seemed unlikely, but she was a dedicated serious member of their religious community, and had never asked for anything before. She had given all her worldly goods to the Church when she entered the convent, much to her older sister's disapproval. She had even given up the little she had left of what her parents had left her. She had spent a good part of it on college, as her parents intended, and acting lessons to further her budding career as an actress. But she willingly gave up what she had when she took her vows of poverty, chastity, and obedience. There was a very small trust left that she couldn't assign to the Church and would go to Melissa or her heirs when Hattie died, and if Melissa had no heirs and predeceased Hattie, only then would the remaining money in the trust go to the Church. Hattie had never touched a penny of it and it was still intact. She had written a will, leaving the small amount in trust to Robbie, and then changed it to Melissa after he died according to the conditions of the trust, and to the Church, if Melissa didn't outlive her. Melissa was not in need of money, but it was all Hattie had to leave her. Hattie had never requested to take money out of the trust and intended it all to go to her sister. But if the mother superior allowed her to use it now, it would be a gift of sorts to Melissa in her lifetime, and put to good use.

The mother superior, Mother Elizabeth, was a stern woman, but she cared deeply for the nuns she was responsible for, and was fair, even if strict. The younger nuns were in awe of her, and afraid of the punishments she meted out for serious infractions, but the nuns who'd been there for longer, and were wise to her ways, knew her better and loved her. She was a role model for them all, a traditionalist, but compassionate as well. Hattie had no idea how the older nun would react to what she had to say. She made an appointment to meet with her early one morning, before Hattie left for work. Hattie had thought of the trust on her drive back to New York after she saw Melissa.

"Peace be with you," the mother superior said as Hattie entered her office, and Mother Elizabeth invited her to sit down. It made Hattie feel like a novice again, or even a postulant. She seemed worried, as the older nun smiled at her. "What can I do for you?" They saw each other constantly, but all of the nuns were busy, most of them were nurses or teachers, and she couldn't remember Hattie ever asking to see her. She quietly observed the way Sister Mary Joseph fingered the rosary beads at her waist as they spoke.

"I'd like to take a trip, Mother," Hattie said in a trembling voice. It had been years since she'd been able to make her own decisions and do as she chose, and she knew this was a big request to make.

"A trip?" Mother Elizabeth looked puzzled. "What kind of trip? A retreat of some kind?" She knew how much the younger nun had loved her years in Africa, and wondered if she wanted to go back for a visit. It wouldn't have surprised her. She had a gift for dealing with young children, and had embraced the ravaged children she had worked with there.

"Not a retreat, Mother. I'd like to go to Ireland."

"For a vacation?" The location surprised her. They had a house in the Adirondacks where they all spent two weeks in the summer. They swam and played tennis and went for long walks. But none of the nuns went to Europe for a vacation, and certainly not on their own. And this wasn't a pilgrimage to Lourdes, Jerusalem, or Rome.

"Not a vacation either." Hattie realized with a sinking heart that there would be no way to convince the mother superior unless she told her the truth, the real reason she wanted to go. "It's kind of a long story. It's something I want to do for my sister. She took care of me after our parents died. I was only twelve and I owe her a lot. She had a baby out of wedlock at sixteen. Our parents, really my mother, sent her to Ireland, to a convent there, to have the baby and put it up for adoption. It was thirty-three years ago. She married eventually, at thirty-two, and had a little boy. He died of a brain tumor six years ago. She never recovered. She gave up her marriage and a successful career, and became a recluse. I saw her for the first time in six years two weeks ago, and we talked about the baby she gave up." Sister Mary Joseph didn't want to malign the convent in Ireland the way Melissa had, so she was careful about what she said. Mother Elizabeth was a staunch defender of the Church, and their sister nuns all over the world.

"A lot of young girls who got in trouble went to Ireland to disappear for a while, or to England to the mother and baby homes there, as they called them. The convents there were well set up to take care of them, and handled the adoptions for them. It was often the best solution for the girls and their parents. They left their babies there and came home, and resumed their lives, and no one knew what had happened," the superior explained, "and they placed the infants in good homes, from what I've heard. The English mother and baby homes were often privately owned and not run as responsibly."

"That's pretty much what happened to my sister at the convent in Ireland. Except now she has lost her son, and the baby she gave up. She tried to contact the convent, to see if she could meet her daughter now, as an adult. She'd be thirty-three years old, but she was told that all the records have been destroyed by a fire. She has no way of finding out where her daughter is. She was adopted by Americans. That's all she knows. And that they were going to call her Ashley. It was all she was told about them."

"I'm sure the nuns in Ireland who handled those adoptions chose good parents for her. She can be assured of that," the mother superior said through pursed lips.

"Even the state has changed their rules about not contacting the children women gave up for adoption. Many people have found their birth parents through the Internet. But there is no way for my sister to find out anything if the records were destroyed." Hattie didn't imply that Melissa believed the fire was intentional, but the superior seemed to know about it.

"I've heard stories that the records were destroyed. I think the nuns in charge of those convents thought it was for the best, to let the past stay buried. Many people never even told their children that they were adopted in those days. And many of those

young girls never told their husbands and subse-
quent children that they'd given up a baby for adoption when they were teenagers. The truth can cause
a great deal of damage."

"My sister says she told her husband before they
got married. And she's alone now. I think it would
help her recover from her losses if I could find out
something about her daughter and put her mind at
rest. Mother, I'd like to go to Ireland and visit the
convent where she gave the baby up, near Dublin,
and maybe some of the other convents, to see if any
of those records survived or any of the nuns remember something about her."

"It's a needle in a haystack, Sister Mary Joe," the
superior said with a disapproving look. "And if you
did find something out, what if it disrupts her daughter's life to have her birth mother show up? The
records were destroyed with good reason, and un-
doubtedly a great deal of thought." But Hattie wondered what they were thinking now. Was Melissa
right? Had they only destroyed the records to protect
the Church? Melissa had called those convents baby
mills, that had been run for profit, not just with good
motives to provide babies for childless couples to
adopt. All of the adopting couples had been rich, according to her sister, and a great deal of money had
ended up in the hands of the Church. But she didn't
say that to Mother Elizabeth, or Hattie knew she'd
turn her down. She didn't want to make trouble for

the convents. All she wanted was to help her sister find the baby she had given up, and had regretted all her life. Or at least find out something about where the baby had gone.

"I'm not proposing to make contact with her daughter, if I'm lucky enough to find out where she is, or where she went. I just want to find the information. It will be up to my sister after that. She may not have the courage to contact her, but at least she would know something about her, who adopted her and where she grew up."

"I'm not sure I believe in raising the ghosts of the past," Mother Elizabeth said. But she could see the distress in Hattie's eyes and how much she cared about her sister. "And how would you propose to pay for the trip? We don't have funds for anything like that, and I can't justify it to the bishop on our books. I suppose your sister would be willing to pay for the trip."

Hattie shook her head. "She doesn't know that I want to go. I don't want to raise her hopes, and then disappoint her if I can't find anything out."

"Which is more than likely," Mother Elizabeth reminded her.

"I have a small trust left from my parents. I wasn't able to transfer it to the Church. I had to follow the conditions of the trust. I left it for the benefit of my nephew when I took my vows, and to my sister, if anything happened to him. I've never touched it, and it could cover the trip."

"And how long would this take?"

"Maybe a few weeks. I could go when all the sisters go to the lake house in the Adirondacks, if you allow it." The superior sat silently for several minutes, thinking, while Hattie waited, praying that she would look favorably on the request.

"This is a very unusual proposal, Sister. I'd have to send you alone. I can't spare anyone to go with you. We need all the younger sisters to help with the older ones at the lake. And I want to remind you of how quickly people jump to criticize the Church, unjustly. There have been stories about those convents, trying to malign them, claiming there was greed and profit involved. I am certain that's not true. Only grateful people donating honestly to the Church. I don't want you getting caught up in any controversy, or becoming confused about our motives and theirs. Those nuns who ran the convents that took those young girls in provided a loving service to all concerned, homes for the babies no one wanted, and a place where the unwed mothers could take refuge, to spare their reputations, and their families'. The couples who were unable to have children of their own went home with an infant in their arms, to give them a solid future and a good life. The motives involved were entirely pure. But I also understand your wish to help your sister find her way back from a very dark place. Losing her son must have been heartbreaking for her. Did their marriage recover?"

Hattie shook her head in answer. "He left her and married someone else. She didn't fight it. She was frozen in grief at the time, and she's alone." Hattie had the feeling that if Melissa had remarried, Mother Elizabeth wouldn't have looked favorably on the request. She didn't want to indulge curiosity or a whim, but she was willing to help heal the broken heart of a mother who had lost both husband and son. And maybe, as Hattie hoped, this would help, although nothing would bring her sister's son back, or turn back the clock for the baby girl she'd given up. But perhaps the truth would free her aching heart. It was the only reason Mother Elizabeth would allow Sister Mary Joseph to go.

The mother superior looked stern for a moment. "I would prefer that you not discuss this with anyone, Sister. We will say that you are going on a mission for the order, and we are sending you to visit a convent in Ireland to carry it out. Whatever you discover, you are not to discuss it with the Sisters here when you come back. This is a personal mission, which is very unusual. But I know how hard you work at the hospital, how much you do for our community, and the miracles you managed, saving children's lives at the hospital in Kenya. I won't agree to anything like this again. Is that understood?"

"Yes, Mother," she said obediently. Her heart was

beating furiously in her chest. She didn't know how she'd done it, but she had convinced her and gotten approval for the trip.

"And anything unpleasant you discover, if that should happen, remains between us. You may go when we move to the lake house, and I want you back in two weeks, three weeks at the absolute most. And I want you to report in to me periodically while you're away. Don't just wander around Ireland like a free spirit. You're to stay at the convents you visit, not in local hotels. I will give you a letter from me, sanctioning your mission, but not explaining what it is. Remember who you are, and where your loyalties lie now. *We* are your family. You are engaging in a compassionate mission for your sister. But she is no longer your primary allegiance. We are Sisters in Christ, as you are also with the nuns in the convents you'll be visiting. You must remain loyal to them too. This is not a fact-finding mission, to criticize what happened in those convents long ago. You are looking for information about the child your sister gave up, and that's all. Keep that in mind when you go."

"Yes, Mother, I will." But from what she said, Hattie could easily figure out that the mother superior had heard things about those convents too. Most of it had happened before her day, but they must have still been in operation when she was young in the order herself. No matter how pure they were supposed to be, there were always rumors and gossip in the Church. Even those committed to the religious life were human too. It had been true when the rumors began about guilty priests. It was human nature to talk. And even convents weren't exempt from gossips. In fact sometimes quite the reverse. And there had been whispers about the mother and baby homes for years.

Hattie left her office a few minutes later, and nearly flew. She kissed the mother superior's hand before she left the room, and smiled broadly all the way to work. There was no one for her to tell. She didn't want Melissa to know what she was doing, in case nothing turned up other than what Melissa already knew. And she had promised not to tell her fellow nuns. Only she and the mother superior would know what she was doing.

The nuns were talking about their upcoming vacation at the lake at dinner that night, and Hattie quietly said she couldn't go. She said that the mother superior was sending her on a mission for the length of their stay and the others were all sorry for her to miss out on their vacation, but they praised her for the sacrifice she had agreed to make. Hattie felt guilty lying to them, but was thrilled to be going. And she prayed she'd find something out to soothe her sister's aching heart after so many years.

She called the bank the next day, and identified herself as Harriet Stevens, which felt strange. She hadn't used that name in eighteen years. She explained that she needed to make a withdrawal from her trust. The amount that was available to her in her lifetime had been accruing interest for years. She was startled to learn that the amount had increased considerably. It wasn't a large fortune, but it was more than enough for the trip, and quite a lot more. The banker asked if she wanted it put in a checking or savings account, but she didn't have either. As a nun, she didn't need a bank account, and wasn't allowed to have one. She agreed to come in and open a checking account, and transfer some of the money into it that she would use to pay for her plane ticket, and have cash for her expenses on the trip. She was planning to be frugal, and would be staying at convents anyway, so she wouldn't have to pay for meals or hotels.

By the time the Sisters left for the lake, which was a complicated exodus with several elderly nuns in wheelchairs, and the younger nuns excited about swimming and fishing and playing tennis for two weeks, Hattie was ready for her trip. Except for the oldest nuns, they would be out of their habits for the entire time at the lake. And Hattie planned to wear ordinary clothes traveling in Ireland too.

Hattie was packed and ready the night before they left. She packed two of her habits in case the nuns in Ireland were sticklers and insisted on it, and for the rest she had packed simple clothes, plain shirts, sneakers and jeans, and a jacket if the evenings got cool.

She helped them onto the buses the next day, and the mother superior gave her a long look, and a hug.

"Take care of yourself, Sister Mary Joe. And good luck." She sounded sincere when she said it.

"Thank you, Mother, for letting me go," Hattie whispered to her. In many ways, being in the convent was an extension of her childhood, which was why she had taken refuge there, after her early forays as an actress. She had rapidly discovered that that world wasn't for her, and this was the safest one she could think of. She couldn't rely on her sister to shield her forever. Melissa had never understood it, but it suited her well. She had been cured of wanting the career she had dreamed of, and being a nurse suited her better. The order had chosen well for her. The past eighteen years had been a rewarding life she never regretted. She was a little frightened now thinking of being out in the world again, on her own. She was doing it for Melissa. Nothing else would have given her the courage to travel alone to Ireland. She lived entirely surrounded by women, except for a few priests, and it was comfortable. In her nursing habit at work, she knew she was almost invisible to the doctors at the hospital, and the male patients she nursed. They forgot she was a woman, and an attractive one. They no longer wore the habit when they weren't working, on weekends, but she wore a starched pure white habit at work, and had worn it in Africa too. And she wore jeans and T-shirts at home on her days off. Leaving for the airport that night, she felt naked in jeans, a shirt, and blazer, with her red hair cut short. She was no longer used to blending in with other women and hadn't thought of herself that way since she was twenty-five.

She had purchased a seat in economy on a less expensive airline for the flight to Dublin. And she would be going from convent to convent, so she wouldn't be alone in hotels. So she felt relatively safe. It was the first time she would be traveling alone since she entered the order. When she went to Kenya, she had gone with a group of nursing nuns, and a priest to chaperone them. And once in Africa, she lived in the confines of a religious community.

She felt strangely free after she checked in, wandering around the airport, waiting to board her flight. She had called Melissa the night before, and told her that she would be out of touch for a few weeks. She said she was going on a retreat, and Melissa sounded annoyed.

"I don't see you for six years, and now you're abandoning me to go on a retreat?"

"I won't be gone long," Hattie reassured her, touched that Melissa cared. They felt closer again after her visit to the Berkshires. Everything Melissa had shared with her had spawned this trip. And just as the mother superior had said, she was on a mission, but not the one she claimed to the other nuns, or the retreat she told Melissa she was going on. Her mission was to find Ashley, a needle in a haystack, as Mother Elizabeth had said. Hattie was praying she'd be lucky, or that some miracle would occur and that she'd find some piece of information to put Melissa's heart and mind at rest. Finding Ashley, or some trace of her, was all she cared about, hoping to bring mother and daughter together. That would have been the greatest gift of all, and Hattie's fondest wish.

As the plane took off, headed for Dublin, her mission had begun. Hattie closed her eyes and prayed with all her heart and soul that it would be a success.

Chapter 5

When the plane landed at Dublin Airport, she only had a carry-on, and walked outside the airport to catch a bus to Port Laoise an hour outside Dublin. She had exchanged emails with the office of the convent, and they had agreed to let her spend the night, and told her which bus to take to get there.

The scenery was plain. It could have been anywhere, as they rolled along, and it occurred to her that this was the same road her sister had been on when she had come to Saint Blaise's. Melissa must have been terrified as a pregnant teenager, banished from her home, and sent to a foreign country to give birth and relinquish her baby. Hattie's heart ached for her as she thought about it, and how devastated she must have been. It made Hattie want to put her arms around her and hug her. She had only been ten years old at the time, with no understanding of what her sister had gone through, although she had overheard her fighting with their mother, and knew that Melissa was pregnant and had to go away. Hattie had been sworn to secrecy by their mother after she heard.

She had seen Melissa crying uncontrollably the day she left, and begging their parents to let her stay. Their mother's face had been hard, and she kept telling Melissa she was a disgrace. After she left, Hattie went to her room and cried too. She was going to miss her sister for the seven or eight months they said she'd be gone, nearly a whole school year. But Melissa was going to go to school at the convent in Ireland so she didn't miss a year. It was her junior year in high school. Melissa had always wanted to go away to college in California, but in the end, she went to Columbia, so she could stay home and take care of Hattie. Her dreams of California went out the window when first their mother and then their father died, within a year of each other. Their mother died of stomach cancer, and their father of what the doctor called "liver trouble," which years later, Hattie realized, meant he was an alcoholic. He had kept it quiet, and Hattie never suspected it, but Melissa knew. She saw him drinking at night, and their mother accused him of being an embarrassment and a failure, a useless husband and a bum, when he got fired from jobs again and again, while his inheritance from his parents continued to dwindle. He still had enough to support them and pay for private school for his daughters, but their mother worried that the money wouldn't last forever. Hattie was aware even as a child that being married to their mother couldn't have been easy. She was openly critical of him and demeaned him in front of the children. It was one more thing for Melissa to hate her for. Her father came from a good family, but had never been successful at anything, including his banking jobs, and went through most of his money. He left his daughters enough to get by on, if they managed carefully and weren't extravagant. And he left a sizable life insurance policy that lasted until Hattie went into the convent, and Melissa's books took off. After that the insurance money was gone, and except for the small trusts both sisters had received, which Hattie still had and had never touched until now.

Their mother came from a less wealthy background, and her parents had left her nothing when they died in an accident, so she had to drop out of college and go to work as a secretary. But she had been beautiful and sexy when she was young, and caught their father's eye when she worked at the same bank he did. His family never approved of her, and she was bitter about that too. He still managed to support them on what was left of his inheritance, despite his drinking and the jobs he lost, but he couldn't provide the easy life and luxuries his wife had hoped for when she married him. But she never had to work during their marriage. They had also inherited his parents' Park Avenue co-op apartment, where they lived until Melissa sold it after their parents' deaths and moved to a small West Side apartment with Hattie. Melissa had handled their finances well.

Their father was a gentle man, but they led a small life, while he drank heavily at night, and all day between jobs. While her parents were alive, Hattie hid in the room she shared with her sister so she didn't have to hear their parents fight. But Melissa knew it all. Her mother blamed her father for Melissa's pregnancy, and said that if he was a better father, supervised his daughters better, and was sober, it wouldn't have happened. Melissa tried to tell him it wasn't his fault. She was just looking for love, but he refused to discuss it with her and let his wife decide what to do about it. He paid to send her away, and when she came back, he acted like nothing had happened. Her mother told Melissa it was her fault she had gotten stomach cancer, from all the worry and shame she caused her. People whispered about them, because of his drinking. And to her dying day, she blamed her husband and oldest daughter for her illness. He died less than a year later, and was in a coma for the last month of his life, after a drinking binge, so the girls never got to say goodbye, and tell him they loved him. As an adult, Melissa felt her mother's own venom had killed her. She had been a bitterly unhappy, dissatisfied woman all her life. Melissa wrote about her in her books, and about the weak father who had given up and died. Both girls felt sorry for their father. He had been a frightened, defeated, sad man, a failure in life and in his wife's eyes. It had made Melissa a fighter, and made Hattie long for a safe haven, which she had found at last when she took her vows. Nothing could touch her in the convent.

When they got to the bus terminal, Hattie took a cab to Saint Blaise's, and it loomed out of the darkness like the prison Melissa had described. It made Hattie shudder. She couldn't even imagine what it must have felt like to Melissa as a frightened teenager far from home for the first time, facing unknown terrors and agony in the months to come.

Hattie had already missed dinner when she rang the convent bell, and an elderly nun with a cane came to answer. She had a kind smile, and Hattie explained who she was, and the old nun looked startled.

"I thought you were a nun."

"I am, Sister. I'm sorry. We don't wear the habit most of the time now. I've got it with me in my suitcase."

"Things must be very modern in America," she said, and hobbled into the dark hallways with Hattie behind her. "You're up the stairs, third floor, first room to the right. The door is open. The WC is at the end of the hall. Mass is at five-thirty, breakfast at six-fifteen in the refectory."

"Thank you, Sister," Hattie said, as she walked up the stairs with her bag. It looked like a perfect setting for a ghost story or a horror movie. The room was grim and bare when she walked in and closed the door softly behind her. The place was every bit as dismal as Melissa had said, although she said that the girls lived in dormitories, with as many as twenty to a room, and Hattie wondered if they even existed anymore. It was a home for older nuns now, and Hattie doubted that they housed them in dormitories, but more likely in cells like the one she was in.

She lay in bed that night, thinking of her sister, no longer surprised by how angry she had been at their mother, and how bitter about the experience ever since. She had been a happy young girl before that, although somewhat introverted and bookish, and an angry woman when she returned, seething with rage at her mother.

Hattie set the alarm she had brought with her for five A.M., and when it woke her, she showered and dressed in her habit. Although it was August, the convent was damp and chilly. There were only two other nuns on her floor. She arrived at Mass promptly at five-thirty, slipped into a pew, and quietly observed the community of nuns who lived there, some of them her age, others much older, and a few earnest-looking young ones, about thirty-five in all. The elderly nuns who lived there now no longer came to Mass at that hour and were exempt, and there were many of them, she had been told.

Breakfast in the refectory was a silent meal, according to ancient tradition, and a far cry from the convent where Sister Mary Joseph lived. She was used to the babble of conversation at breakfast, before everyone rushed off to their day at work in schools and hospitals around the city.

She had an appointment with Saint Blaise's mother superior at nine A.M., and went back to her room for two hours to pray. She hoped for some little wisp of information that she could use to warm a trail toward Melissa's daughter, but the meeting was discouraging. The mother superior was a woman in her early sixties who had only been there for two years, and said she knew little about the adoptions that had taken place so long ago. She confirmed that there wasn't a shred of the records left, and told Hattie that there was no way to reconstruct them now, since there had been no copies of the records and documents, to protect everyone's privacy, including her sister's.

"They didn't want it leaking out about who had been here. And the adoptive parents wanted confidentiality too. It served everyone's interests to keep it all secret, and dispose of the records once they no longer served any purpose to those concerned," she said firmly, obviously convinced.

"But what about the girls who wanted to know what had happened to their babies, or the children themselves once they became adults? It's inhumane that they have no way of finding anything out."

"They gave up their babies, and signed away all right to know," the mother superior said coldly.

"As children themselves, the young mothers had no idea how it would impact them later. I believe that in some cases, it ruined their lives. Are there no nuns left who were here at the time and might remember something?" Hattie asked, feeling desperate. The needle in the haystack was proving to be as elusive as she had feared.

The mother superior was pleasant but firm, and offered her no hope. Hattie changed out of her habit and went for a walk afterward to clear her head, and figure out what to do next. There were three other convents on her list to visit, one only two hours away, but Saint Blaise's was where Melissa had been, and it frustrated her that the trail here was so cold. She was hoping that even one nun from the old days might have been transferred to one of the other convents where adoptions had taken place, and still be there, and might remember something about Melissa and her baby, and her adoptive parents. It was a long shot, to say the least. But it was all she had to go on, with no information at Saint Blaise's.

She wandered into the neighboring village on her walk. It was still early and the shops weren't open yet, but the librarian was sweeping off the front steps of the library and had just opened the doors. Not knowing what else to do, Hattie walked in, and smiled at the librarian when she came to the desk after her sweeping. She was a tall thin woman with a sharp face, who glanced at Hattie with suspicion, and recognized immediately that she was a stranger in their midst. She looked old enough to have been there when Saint Blaise's was an adoption mill, and Hattie decided to be bold and take the chance, and dove in.

"Have you worked here long?" Hattie asked her, trying to sound casual.

"Long enough. Why do you want to know?"

"I'm curious about Saint Blaise's," Hattie said, getting right to the point. "A friend of my mother's adopted a baby here."

"A lot of people did. Americans mostly. Rich ones, and even some movie stars. Everybody around here knows that. It's not a secret." No, but everything else about it was. "You're American," she added. "Was your mother's friend a movie star?"

Hattie smiled at that. "No, but they had money. I understand people paid the Church a fortune for those babies." As she said it, she could see the librarian bristle.

"Are you a reporter?"

"No, I'm not." She thought of telling her she was a nun, but decided it was a bad idea.

"Every few years, someone goes on a witch hunt about those adoptions. Ever since that traitor wrote a book about it, and left the Church."

"There's a book?" Hattie asked her. The only one she knew of was the one Melissa had mentioned, written by a reporter. But when Hattie had asked her sister about it, she couldn't remember the author or the title and said she had thrown it away.

"It's garbage. All lies. Banned by the Church," the librarian answered. "She was one of the nuns here back then, and then she turned on them. You're not a Catholic, are you?" she asked Hattie accusingly.

"Yes, I am," Hattie said simply.

"Then you shouldn't be snooping around what doesn't concern you, and happened a long time ago, and trying to vilify the Church. They did a good thing for all those unfortunate, sinful girls, and put the babies in good homes. That's all that matters. The rest is nobody's business."

"What's the name of the book?" Hattie persisted.

"*Babies for Sale.* Catholics aren't allowed to read it. And a good Catholic wouldn't want to."

"Thank you," Hattie said politely, and walked out of the small library as the woman stared at her angrily.

Hattie walked farther into the village and stopped at a bookstore. A young girl was dusting off the books as Hattie walked in and asked if she had a copy of the book the librarian had mentioned. She wondered if it was out of print. The girl said she'd check in the back, and returned a few minutes later with a dusty copy. She grinned mischievously.

"We're not supposed to have it. It's banned by the Church, but the owner likes keeping books like that in the back. I think it's about some scandal around here." Hattie paid for it, put it in her purse, and walked back to the convent. She sat in the garden reading it, as younger nuns brought the elderly ones in wheelchairs outdoors to get a little morning sun. Hattie was so engrossed in the book she barely noticed them. The book was written by a woman named Fiona Eckles, and the blurb on the back said that she had questioned her vocation after serving at Saint Blaise's as a nurse and midwife, and ultimately left the Church. It said she taught literature at Dublin University now. In the photograph, she looked to be in her late sixties, if the photo was recent. The book was only a few years old. It said it had taken her years to write about it. The few pages Hattie read corroborated what her sister had said about Saint Blaise's and the adoptions that took place there.

Hattie called Dublin information on the cellphone she had rented at the airport. She got Fiona Eckles's phone number, and left her a message. She was packing her bag when the author called her, and Hattie asked if she could meet with her, about her book.

Fiona Eckles hesitated for an instant, and asked if she was a reporter. Hattie said she wasn't, but that her sister had been at Saint Blaise's in the late 1980s.

"I was there then, but I doubt if I can provide much information. I delivered the babies, but I was never privy to the records or the names of the adopting parents." She said she'd had calls like this one before, from women desperate for information about where their babies had gone. "My fellow nuns covered their tracks pretty well. That was part of the deal. Some of the couples who adopted were very well known. We recognized the movie stars, but not the others. It was a booming business for a while. The Church doesn't want anyone talking about it. If I hadn't left, they probably would have excommunicated me," she said with a wry laugh. "I couldn't stay after what I'd seen." Hattie wondered if she knew Melissa or would have remembered her. She had brought a photograph of Melissa at sixteen, just in case. She kept several photographs of her and their parents at the convent in New York.

Fiona agreed to meet with her at six o'clock that night, in a hotel lobby in Dublin. After the call, Hattie walked around the convent, to get a better feel of it in the daylight. It was just as grim and depressing as it was at night. She left a note for the mother superior, thanking her for allowing her to stay, with a small donation for the convent. She picked up her bag then, and called for a taxi to take her to the bus terminal. She caught a bus to Dublin, and checked in to a small hotel in time to meet Fiona Eckles at the Harding Hotel for a drink. She couldn't wait to meet her now and hear what she had to say. She felt mildly guilty for staying at a hotel, but didn't have time to contact a convent, despite her promise to Mother Elizabeth.

Hattie recognized the woman easily from the photograph on the book. Fiona Eckles had short snowy white hair and bright blue eyes. She had a ready smile and laugh lines around her eyes. She looked like a happy person, not a tortured soul, and like a well-dressed grandmother in a navy linen suit. She had a trim figure. Hattie thought she might be seventy by then, and nothing about her style or demeanor suggested that she'd ever been a nun. She could have been a banker or an executive, and had been a college professor now for many years. She wrote nonfiction, and had published a total of four controversial books, the most recent one about wayward priests. It had been a bestseller. The writing style was simple, clear, and direct.

"I hope I can help you," Fiona Eckles said kindly when they sat down, "but I doubt I can. I delivered hundreds of babies, maybe a thousand, while I was at Saint Blaise's. The uncomplicated ones. The high-risk cases went to the hospital, and were seen by a doctor. And I had very little contact with the girls until they were in labor, and I knew nothing at all about the adopting parents, and never met them. Except the movie stars of course. There were a number of those. We all recognized them, and it always provided a buzz around the place when one of them showed up. We knew who they were even when they used false names."

"My sister was there in 1988," Hattie said, after their initial introductions, and they each ordered a glass of wine.

"I was there then, delivering babies night and day."

"My sister calls it a baby mill."

"She isn't wrong," Fiona Eckles said with a small sigh. "In the end, I thought that too. They brought them in, they made them work and go to school, delivered their babies, and charged their parents a hefty fee for keeping the girls there for several months. Then they took their babies, collected a huge fee from the adopting parents, for the Church of course, and sent the girls home two weeks after they delivered as though nothing had happened. No therapy, no counseling, just in the stirrups and out the door, while a lot of money changed hands, from wealthy people who couldn't have babies of their own. I guess it suited everyone's needs at the time. But I know from talking to them when they were in labor that a lot of those girls didn't want to give their babies up, but they had no other choice. Their parents wouldn't let them come home until they did.

One girl went on a hunger strike and nearly died, and refused to sign the papers. She did in the end, though. They all did. It broke my heart to see the look on their faces when we took the babies away minutes after we delivered them. I tried to at least let the girls see them, and hold them when I could get away with it. Our orders were to take the babies away immediately, with no contact between mother and child, after everything they'd been through. We practiced natural childbirth, so there was less liability for us. The adoptive parents were usually waiting in the nursery. That was the end of it for the girls from that point on. They had no contact with their babies, no chance to hold them or say goodbye. It was very traumatic for most of the girls. All of them probably.

"After a while, I just couldn't do it, it was too painful to watch, worse than labor and delivery. I let the nursing nuns take the babies from them. I couldn't. I gave up midwifery and the Church when I left. In a way, it destroyed me too. I recovered, but it took a long time, and I never really forgave myself for being part of it. We had very strict orders about our protocols. That's why I wrote the book. I wanted to make people aware, and maybe to get absolution. The Church claimed we were providing a noble service, but they never admitted how much money they made. I think we'd be even more horrified if we knew how much they made in all those years."

"Were there local girls there too?" Hattie asked her.

"Very few. Most of their parents couldn't afford it. There were a few socialites and aristocrats from London, the occasional French girl, or Spaniard or Italian, but mainly Americans. They could pay more to send their daughters away, and the Americans who adopted the babies liked adopting from other Americans. It was mainly a business for the Church."

"Why did they burn the records?" Hattie asked in a sad voice. She hated to think of what her sister had been through.

"Why do you think? So no one could be contacted, no one would talk. The girls' parents didn't want anyone to know their daughters had given birth out of wedlock. And a lot of the adopting parents often pretended the babies were their own. They disappeared for six months, and then suddenly reappeared with a baby. Burning the records protected everyone, including the Church for what they'd made. They did it for decades, long before I got there, and when I realized what was happening, and how it was handled, I finally gave up and left. It took me another year to give up my vows and ask to be released. It soured me forever on everything I believed about the goodness and innocence of the Church. I didn't want to be part of it. It turned my years as a nun into a travesty. I felt as though I did more harm than good and had been part of a cabal to coerce those girls into giving up babies they wanted. Their parents didn't even show up to pick them up after what they'd been through. We just put them on a plane and sent them home, two weeks after delivery. Stand 'em up and out the door. Next. It was heartless and profitable. Be careful," she warned Hattie, "if you read too much about it, it may do the same to you. I didn't want to be part of a church that did things like that for pure profit. Maybe, if they'd done it for free, out of ignorance and some archaic beliefs, I could have forgiven them. But not for profit to the degree it was. I'm sure there were some innocents involved, but the nuns who ran Saint Blaise's then knew what they were doing. They didn't care at all about the girls, just about the babies they could sell to rich, desperate couples. The truth is ugly," she said in a matter-of-fact voice, but her eyes were sad when she talked about the girls.

Hattie showed her the photograph of Melissa at sixteen then, and Fiona shook her head. "I'm sorry, but I don't remember her. The only thing I remember about that year is who the movie stars were that we gave babies to. I think there were three major stars that year." She named them, and Hattie was startled by who they were. All three were very famous Hollywood actresses. "If you do some research, you might dig something up that way. See who adopted daughters. It might be a backhanded way to find your sister's child, if she was adopted by a major Hollywood figure. If not, I don't think there's any way to track her down. There are still some nuns around who were part of it, but most of them are ancient now. The really old ones have died, and they've spread the living ones around. I tried to find them when I wrote the book, but I found very few, and none of them would talk to me. The Church tried to discredit me, and claimed that I was psychiatrically unbalanced, but they didn't get far with that. The bottom line is that it's not a pretty thing the Church did, however good their original intentions were, and they don't want anyone to know about it. It's been swept under the rug, and they won't tolerate anyone uncovering it now. It doesn't make them look good. That's why they burned the records. They had too much to hide to preserve them." It was a wartime tactic, and it worked. All evidence that might have led to Melissa's baby had turned to ash in the fire.

They talked for a while then about the future of the Church, and Hattie's work in Africa. Two hours after they had met, Hattie and Fiona Eckles parted, and Hattie thanked her for all the information she'd provided.

"Check out those movie stars, and see if you can find anything out that way," Fiona encouraged her. "It's worth a shot."

"I will," Hattie promised, and stopped at an Internet café on the way back to her hotel. She signed on, and googled the names of the three actresses Fiona had mentioned. The first one had been dead for fifteen years, but it mentioned that her daughter was an actress too, and had starred in a recent film. She was the right age. The other two stars were still alive, one had retired recently, the other was still working, and nothing was said about their children. But all three were leads that Hattie intended to follow up on. If Melissa's baby hadn't been adopted by a famous actress, the trail would end there. But in the meantime, there was always hope that Ashley had been one of the lucky ones adopted by a famous mother, which would make her easier to find. Hattie printed out the information and went back to her hotel.

She had nightmares that night about her sister as a teenager, screaming in pain during the delivery, and nuns running away with her baby while she tried to crawl after them and couldn't. Hattie awoke in the throes of a rising wave of panic, crying for Melissa. And like Fiona, it made her feel guilty by association. How could nuns do something like that? The venal cruelty of it all overwhelmed Hattie and made her suddenly ashamed to be a nun. She wanted to throw her habit away. She wanted to go home to the safety of her convent, but she couldn't yet. She was on a mission, and had a job to do. She knew she had to follow it through to the end. She didn't know if she would ever tell Melissa all that she had learned. But she loved her as never before for all that she'd endured. And Hattie knew what she had to do next.

She couldn't go back to New York, at least not yet. She had to go to L.A., and track down the two living actresses, and the three adopted children if they had been born in 1988.

In the morning, she exchanged her return ticket to New York for one from Dublin to L.A., with stops in London and Chicago on the way. She hated L.A., after her one visit there as a young actress, but it didn't matter. She would have gone to the ends of the earth now to find Ashley for her sister. And Fiona Eckles had given her the only leads she had. It had been a stroke of luck finding her at all, and learning about her book from the librarian. And lucky too that the book shop had a copy, and Fiona agreed to see her.

Hattie sent an email to Mother Elizabeth saying that she was on her way to Los Angeles to gather more information. And all she could do was pray that the needle in the haystack she was seeking might be there. Once she found her, if she did, she was going to give Melissa the information, and it would be up to her to decide what she wanted to do next. And that was only if the leads Fiona had given her panned out, and if the needle in the haystack turned up. It was going to take more than luck for that to happen. It was going to take a miracle. Hattie closed her eyes and prayed as her plane to L.A. took off. The trip to Dublin had been productive after all.

Chapter 6

Hattie slept fitfully on the flight from Dublin to L.A. They changed planes at Heathrow, and she had a screaming baby next to her for most of the flight. She was tired and felt physically sick when they landed in L.A., after their stop in Chicago. She had been to L.A. for a screen test when she was young, and had hated it so much she had sworn she'd never return. But she was here now for Melissa, and forced all other thoughts from her mind. She would have done anything for her sister. She felt as close to her now as she had when they were young girls.

She took a bus to downtown L.A., and checked in to a hotel on Sunset Strip. The area looked questionable, with homeless people on the streets, but the hotel was cheap. And she knew none of the convents in the city. It was simpler to stay at a hotel. She changed into her habit, thinking it might protect her when she left the hotel for dinner at a diner nearby.

She always felt safe and invisible when she wore it, and the waitress poured her a free cup of coffee because she was a nun, and wouldn't let her leave a tip.

She used the business center when she got back to her hotel, dazed by the time difference and the long trip. She researched the three actresses online, and saw that the actress who had recently retired had a thirty-three-year-old son. So Fiona hadn't been wrong. She had obviously adopted a baby the year Ashley was born, but it was a boy. The young actress whose famous mother had died lived in Beverly Hills and was the girlfriend of a punk rock star. Hattie found her phone number and address online, on a website that listed celebrities and their private information, which was not unusual to find online, home addresses and phone numbers. She stared when she saw the information. The girl was beautiful in photographs, but looked nothing like Melissa.

The third actress whose name she had gotten from Fiona was still working, very famous, currently making a film, and she had a daughter, also thirty-three years old. The fan website said she worked for an organization that provided legal and medical assistance for abused inner-city children, and had a degree as a social worker. Her husband was an entertainment lawyer with a well-known firm, and she had two children. There was no photograph of her, and the little Hattie read about her made her sound like a normal, well-educated woman with a good heart. The brief article about her said that she had graduated from the School of Social Work at Columbia University, where Melissa had gone to college. But neither the social worker nor the young actress were named Ashley, so they probably weren't the right ones. But Hattie wanted to meet them anyway. They were the only leads she had.

Hattie jotted down both phone numbers, still amazed by how easy it was to get the contact information for celebrities. They really had no privacy. She decided to call them in the morning. She wanted to try the actress first. She went back to her room then, lay down on the bed in her habit, fell asleep, and didn't wake up until the sun was streaming into her room at nine o'clock the next day. She didn't remember where she was for a minute, thought she was in Dublin, and then remembered that she was in L.A.

Hattie went back to the coffee shop, in jeans and a T-shirt this time, had coffee and toast, and went back to her room to make the calls. She had thought about it that morning. She had told Mother Elizabeth that she wouldn't try to meet the girls herself, but now that she was there, the temptation was just too great.

The young actress's name was Heather Jones. Hattie dialed her number, expecting to hear voicemail, or an assistant, and a young voice said hello. Hattie was shocked for a minute, and on the spur of the moment claimed to be a reporter wanting an interview.

"From where?" The voice sounded blasé and not particularly interested, but she didn't hang up, and Hattie thought frantically and said it was an Internet magazine for teens, and invented a name. She said it was new, and their readers were crazy about her. Heather Jones giggled then and sounded pleased. "Do you want to send me a Q and A?" she asked casually, and Hattie scrambled for what to say next.

"I'd rather meet you in person. It won't take long." And much to her amazement, the girl trustingly agreed, and gave her an appointment at four o'clock that afternoon, at her home in Beverly Hills. It had been easier than Hattie had dreamed. She had no idea what to say to her, or how she'd bring up the subject of Melissa, but she was in it up to her neck now, and was determined to follow through.

She tried to reach the second young woman then, whose number had been on the Internet. Her name wasn't Ashley either. When she got voicemail, Hattie left a message.

She took a cab to the house in Beverly Hills, and arrived on time, and felt as though she were living a movie. It reminded her of her brief stay in L.A. eighteen years before. Heather Jones's famous rocker boyfriend was lounging at the pool, when a maid opened the door and led Hattie past the pool into the living room, where Heather was on the phone, waiting for her. She ended the call as soon as Hattie walked in, desperately afraid that they would ask her for credentials she didn't have, but Heather Jones smiled at her and offered her a drink, which Hattie declined. The actress lay down on the couch, and invited Hattie to take a chair facing her.

"You'll be using existing art?" she asked her blithely. "We just did a PR shoot, my assistant can send you whatever shots you need."

"That's perfect, thank you," Hattie said, feeling dazed. It was all so Hollywood and everything she had run away from. She was a nun, not a reporter, but she reminded herself that she was doing it for her sister. She was trying to think of questions to ask her that teenagers might be interested in. She asked her about her early career, the movies she'd been in, which one meant the most to her, what her dreams were for the future, and what message she might want to send to her teenage fans. The actress loved talking about herself, and it wasn't difficult to keep her engaged. Then finally, Hattie slipped a pertinent question into the mix at the end.

"How do you think it affected you, knowing that you were adopted? Did you feel closer to your famous mother, or competitive with her?" The actress stared at her for a moment as though Hattie had spoken to her in Chinese.

"Adopted? What are you talking about? I wasn't adopted. Is that on the Internet?" She looked shocked. "I was born in Italy when my mother took six months off between movies to have me." And then had obviously come home with a baby, claiming she'd given birth to it abroad, while taking a break in Italy where no one had seen her. She was one of the children who had never been told she was adopted. "I don't know where you heard that. Everyone says I look like my mother, but we were always very different. As you know, my mother had a terrible substance abuse problem. It made me determined *not* to be like her. I wanted to have her talent, but not her problems. She died when I was seventeen. She OD'd in our swimming pool. I found her. I've never done drugs and I don't drink because of it. And as you know, Billy Zee, my first husband, had a problem with heroin addiction, which is why I left him. In fact, I'd like to remind your readers never, ever to mess with drugs. I want you to put that in the article. That's the most important thing I have to say." She was so earnest that Hattie was touched. She wasn't a very interesting subject, but she had a poignant naïve quality, despite her striking good looks and the skin-tight white jumpsuit she was wearing.

"Of course, I'll put that in, in bold type," Hattie assured her. "I want to thank you for your time, and your message to our young readers," Hattie said, trying to sound sincere, and feeling slightly guilty.

"When will it run?" Heather asked, standing up.

"I'm not sure. Probably in the next month." Hattie

felt like a supreme liar, and she had stared at Heather Jones throughout the interview. Her birth year was right, and even the month, but Hattie was almost sure that she was no relation to Melissa. She had probably been born at Saint Blaise's, but to someone else, and never knew she'd been adopted, and never would, with no records now to prove it, and her adopted mother long gone.

Her boyfriend strolled into the room then, put an arm around Heather, pulled her close, and kissed her, as a maid appeared to escort Hattie out. Heather waved with a sensual smile as Hattie made her exit. The maid called a taxi for her and it came within minutes as Hattie waited on the street outside Heather's house. She felt as though she had gone over Niagara Falls in a barrel, but she didn't think she'd found Ashley. Nothing about her felt right.

She went back to her hotel and fell asleep again. She awoke to the phone ringing in her room. It was the other young woman she had called earlier, the social worker, who said she had just gotten the message when she got home from work. Hattie was half asleep, still jetlagged, and decided to try the interview ploy again, since it had worked so well the first time. This woman's name was Michaela Foster, not Ashley. She was the daughter of the famous actress Marla Moore, whom even Hattie knew by name. She told her she was calling for an interview about her humanitarian work with inner-city children.

"I think there's some mistake," Michaela Foster said politely. "I don't do interviews, I'm a social worker. You were probably looking for my mother, Marla Moore. She's working on a film right now. If you call her PR people at ICM, they'll set it up when she gets back if she's interested. She's on location in Quebec." She was about to hang up when Hattie stopped her.

"No, we really wanted you. What you do is very interesting. I'm writing an article about the children of famous women and the careers they choose. Were you ever drawn to acting?" Hattie tried to keep her talking, and snag her interest.

"Never. I know what hard work it is. And I've never wanted to be in the limelight. My mother and I are very different, and I'm adopted," she said in a cheerful, matter-of-fact tone, clearly comfortable with who she was, and well aware of her origins.

"I'd really like to meet you," Hattie persisted, feeling like a stalker.

"If you're interested in the work we do, you should really speak to my boss or my team, not just to me." Michaela hesitated for a moment and then sounded startled and a little confused, but she went on. "Why don't you come to my office tomorrow afternoon. It's important to make the public aware of the needs of inner-city kids. There are people living well below the national poverty level right here in L.A." She sounded intelligent and dedicated to her work. There was something about how direct she was that re-minded Hattie of Melissa, but she told herself it was wishful thinking.

"Thank you," Hattie said, feeling breathless, and like a liar again. The young woman on the phone sounded lovely, like a real person. She knew she was adopted, which would make things easier for Hattie, if she decided to tell her about Melissa. She wanted to make a clean breast of it soon, and not string this woman along with a false interview, as she had Heather, who had lapped it up, and wasn't nearly as bright. Heather's ego was in evidence at all times.

Hattie lay awake all night, thinking about what she would say, and how to do it. By morning, she was exhausted, and by that afternoon, she was a nervous wreck. She went to the address Michaela Foster had given her. Her office was in a bright modern building in a renovated area that had been a slum only a few years before, but was being gentrified. Hattie gave her name to a young receptionist, and a few minutes later Michaela came out to greet her. She had a warm, gentle smile, and Hattie was shocked for a minute. Michaela looked strikingly like Hattie and Melissa's mother, although in a much friendlier, more upbeat, younger version. She exuded charm and hu-mility and was clearly very intelligent, with natural beauty. Hattie sat staring at her, and didn't know what to say.

"I've asked my team to be available, if you'd like

to chat with them," she said easily, making Hattie feel welcome, and guilty for her lies to get to her. And the promise to Mother Elizabeth she was about to break. Hattie wanted to seize the opportunity she had while she was there.

"That won't be necessary," Hattie said in a low voice. "Mrs. Foster, Michaela, I have a story to tell you. It may sound crazy, but it isn't. If you're who I hope you are, I've been looking for you, and my sister has been searching for you for years. We thought your name was Ashley," Hattie said, feeling foolish, and Michaela Foster looked surprised.

"That's my middle name. My mother wanted to name me Ashley, but my father preferred Michaela, so they compromised, and Ashley is my middle name. Where have you been looking for me, and why?" She looked puzzled.

"Mainly in Ireland. I came from there two days ago."

"I was born in Ireland," she said, looking intrigued. "My parents adopted me there, and brought me home. I think foreign adoptions were easier then. It's more complicated today."

Hattie jumped in without waiting any longer. "My sister, Melissa, gave birth to a baby girl there, she was unwed and just sixteen. My parents sent her to Ireland to spend the pregnancy in a convent, and give the baby up, which she did. She always regretted it. Sixteen years later, she married and had a son.

He died of a brain tumor at ten, six years ago. They divorced, and she's alone now. Her husband knew about the baby she had at sixteen. She reached out to the convent to find out where the baby was, who had adopted her, and where she grew up, in the hope of meeting her one day. The nuns told her that all the records had been burned and destroyed, and there was no way to trace any of the babies, birth mothers, or adopting parents."

Michaela was staring at Hattie too, as though she'd seen a ghost. "I called them too. Saint Blaise's. My mother was always very open with me about the fact that I was adopted. I always knew, she never hid it from me. She and my father were older parents. She was forty, and he was sixty-two when I was born. He died when I was three. He was a famous producer and I never knew him. I don't remember him at all. My mother is a wonderful person, an honest, incredibly talented woman. She was always very candid about the fact that she realized that the adoption had been a mistake. She thought she'd be more maternal, but she wasn't. And she felt she was too old for motherhood by the time they got me. And then my father died suddenly. She has a huge career and she's busy. Even now, at seventy-three, she makes about two movies a year, more if she can. The adoption was my father's idea, and she blames herself for not being around more when I was young. She says she's not maternal, but she's better at it than she gives herself credit for. I love her very much and she loves me. She's been a wonderful mother.

"I've wanted to know more about my birth mother from the time I was in my teens. My mother encouraged me to find out. She knew that my birth mother was American, and from a good family in New York. But that was all she knew. When I was eighteen, I called Saint Blaise's, and they told me about all the records being destroyed. There was nothing I could do after that, so I gave up, and figured I'd never know who she was or anything about her."

"My sister decided the same thing. She admitted to me recently that giving you up was the worst thing she ever did, and in some ways it ruined her life. Her parents forced her to do it, and she never forgave them for it. I think she called the convent a couple of times, and got the same answer. It was a dead end. I want to help her, so I went there myself a few days ago. It's an abysmal place. The worst part of it is that they destroyed the records intentionally, and thought they were doing the right thing, to protect everyone's privacy, and themselves.

"The only reason I got your name is because I came across a woman who was a nun and a midwife there. She left the Church since then, but she remembered that your mother adopted a baby the year that my sister's baby was born. It was a wild long shot, but I decided to come here to try and find you, and hope we got lucky. It's a miracle if you're really my niece. My sister doesn't know I'm here, she doesn't know I went to Dublin to go to Saint Blaise's in person. She told me details recently that she'd never told me before, and I realized that the greatest gift I could give her was to find her daughter. You, hopefully. So here I am. You look remarkably like my mother, and I hope you're the baby we've been looking for." There were tears in Hattie's eyes when she said it, and in Michaela's as she listened to the story. It didn't come as a shock to her, it came as a relief, and she suddenly had the feeling that she was complete. "And by the way," Hattie added with a wry grin, "as a further surprise, I'm not a reporter, I'm a nun."

"You're a nun?" Michaela looked shocked at first and then she laughed. "You don't look like a nun, or act like one."

"But I am. I left my habit at the hotel. My order doesn't require me to wear it in daily life. And I couldn't pose as a journalist, and show up in the habit."

"I guess not." Michaela grinned.

"Would you be willing to take a DNA test?" Hattie asked her and she nodded, thinking.

"My mother is very open-minded and always encouraged me to find my birth mother if I wanted to. But I don't want to tell her about this though until we're sure. I think in some way, it will be a shock to her if what she calls my 'real' mother turns up. She's my real mother and has been all my life. But there's room in my life for the woman who gave birth to me. I can only imagine the trauma it must have been for a sixteen-year-old girl to have a baby and give it up."

"I don't think she ever recovered from it. There's a sharp side to her. And losing her son nearly finished her off."

"Where does she live? In New York?" Hattie had said that she lived in New York, so Michaela thought her birth mother might too. "She lives in the Berkshires, in Massachusetts. She has become a recluse since she moved there four years ago, two years after her son's death. And she's divorced."

"What does she do?"

"She's a very talented writer, she wrote under the name Melissa Stevens. She gave it up when her son got sick, and hasn't written since, and says she won't."

Michaela looked shocked again. "I've read her books. They're brilliant, but very dark and depressing."

"She's been through a lot. I'm not going to tell her until we're sure. I can help provide a sample for the DNA test, if that's helpful. I think we should keep it between us, until we know. I don't want to get her hopes up and disappoint her."

"I want to meet her," Michaela said, looking earnestly at Hattie, "and for my kids to meet her. I gave up on finding her years ago. It seemed hopeless after they told me about the fire. Why did they want to hide the records? Just to protect everyone's privacy? My mother never made a secret of adopting me."

"Others did." Hattie thought of Heather Jones. She took a deep breath then. "The Church made a lot of money on the adoptions, which they don't want people to know. They had a booming business with it for a long time. The girls who had their babies there came from families who could afford to send them away, and all of the adopting parents were rich and could pay anything for the babies they adopted. There are plenty of convents who took care of poor girls having babies out of wedlock. But there were a handful of convents in Ireland that turned it into a high-priced, very lucrative business, which some people frown on. It was for the benefit of the Church. My sister and parents, and your adoptive parents, were part of it, and others like them. The nuns were particularly proud of the movie stars who came to them for babies, which is how I learned about your mother, and about you. If she wasn't a movie star, the ex-nun I talked to wouldn't have remembered her and I would never have found you, so I guess we're both lucky. Do you think she'll be upset?"

"Probably more than she'd expect, at first, but she'll be gracious about it. She gave me everything I needed, an education at the best schools, nannies to take care of me when she was on location, beautiful homes to live in, vacations in terrific places. I never lacked for anything. She just wasn't around a lot of the time, but I wasn't unhappy. It was part of the territory of having a famous movie star mother. I was never mistreated or neglected," she reassured Hattie, who believed her, and she seemed very forgiving of her adopted mother's faults. "She never remarried after my father died, so I didn't have to compete for her attention."

"She sounds like a wonderful person," Hattie said admiringly.

"She is. And she'll be happy for me once she gets used to the idea. How soon can we do the DNA test?" she said, looking excited. Hattie already knew it was a simple mouth swab and they needed a DNA kit from the doctor.

"How about tomorrow?"

"Fine. I'll call my doctor."

"I can do it too if that will speed up the process."

"I'd like you to come and meet my kids and my husband tomorrow," Michaela said warmly. "How long will you be here?"

"As long as I need to be," Hattie said quietly, basking in the warm glow of the hope that she had actually found Ashley. It seemed too good to be true. The needle in the haystack had shimmered in the sunlight of truth, and she had found it, with Fiona Eckles's help. It really was a miracle, for them all. She had Fiona to thank for putting her on the right track.

After promising to come for dinner the following

night, Hattie called Fiona from her hotel. It was late in Dublin, but Fiona had said that she worked late at night, so she called her and told her what had happened.

"And where does that leave you now?" Fiona asked her, as Hattie wondered what she meant.

"An aunt, I guess, if the DNA test shows that she's my sister's child."

"And how are you feeling about the Church?" Fiona asked her pointedly.

"I'm not sure. I have no respect for the nuns who were involved in it, particularly those who burned the records, and ruined countless lives when they did. Others won't be as lucky as we were, thanks to you, and a famous adoptive mother, which made it easier to track her down."

"Don't forget, those nuns had the blessing of the Church for what they did. They weren't protecting anyone's privacy, they were covering their tracks and the money they raked in for the Church, so no one could criticize them for it. And they forced the girls to give their babies up, with their parents' blessings."

"What are you saying?" Hattie asked her, looking worried.

"I'm saying that a vocation is a delicate thing. It's made of spun glass. Mine was shattered forever by what I saw and what I learned at Saint Blaise's."

"I think mine is still intact," Hattie said quietly. "This was only about my sister for me, nothing else."

She wasn't on a witch hunt to condemn the Church, like Fiona had been with her book.

"It's about all of us, Hattie. It's about integrity and honesty, and pure motives. Even the Church has feet of clay sometimes. In the end, I couldn't accept that. I felt as though I had committed myself to a life of hypocrisy that was all about money, not about helping those childless couples and poor girls who were too young to know what they were doing and the price they would pay later on. Look at your sister, and what you say it did to her."

"My vocation is strong," Hattie said, wanting to convince herself as much as Fiona.

"Then I'm glad for you. Mine wasn't. I had to leave after all I knew. Maybe I was never meant to be a nun. I went in for shaky reasons, after a broken engagement, when I got jilted at the altar. That isn't good enough to last for an entire life." Hattie knew why she had gone into the convent, and she hoped the reason was good enough to carry her all the way. There was no question, what she had learned about Saint Blaise's had shaken her respect for some of the decisions that people in the Church made, but not her faith. She had sought the convent as a refuge and safe haven, and it still was for her.

She thanked Fiona again for the invaluable information that had led to Michaela, and hung up thinking about what the ex-nun had said. Hattie could only conclude that Fiona's vocation had been fragile, and not strong enough to withstand all that she'd seen at Saint Blaise's, and her role in it. Hattie had no part in that. There was no blood on her hands. She had only been a child when it was happening. But Fiona's words kept echoing in her head . . . a vocation is a delicate thing . . . like spun glass . . . and in her heart of hearts, Hattie knew just how true it was.

Chapter 7

Both Michaela and Hattie had the mouth swab for
the DNA kits the next day. Michaela went to her doctor, and Hattie to a lab at UCLA and made the request. Melissa would have one too eventually, which
would be conclusive, but this would give them some
significant idea if they were related, and on the right
track. Hattie didn't want to give Melissa false hope
and then break her heart again.

She went to Michaela's house for dinner that
night, and met her husband and their children, Andrew and Alexandra. David Foster was a handsome
man in his late thirties, with dark eyes, dark hair, a
cleft chin, and looked like a movie star. Michaela said
he had done some acting and modeling before he
went to law school and became an entertainment
lawyer. He worked for a prestigious firm. He seemed
to be very much in love with Michaela, and was great
to his kids.

The children, Andrew and Alexandra, were adorable, and very well behaved. They were six and four, and all together they looked like the poster for the perfect family. Michaela had dark hair like Melissa, and had the same tall, lean build. Her features were more like her grandmother's, but when she moved, Hattie was instantly reminded of Melissa. She found it hard now to believe they weren't related. It seemed so obvious to her.

The children loved playing with Hattie before and after dinner, and she was falling in love with the idea that she might be their great-aunt, although she felt a little young for that. Hattie was only ten years older than Michaela, since Melissa was so young when she had her.

Michaela had explained everything to David the night before. He knew of his wife's attempts to find her birth mother, and it seemed right to him that somehow they had found each other, if indeed Hattie was correct and she had miraculously found Melissa's long-lost baby girl. Hattie thought about them the next day all the way back to New York. She and Michaela had agreed that Hattie would not say anything to Melissa until they got the DNA results back. And Michaela was waiting to tell her adoptive mother too. She was on location anyway, and wouldn't be back in L.A. for a month. It wasn't the kind of news Michaela wanted to tell her on the phone.

Hattie and Michaela promised to stay in touch

while they waited for the test results to come in. And when Hattie wasn't thinking of them on the plane to New York, she was thinking about everything Fiona Eckles had told her, and what she had seen of Saint Blaise's herself. It validated everything Melissa had told her the last time they'd seen each other, when Hattie visited her at her new home.

Hattie had a deep sense of shame being associated with a church that would use people for gain, and exploit their griefs, leaving young girls forever damaged by giving up their babies in such a cruel way. It went against everything she believed about the Church, and she wanted time alone now to give it more thought.

She had been gone for barely a week, but she had seen and learned so much, in Dublin and Los Angeles. She felt like a different person as she flew back to New York. The nuns were still at the house at the lake, and weren't due back for another week. Hattie could have joined them there, but didn't want to. She needed time to absorb all that she'd seen and heard. She wasn't ready to see Melissa again either. There was no way she could have kept from her the fact that she'd met Michaela, and was almost sure she had found her daughter.

All she wanted now was to return to the convent that was her safe haven. She knew she would be at peace there. It was like climbing back into the womb for her.

She emailed Mother Elizabeth when she got home to the convent, and told her she was staying in New York to recover from the trip. It led the superior to believe that the journey had been disappointing, which didn't surprise her, and she was sorry for Sister Mary Joseph and the long trek she assumed she had made for nothing. It had been a loving gesture to her sister, even if it had come to naught, and this way she could tell herself she had done all she could to help her.

Hattie spent the next week in prayer, giving thanks to the merciful God who had led her on the right path to find Melissa's daughter. The DNA test seemed almost superfluous. She was sure she'd found the right person. But what was tormenting her was the suffering of the young girls, and that most of them would never be able to find even a trace of the infants they had given up. It seemed so profoundly wrong.

She was very quiet the night the nuns came home from the Adirondacks. They looked tanned and relaxed, and were full of tales of what they'd done and the fun they'd had. They were like a girls' school returning after going to camp, which was what it was. It was all innocent play, and healthy pursuits in the sun and fresh air, that would have done Hattie good too, if she'd been in the mood to join them.

Mother Elizabeth invited her to her office after dinner that night.

"I take it the trip wasn't a success," she said solemnly, as Hattie sat across the desk from her. The superior looked deeply sympathetic, knowing how much it had meant to her.

"Not at all, Mother," Hattie said with a slow, peaceful smile and a light in her eyes the superior had never seen before. It was a kind of blissful joy. "I think I found her. It's a miracle really. We had a DNA test to see if we're related, and we're waiting for the results."

"How on earth did you find her?" She looked genuinely shocked, remembering that Hattie had said she wouldn't try to meet her, but it sounded like she had.

"One of the nuns who had been a midwife at the same time my sister went there left the order and wrote a book about it. What she saw at Saint Blaise's caused her to ask to be released from her vows. The book is shocking in its painful nakedness. I met her. She didn't remember my sister. But apparently, a lot of the adoptive parents were from Hollywood, some were famous actresses, and almost all were from the States. Three movie stars adopted babies that year. She remembered that with perfect clarity and who they were. It's why I went to L.A. One of them adopted a baby boy, and the other two baby girls. I'm almost sure that one of them is 'Ashley,' the infant my sister gave up. Marla Moore, the actress, adopted her. I don't think she was a fantastic mother, but the young woman seems to have had a good life. She's a social worker in L.A., working with inner-city kids, and her husband is an entertainment lawyer. They have two adorable children, a four-year-old girl and a six-year-old boy. And I did meet with them, although I told you I wouldn't. I couldn't determine if she was the one unless I did." Mother Elizabeth nodded and didn't comment. "She contacted the convent fifteen years ago, wanting to find out what she could about her birth mother, with her adoptive mother's agreement. They told her about the fire, and that all trace of the adoptions had been destroyed. She gave up after that, just the way my sister did. If I hadn't found the ex-nun who wrote the book, I would never have found her. It was a long shot, but I think it's going to pan out, and she'll turn out to be the right one."

"Have you told your sister yet?" Mother Elizabeth asked her, pleased for her. She could see that there was more to the story that Sister Mary Joseph hadn't told her yet. She was sure there was a reason why she hadn't joined them in the Adirondacks, although she'd been back in New York.

"I want to wait for the test results. If I'm a match with this young woman, then it's almost a sure thing my sister will be."

"So why do you look troubled, my child? Your eyes say there's something you're not telling me. Are you afraid it won't be a match?" Michaela also had the right birthday, which could be a coincidence.

"Not so much. It's everything I heard and saw in Dublin that upset me deeply. How could they do what they did? Made money from all of them, and consciously destroyed all evidence that would have helped mothers and children to find each other again one day, or at least the mothers could find out what had happened to them."

"I'm sure they thought they were doing the right thing. Open adoptions were unheard of then, or very unusual, as was finding birth mothers on the Internet. Those were all highly confidential matters back then. It was considered information that could have ruined people's lives if it got out."

"That doesn't explain why all the girls who went there were from families who could afford to pay the fees to the Church. There were no poor girls there, and no locals for that reason. And the adoptive parents were all very rich Americans. They were taking full advantage of the situation and ran it like a business."

"It sounds that way now, but it was probably efficiently run, which is to their credit, and everyone's benefit."

"It was more than that, Mother. It was highly profitable. My sister calls it a baby mill, and after what I know now, having been there, I think she's right. And after talking to the author of the book I read by the ex-nun who was a midwife there, I have serious questions about the Church, and the people who ran it.

They didn't even let the girls touch or see their babies when they were born, or hold them. It must have broken their hearts," just as it had Melissa's. Giving her daughter up was still an open wound for her.

Mother Elizabeth sighed as she listened. "Women who have been released from their vows are never a strong source to solidify one's faith," she reminded Hattie, who thought about it and nodded.

"What she saw and experienced there drove her out of the Church."

"Maybe she would have left anyway. A weak vocation won't hold you forever. It's like a weak bridge, sooner or later it breaks, and if you're standing on it, you fall into the abyss. Did she try to influence you?"

"Not at all," Hattie said, although she knew it wasn't entirely true. "She just shared that it had been a test of faith for her."

"Which she failed," the mother superior pointed out. "She didn't stay and respect her vows. She abandoned them."

"I think she was very deeply marked by what happened there, and her part in it."

"We must all learn to forgive, ourselves as well as others. Our Church isn't perfect, nor the people in it, nor any of us. I have to believe that the nuns who ran Saint Blaise's and the convents and mother and baby homes like it had the very best of intentions while they did it. Who can blame them for only accepting stable, financially sound adoptive parents? At least the babies they adopted would be safe and never have to struggle. They didn't make large donations to the Church in order to abuse them. And if you've found your niece, she sounds like she had a good life with her movie star mother, an enviable life. Who wouldn't want that for a child they were giving up? And you forget that the girls who went there, like your sister, were barely more than children themselves, teenagers at best. What kind of life could they have given their children? A life of shame and disgrace, ostracized and shunned by their communities and the world, and even their own families. I think the nuns at Saint Blaise's made the best of a bad situation, and it sounds like they did it quite successfully, for the benefit of the Church as well. You need to put this behind you now, Sister Mary Joseph, and thank God you found the girl, if she's the right one. I'm sure your sister will be very grateful, particularly to know that she was adopted by people who took good care of her, and she had a good life." The superior refused to see the sordid side of it that had shocked Hattie and Fiona Eckles deeply. "You cannot let this shake your faith in everything you believe in and have dedicated your life to. You have a strong vocation. In the life of every religious, at some point, there will come a challenge that will try to break them. You must resist that, and come out of it stronger, better, and more dedicated." Hattie was chastened into silence, could only nod, and kissed the superior's ring before she left her office, feeling like a schoolgirl who had been sent to the principal's office to be reminded of the tenets and beliefs of the school. But even after Mother Elizabeth's speech, Hattie hated everything she now knew about Saint Blaise's and felt it was wrong. And like Fiona Eckles, her faith had been shaken by it, and possibly her vocation.

The next day Mother Elizabeth suggested to her that she spend more time in prayer until she felt better. Her trip out in the world and the people she had met there had obviously upset her.

She spent her lunch hour at the hospital in silent prayer that day, and stayed longer in chapel than the others at the end of the day. She stayed after Mass in the morning and skipped breakfast, and went to confession. But no matter what Hattie did, the test of her faith was getting the better of her. She had never fought as hard to strengthen her beliefs and cling to them, and she felt as though she were hanging onto the edge of a cliff with her bare fingers and below her yawned the abyss, waiting to swallow her.

"You're wrestling with the devil himself," the mother superior said when she called her to her office again. She could see that the younger nun was still having a hard time. She had hardly smiled since she got back from her trip, and she was spending all her spare time on her knees in church. She scrubbed the kitchen floors every night as penance, but nothing helped. No amount of self-denial or ardent prayer had brought relief. Hattie wondered if the superior was right, and the devil had her in his grip. But the only devil she could see were the nuns who had been at Saint Blaise's while the girls were there, and what they had done to eliminate every trace of where their babies went.

As she continued to pray about it, the results of the DNA tests came back, and there was no question, she and Michaela Ashley Moore Foster were a match, and Melissa would be too. The index of the test was high, which was very good. For Hattie and Michaela, it was cause for celebration. She called Hattie at the convent. They had both gotten the emails with the results at the same time. Michaela sounded jubilant and Hattie smiled for the first time in weeks.

"When can I meet her?" Michaela was eager to meet Melissa now.

"I'll go up and see her as soon as I can, and tell her," Hattie promised. Melissa still had no idea that Hattie had been to Dublin, and Saint Blaise's, and had found Michaela Ashley. Hattie was smiling from ear to ear and Michaela said she had cried when she read the results. Her mother was still on location, but she had decided that she wasn't going to tell her until after she met Melissa, so she could be more reassuring about her, and assure her mother that Melissa was a decent person. "I'll try to go up this weekend, if I'm not working. And if I am, I'll try to trade my shifts. I can go up and back in a day if I have to. I did last time."

"Thank you," Michaela said, profoundly moved by what was happening. "Should I call you Aunt Hattie now?" It had been strange asking for her as Sister Mary Joseph at the convent, since she had introduced herself as Hattie Stevens when they met, and had been wearing normal clothes. Michaela was still surprised that she was a nun.

"You can call me anything you want," Hattie said, and promised to call her as soon as she had told Melissa. It was a moment Hattie was savoring, the opportunity to help heal her sister's wounds of the past.

Mother Elizabeth saw her face after the call. Sister Mary Joe was beaming.

"It's a match," was all she said, and the superior understood immediately.

"Congratulations. That should cheer you up." She knew how she had been struggling.

"I'd like to go up and see my sister this weekend," she said hopefully, and the superior nodded.

"Of course, you have my permission. Stay overnight if you'd like to. That's a long drive to do round trip in one day."

"Thank you, Mother," she said gratefully. All she wanted now was to see the look on Melissa's face. It would make everything worthwhile, no matter how much the trip to Dublin had challenged her faith ever since. It was a small price to pay compared to what her sister had been through.

*   *   *

Melissa was sanding the fifth door when Norm came by at the end of the day. He had promised to bring her more fine-grained sandpaper. She had seven more doors she wanted to do, and was just halfway through the project. He'd gone to Maine for a few days with friends to go sailing, and she missed his impromptu visits. He was the only person Melissa saw and spoke to on a regular basis. He'd been dropping by more frequently since the fire.

"How was Maine?" she asked him.

"Great. Perfect wind conditions for sailing and fresh lobster every night." To his knowledge, she hadn't been on a vacation since she'd lived there, and he wondered why she never went away. But she had nowhere to go, and no one she wanted to be with, so she stayed at home and worked on the house. "I'll bring you some lobsters from Boston the next time I go," he promised, and she laughed at the suggestion.

"I wouldn't know how to cook them."

"I'll cook them for you." It was the first time in four years he had suggested a meal with her. Usually they shared lemonade or iced tea on the porch, or a cup of coffee in winter. He had never invited her to dinner, but she seemed friendlier since the fire, so he risked it, and she didn't seem to mind his suggesting a meal or offering to cook for her. "What did you do while I was gone?"

"Two more doors." She smiled at him.

"You need to get out of here once in a while," he said cautiously.

"Why? I'm happy here."

They sat on the porch for a while, and she poured him a glass of wine. She was wearing shorts, and he couldn't help noticing her long legs and the graceful way she moved.

Everything was back to normal since the fire, except for the people who had lost their homes. They'd both read in the paper that the arsonist was back from his psychiatric evaluation and had been declared fit to stand trial as an adult, which was legally fair but unbearably sad. He had ruined his life along with those of the people he had harmed when he set the fire. He would certainly go to prison, at seventeen. Melissa felt sad every time she thought of it, and sorry for him. He had never had the chance for a decent life, and he surely wouldn't now.

It was after six o'clock when Norm left. He said he was having dinner with friends at the tavern that night. He didn't ask her to join them, and knew she wouldn't have anyway. She was like a wild horse, always skittish. It had taken years for her to get comfortable with him, while they worked on her house together.

She was putting their glasses in the dishwasher after Norm left, when Hattie called her. They hadn't spoken since her supposed retreat. Hattie had been avoiding her until she got the results of the DNA test.

"What have you been up to?" Hattie asked her, as though they spoke all the time.

"Sanding some doors, clearing away brush in case there's another fire."

"Don't you have people to do that?"

"I like doing a lot of it myself. How was your retreat?"

"Interesting. I'll tell you about it when I see you."

"I can hardly wait," Melissa said sarcastically, and they both laughed.

"I have some time off this weekend," Hattie told her.

"Do you want to come up?"

"I'd love it. I have permission to spend the night." Her saying it that way made Melissa wonder how she stood living such a restricted life, needing permission for every move she made. But that was the life she had chosen. She had given up her freedom forever. Melissa couldn't have tolerated anyone telling her what to do, and never had.

"You're welcome to stay."

"I'll be there by lunchtime. I'll get an early start," Hattie said, barely able to contain herself. "Do you need me to bring anything?"

"Just you." And the best news she'd ever had, Hattie said to herself. She couldn't give her Robbie back. But she had found Ashley. Michaela Ashley. Hattie couldn't wait until Saturday. She was counting the hours.

Chapter 8

Hattie left the convent at seven A.M. on Saturday morning, and kept her foot on the gas all the way from New York. There was no traffic at that hour, and she kept the convent station wagon right at the speed limit the entire time. She couldn't wait to get there and see Melissa's face when she heard the news. Hattie was wearing jeans and a sweatshirt. The morning had been cool when she left the city. It was the end of summer, and what a summer it had been. Hattie's spirits had risen ever since they got the results of the test. Michaela had called every day, wanting to know if Hattie had told her yet, and she had to keep reminding her that she wouldn't see Melissa until Saturday.

She made it in just under four hours, which was some kind of record. Melissa was pushing a shiny green wheelbarrow full of twigs and branches when Hattie drove up and stopped the car. She got out quickly, and hugged Melissa, who looked happy to see her. Hattie pointed at the wheelbarrow.

"You look like a farmer." She laughed at her, and Melissa grinned.

"That's what I am. I've got six boxes of apples for you to take back to the convent. I've got tomatoes too, if you want them."

"They'll love it."

"Do you want a cup of coffee?"

"Actually, I'm starving," Hattie admitted, as she followed her up the steps to the kitchen. She'd left the convent before breakfast. And as soon as they walked in, she could smell cinnamon buns in the oven. Melissa had bought them for her again. She put two on a plate, set them on the kitchen table, poured the coffee, and a minute later they sat down.

"You look happy," Melissa commented, as Hattie took a single bite of the bun and set it down.

"I am. Mellie, I have something to tell you," she said, as her older sister raised an eyebrow in interest. "I didn't go on a retreat. I went to Ireland, to Saint Blaise's."

A cloud crossed Melissa's face instantly at the words. "Why? We already know they destroyed the records. Why did you do that?"

"Because I hated the look in your eyes when you talked about it the last time I saw you. I thought that maybe, as an insider, I could talk to some of the nuns, and find someone who'd been there when you were, and might remember something useful."

"And did you?"

"Not at Saint Blaise's. They have a new mother superior, who gave me the party line. God, what an awful place that is. It made me cry, thinking of you there. It's a home for old nuns now. I walked around, but no one told me anything, or had been there then. They've all died or been dispersed. But I discovered that there's a book about the convent, about the adoptions they did there, and what it was like then. It's called *Babies for Sale* and it was written by an ex-nun. I'll give it to you," she promised. "Her name is Fiona Eckles. She's a professor of literature at Dublin University now. She was a midwife at Saint Blaise's then, when you were there. She's been released from her vows. Her name was Sister Agnes. She didn't remember you. I showed her a picture of you at sixteen."

"I don't think I remember her either," Melissa said, frowning. "There were two or three midwives. It was a pretty grim experience. To lower their liability, and reduce the risk for mothers and infants, they gave no drugs, no spinals or epidurals, nothing for the pain. All deliveries were natural. I guess it covered them nicely, no matter how bad it was for the girls. As far as I know, they only had one bad incident, a girl who bled to death in minutes. They didn't even have time to call the doctor. When they finally

did, she was dead when he arrived. She was fourteen. It was terrible. I think the placenta separated or
something.

"Maybe I knew Sister Agnes by sight, but I don't
remember her. We only saw the midwives when we
delivered. I was in so much pain, I don't remember
anything except wanting to die on the delivery table.
I couldn't believe how civilized it was when I had
Robbie. It was night and day. I had an epidural with
him. At Saint Blaise's, it was all very primitive and
basic. You went through as many hours of labor as it
took, you pushed the baby out, and they took it away
and didn't even show it to you. They sewed you up,
and as soon as you could stand up, they put you on a
plane and sent you home. So what did this Sister
Agnes say?" She spoke in a monotone, remembering
clearly the horror of it all.

"She said all the same things you did about the
place. She asked to be released from her vows when
she left. She gave up being a midwife too. She didn't
remember much about the girls. She said it was a
factory, a baby mill for profit, for the Church, just as
you said. I think it turned her against the Church forever. Her book about it is very harsh, deservedly so.
What she remembered were the names of some of
the adoptive mothers, the famous ones. Apparently a
lot of Hollywood stars adopted babies there. She remembered three major movie stars who adopted babies the year you were there and she told me their

names. It was a long shot, but the only one I had. I figured that our only hope of finding your baby was if one of them had adopted her. So I went to L.A. after I spoke to Fiona Eckles. One of the movie stars had died years ago. Her daughter is an actress and doesn't know she's adopted, and I'm happy to say you're not related to her. She's a first-class narcissist living with the lead singer of a punk rock band. I pretended to interview her for an online magazine."

Melissa laughed when Hattie said it. "Oh my God, you're crazy! When did you do all this?"

"When I told you I was on the retreat. I was playing Sherlock Holmes. I got a three-week leave to do it."

"Why didn't you tell me? I would have gone with you." Hattie wasn't sure that was true, but she didn't argue with her.

"I didn't want you to be disappointed if nothing turned up. The second famous actress adopted a baby boy, so that was a dead end. Marla Moore was the third actress. She was forty years old when she adopted a baby at Saint Blaise's, and her husband was sixty-two. He died three years later. They were too old to adopt through normal channels in the States, so they went to Saint Blaise's. They adopted a baby girl, who is a social worker now, married to an entertainment lawyer. They have two very sweet children, Alexandra, who is four, and Andrew, who's six. Her name is Michaela Ashley. Ashley is her middle name. Marla's husband didn't like the name, so they gave her the first name of Michaela." Hattie was crying by then, and so was Melissa. "She looks so much like Mom that it's scary. She's a beautiful girl. We had a DNA test, and we just got the results a few days ago. I'm related to her genetically, so she's your baby, Mellie. She tried to find you when she turned eighteen, and they told her the same thing they told you, that the records were destroyed in a fire. She gave up after that, but she always wanted to find you. She wants to meet you now." Melissa had leapt to her feet by then, with tears running down her face, which had gone pale, as she stared at her sister.

"You found Ashley?" she said in barely more than a whisper, shaking from head to foot until she had to sit down. Hattie put her arms around her and hugged her.

"Michaela Ashley," she said, choking on a sob too. "She's so beautiful and so nice, wait till you meet her. And she looks like you and Mom. She moves like you, and has your eyes and hair."

"Were they good to her?" Melissa wanted to know.

"Marla Moore doesn't sound like the mother of the year, but Michaela said she had everything she could have wanted, and kind people around her. Marla was on location making movies a lot of the time. She was all in favor of Michaela finding you, if she wanted to, but the records being destroyed made it impossible. I hate to think how many people have tried and given up." Melissa nodded, since she had too.

"When can I see her?"

"She said she'd come to New York to see you and bring the kids. You could invite them here if you want."

"Does she hate me for leaving her?" Melissa's eyes looked huge as she questioned her sister.

"Not at all. I told her you were sixteen. She's not angry. She seems like a very well-adjusted woman. She works with inner-city kids in L.A. They have a good life, live in a beautiful home, and are responsible people. They're a sweet couple. I think Marla took good care of her. She's apparently not a very maternal person, but Michaela loves her, and seems very forgiving. She thought there was no hope that she'd ever find you."

"I thought so too. I can't believe what you did," Melissa said to her, overwhelmed with gratitude. "You've been flying all over the world, looking for her."

"You always did everything for me. It was my turn. I thought I might have the inside track because of the Church, but I got nowhere at Saint Blaise's. Fiona gave me the only lead when she remembered the three movie stars who adopted in 1988. You were meant to find each other, Mel. You can call Michaela later if you want, or now. She knew I was coming here. She's been calling me all week."

"What if she hates me when she meets me?" Melissa said, suddenly seized by panic. "I'm not as glamorous as her movie star mother. I'm a farmer now, just as you said. I crawl around under the house and up on the roof, and drag tree trunks around with the tractor. I don't even own high heels anymore. I threw them all away. Oh my God, Hattie, I'm a mess." She was laughing and crying at the same time and couldn't stop. And then, finally, she looked at her sister seriously, and her voice dropped to a whisper. "I'm scared."

"So is she. So was I when I went to meet her. She's lovely. And trust me, she has no axe to grind about you."

"Does she know about Robbie?"

Hattie nodded. "I told her. She felt terrible for you. Now you need to figure out when you want to see her. I think it might be better in New York. Coming here and staying with you might be a little intense for the first time. It'll be easier to meet on neutral turf. Like New York."

"New York isn't neutral. I haven't been there since the divorce, when I bought this house. I swore I'd never go back. I have too many memories there, of Carson and Robbie. It's too hard for me." She looked genuinely panicked.

"You're going to meet your daughter, Mel. It's a happy event, not a sad one. You've waited thirty-three years for this. You can do it." Melissa was turning fifty soon, and the last time she'd seen her baby girl, she was sixteen. Hattie couldn't imagine it, waiting that long for something that important that she'd been robbed of as a young girl.

"What'll I wear? I need to buy clothes. All I have is the old stuff I wear up here."

"You can come a day or two early and buy something nice. I don't think she'll care. She's not that kind of person. She's honest and real. She really loves her kids. They're very sweet. They want to meet you too."

"Oh Christ, I'm a grandmother and I'm not even a mother anymore." Her eyes filled with tears again as she reached out to hug Hattie. She felt as though she'd been given an entire world.

"Yes, you are a mother. You have Michaela," Hattie said softly.

"I gave her up." Melissa sounded convulsed with guilt.

"You had no choice, Mel. You're still her mother. She has two mothers now."

"Will her adopted mother hate me? Does she know?"

"Not yet. Michaela wants to tell her after you've met."

"To see if she likes me?"

"No, to reassure her mother that she's met you, you're a nice person, and it's fine."

"It's not fine. I abandoned her. What'll I say when I meet her? 'I'm sorry I gave you up and ran away'?"

"You didn't run away, Mel. You were sixteen and Mom made you do it. You would have kept her if you could have. There was no way you could. In today's world, you could probably do that. But not thirty-three years ago. You did what you had to do. What you were forced to do. She understands that. She's nervous too." But not as nervous as Melissa, who was terrified that her daughter would reject her, and had good reason to. "She's not angry at you, Mel. She's not an angry person. She wants you in her life. She tried to find you at eighteen. She wanted to find you before that, but didn't know how. The nuns at Saint Blaise's didn't make it easy for anyone. This is an incredible stroke of luck to have found her. It was meant to be. Don't torture yourself about it until you meet."

"Maybe I'll have a heart attack and die before," Melissa said grimly, and Hattie laughed.

"No. Maybe you'll have a nice time, and be able to see her from time to time, and you even get two grandchildren in the deal. You have a family, Mellie. A daughter and a son-in-law and two grandkids."

"Does she know I used to write?"

"She's read all your books and loves them. You lucked out here. Now try to enjoy it and relax a little." Hattie had never seen her solid older sister so terrified.

"Will you come with me when I meet her?" she pleaded.

"If you want me to. But I think you're going to get along fine. I was a total stranger who barged into her office with a crazy story, and she couldn't have been nicer to me."

They talked about it for hours, late into the night. Melissa thanked her dozens of times and considered it from every angle, and raised every fear. Hattie spent the night reassuring her. They fell asleep on her bed, still talking, and Melissa looked exhausted when she got up the next day. She had worn herself out, and didn't have the courage to call her daughter. She wanted Hattie to set up the meeting, and she promised she would. Melissa agreed to go to New York to see Michaela, although she dreaded it, and the memories it would revive.

She was still a nervous wreck when Hattie left to drive back to the convent on Sunday afternoon. She looked dazed when Norm came over on Monday and brought her fruit from his orchard and fresh corn. She had sent the six boxes of apples with Hattie for the convent. Norm had brought his pears, which were delicious, and he noticed how odd Melissa looked, and how distracted, and asked if she was okay.

"I had kind of a crazy weekend," she said with a vacant look.

"Are you feeling all right?"

"No . . . yes . . . I just found out this weekend that I'm about to get something I've wanted desperately ever since I was a kid, and now that it's happening I'm scared to death." He couldn't imagine anything that would scare her, but she looked flustered. He had never seen her like that.

"Do you want me to leave?" He suddenly felt as though he was intruding. She was in a strange mood. "Is it something I can help you with?" he asked hesitantly. There was no sign of her sharp tongue, or acerbic comments that amused him but could hurt sometimes. She seemed young and frightened and humbled.

"I've never told you this. I've never told anyone except my husband." He could tell she was about to share another secret with him, like the ones about the son she had lost, or the books she had written. They had an odd friendship that he wanted to grow, but she never seemed ready for that and now seemed totally discombobulated and confused. She hadn't even combed her hair yet that morning, which wasn't like her. She was always neat as a pin, with her long dark hair pulled tightly back, or piled on her head in the heat. Now it hung down her back in a tangled mass.

"I had a baby when I was sixteen," she blurted out and startled him. "A little girl. My parents sent me to Ireland to have her and made me give her up for adoption. All the records were destroyed later, I've wanted to find her for years and never could. My sister just did. She found her in L.A. She's married, a social worker, and has two children. She wants to meet me and I'm scared to death. She has every reason to hate me for giving her up." He looked down at the woman he had admired from a distance for four years, and had no idea what to say about the enormous piece of information she had just shared with him. He did the only thing he could think of, he put his arms around her and held her. He could feel her shaking against him, and he kissed her, as much to calm his own nerves as hers.

Her eyes opened wide when he did, and for a minute, he was afraid she would hit him, or push him away, but instead she melted in his arms and kissed him back, which he hadn't expected. The whole world had suddenly gone topsy-turvy, for both of them. She had lived in self-imposed isolation for more than four years, having lost two children and a husband, having given up everything, with no one in her life, not even the sister she had avoided for six years. And now suddenly everything in Melissa's life had changed. Her sister was back, she had a daughter, and a man in her arms. She didn't know how to react, and burst into tears as Norm held her. She clung to him as wracking sobs shook her, and the tears rolled down her cheeks. Like it or not, she was back in the human race, alive again, and scared to death. It was wonderful and terrifying all at the same time, like a roller coaster. She didn't know whether to laugh or scream.

Hattie called Michaela in California on Sunday night when she got back to the convent. It was late afternoon in L.A. She told her how the announcement had gone with Melissa, and how excited she was about meeting her daughter for the first time, and scared too. She wanted Hattie to set it up, and they agreed on New York in two weeks. David had a meeting there, and the kids had a long weekend from school. By the end of the conversation, it was all arranged. Hattie called Melissa to tell her, but she didn't answer. She was so exhausted by the emotions of the weekend after Hattie told her about Michaela, that she was sprawled on her bed, fully dressed, with the lights on, sound asleep.

Chapter 9

Norm decided to do things right, after what had happened between him and Melissa the day before, when he kissed her. He didn't want it to be a one-time occurrence, or for her to see it as a moment of madness, never to be repeated. He could tell that things were changing rapidly in her life. He had waited four years for this, standing on the sidelines. He finally had the opportunity, and didn't want to treat it lightly. He wanted there to be substance to it, and gravitas.

He called Melissa the next morning. She was still reeling from everything Hattie had told her, and what she'd done for her. She had taken care of her younger sister when they were growing up. Then Hattie had defected, as Melissa saw it, and run away to the convent. Melissa had been angry at her ever since. And now she had done this incredible thing for her, and found the daughter Melissa thought she'd never see again. She was still trying to absorb it when the phone rang, and she picked it up.

"I'd like to cook dinner for you tonight," Norm suggested, and made no mention of the kiss the day before. Melissa was mildly embarrassed by it, but she had enjoyed it. She had decided to ignore it when she saw him again, and treat it as an aberration. Everything was spinning out of control around her. She didn't want her friendship with Norm to do that too. She had no room in her life for a man and a relationship. She couldn't handle that too. Finding her daughter again was enough for now. But he sounded so sweet on the phone, she didn't want to hurt his feelings. "Why don't I come over at seven, and whip up something for you? Things are pretty exciting for you right now. I have a feeling you won't eat if someone doesn't make it for you." She laughed. He was right. She hadn't eaten the night before, and wasn't hungry now. There was too much to think about, which seemed so much more important.

"You don't have to cook for me, Norm," she said kindly.

"No, but I'd like to. Leave it to me, I'll do something easy. We can save soufflés for another time," he said, and she laughed again. Cooking was mathematical and precise to him, like building houses, and he liked that. He had been a whiz at math in school, and terrible at writing and abstract concepts, which had been Melissa's strength, and led to her writing later on.

She ambled around the house all day, feeling disconnected. She wanted to call Hattie, but knew she couldn't reach her at the hospital unless it was an emergency. The idea that she was finally going to meet her daughter was the most exciting thing that had happened to her in years, but also terrified her. Who was the girl she had thought of as "Ashley" for more than thirty years? Would she like her natural mother? Was she angry at her? She had a right to be. Melissa knew she would have to face her daughter honestly, and herself now. How could she explain that she hadn't tried harder to find her? But the trail had been stone cold after the convent burned the records. And Melissa hadn't been old enough to look for her before that, or to want to. It was already too late by the time she called Saint Blaise's to try and find her.

There was so much to think about, and now Norm wanted to cook dinner for her. She didn't think it was a good idea to get in any deeper, but she had agreed to let him come.

She felt drunk and hungover all day, and she was neither. She was drunk on the changes in her life. She thought of it as she stood in the shower, the warm water raining down on her, which woke her up a little.

She put on a simple white sweater and jeans, a little makeup, and looked fresh and felt a little more awake when the doorbell rang, and she let Norm in.

His arms were full of bags from the grocery store, and he was carrying a big box tied with string, with a handle, with air holes punched into it. He set all of it down in the kitchen, and there was a thumping from the box, which smelled faintly of fish and seaweed. He opened it to show her two huge live lobsters, with their claws bound. He had driven to Boston to get them. He had brought a good white wine, and crab salad as a first course. He rolled up his sleeves and got to work as soon as he got there, and Melissa set the table with linen placemats and napkins.

She watched him cook the lobsters, which he managed masterfully. He had opened the chardonnay, and she poured each of them a glass to drink while he cooked. They chatted easily as they always had, and the kiss was never mentioned. She was hoping he'd forget it, and how vulnerable she'd been after hearing about Hattie finding Michaela. It was her life's dream and fondest hope, and now she wasn't sure she was equal to it, and the explaining she'd have to do to justify her actions. All her life she had blamed her mother and said that abandoning the baby was her fault. But was it? Could she have stopped it and refused to go to Ireland, or to give the baby up? What if she had refused to sign the papers? She had let it happen, and now she had to face the person she had hurt most in the process. She just hoped that the people who had adopted her daughter had been good to her. Being a movie star didn't guarantee that, as history had shown with others, famous for abusing their children. She prayed that Marla Moore wasn't one of them.

Norm could see that Melissa was troubled and distracted as they sat down at the table. The lobsters looked huge on the plates where he had set them with lemon and melted butter. She'd put the salad in a bowl, and he lowered the lights after she lit the candles. She smiled thinking that before he had built things in the house, and now he was enjoying the fruits of his labors, and how well it all worked. He had fully remodeled the kitchen, although she had refused all the fancy equipment he'd suggested. It was simple and modern and functional, and there was a cozy place to sit and eat. It didn't look like a rocket ship the way his did, with every kind of technology available. She didn't want or need that.

"You've got some exciting changes happening," he said quietly, as they ate the lobster. It was delicious.

"That's a vast understatement," she said with a sigh, and looked at him. He was a good man. She loved his outdoorsy mountain man look, and realized how little she knew about him. She knew he was from Boston, had gone to Yale and dropped out, and had been married and had no children, but she knew none of the details. He never talked about them, and she hadn't asked, not wanting to share her own history in any intimate way in exchange. He knew about both her children now, and the fact that until recently she no longer had any. In her own eyes, she wasn't a mother anymore after Robbie died. And now she was about to be again, with the reappearance of Ashley in her life—Michaela. She had to correct herself every time she thought about her.

And as though he sensed what she was thinking, he talked about himself during dinner, more than he had before. It wasn't relevant before this, but with the kiss the day before, it could be.

"I haven't been seriously involved with anyone in a long time," he said quietly. "I've been divorced for eight years." She knew he had just turned fifty. They were almost the same age, since she was forty-nine, about to turn fifty herself. "We were married for nine years, and I think we were both surprised it lasted that long. My wife was an ambitious woman. My family was in politics and so was hers, and I think she thought that she'd get me headed in that direction eventually. My grandfather was the governor of Massachusetts when I was a boy. My father was a senator. I hate politics and everything it stands for. She's married to a senator from Texas now, which is everything she wanted from me and I didn't give her. I told her what my plans were before we got married and she didn't believe me. I wanted a simple country life. We moved here the year after we got married, and I started my construction business. She hated every minute of it, and was in Boston all the time. We tried to have kids for a while, and once we knew that wasn't going to happen, she lost interest in our marriage. In her mind, she was trapped with a rustic carpenter, and she hated me for it. We hardly saw each other for the last four years we were married. She was away most of the time, in Boston or New York. For the first five years we were trying to have kids, which was hard on her. It's a depressing process when it doesn't work, and we tried everything. She blamed me for it, but it turned out to be her. I was okay with it, but she wasn't. She wanted to adopt, and I wouldn't. I love children, but don't need my own to be happy. My brother, Ted, has five boys and I love being an uncle. It's enough.

"My brother is a lawyer in Boston, and so is his wife. They both went to Yale, undergrad and law school. Everyone in my family did, and graduated, except me. I'm severely dyslexic and struggled as a kid, I'm better with my hands, and at math. My wife hated the fact that I had no political ambitions, building houses didn't count for her as an occupation. She thought it was blue-collar work and was ashamed of it. I'm proud of every house I built or worked on." He smiled at Melissa and was proud of hers too, and so was she. She had enjoyed their collaboration for four years. "So that's me," he said comfortably. "What about you?" he asked her. "Do you miss writing books?" Now that he knew she was a bestselling published author, which impressed him. The written word always did, since it was hard for him. He was good at other things, like his construction business, which was very successful locally.

"Never." She answered his question immediately. "You have to sell your soul to be a successful writer. I did that for ten years. And in my case, I needed to be angry to do it. I'm not angry anymore. I don't need to write and won't again. My books and our son held our marriage together and made it work, since my husband was my literary agent. He made some great deals for me. That's all over. I don't need it, and everything you have to do to stay on top. My life is better now." She had that in common with him. They could have had bigger lives, and didn't want them. She'd had all that for a while, and Robbie had been her excuse to give it up. She realized now that in some ways she'd been relieved to stop.

"What were you angry about?"

She thought about it for a minute before she answered. "Everything. Everyone. My parents. My mother, for sending me to Ireland and forcing me to give up the baby. She was a hard, unhappy woman with a sharp tongue. I've been more like her than I want to be since my son died. I guess she was angry too, at my father. He was a weak man, from a successful family with money. He lost most of it and couldn't keep a job. He was an alcoholic, but a quiet one. He let her do whatever she wanted to keep the peace, and took a beating from her every day. She died when I was seventeen, less than a year after I came back from Ireland, which I never forgave her for. And he died a year later, of cirrhosis. I took care of my sister then. She's six years younger. She was like my own child. She wanted to be an actress, and threw all of it out the window and ran away to become a nun. I never understood it, and I hated nuns because they took my baby away. So after that, I was angry at her too. I was angry at life when my son got sick and died. I'm not angry at my ex-husband. I don't blame him for leaving me. There was nothing left of me by then, and he was in pain too. He's married to a quiet, unexciting woman, a writer too, but she's a nice person and she suits him. I hope he's happy. We don't speak. I email him once a year. I haven't seen him in years, and don't want to. So I guess you could say that anger has fueled me, and my writing. I don't want to live like that or be angry anymore. That's all writing was for me, a place for me to vent. The books were very dark, and for some reason, people loved them. They thought they were brilliant, and so did the critics. They were just the rantings of an enraged woman, mad at life."

"They're a lot more than that. I've read them. They're dark, but there's a soft underbelly to them, a tenderness and poignancy that shines through. They made me cry when I read them."

"For the characters?" She looked surprised. "Some of them are pretty awful people."

"I cried for you. I could feel your pain when I read

them." What he said touched her deeply and she was silent for a minute. "So we've both taken refuge here," he commented to fill the silence. "I'm not hiding. I really love it," he said, as they finished the lobster. They had eaten every bit of it, and the melted butter had been delicately flavored with truffle oil. She had noticed and loved it.

"Neither am I," she said, and then thought better of it. "Well, maybe I am hiding. Or I was. I'm not hiding now. And life has a way of finding you wherever you are anyway. I'm stunned that my sister found my daughter. I had no idea she was doing that. She got lucky, and so did I."

"Some things are just meant to be. You can't stop them, both good and bad." She knew it was true. Hattie had just demonstrated that.

"I'm glad my sister and I are close again. I missed her. I just couldn't understand why she'd want to be a nun, and not an actress. But it seems to suit her." He smiled at that.

"Maybe for the same reason you'd rather be a carpenter or a 'farmer' instead of a writer, and I'd rather build houses than be a politician. We've made choices, and those choices have made us who we are. I'd rather go to prison than be in politics," he said, and Melissa laughed.

"Some people do both." He laughed too. He had always liked their exchanges, even when she was tart or sharp with him. There was usually a reason for it, and if angry, she expressed it well. But she could be kind at times too. And he loved talking to her now that they were both revealing more of themselves. She was everything he had guessed, and more. He was a good judge of people, and tolerant of their quirks and flaws. More than she was.

She often said that she was allergic to stupidity, and hated people who didn't keep their word, or lied. She held herself to a high standard and expected that of others. He knew she was a hard worker, they had that in common too, and the no-frills life they had both adopted, although her home was supremely comfortable, in part thanks to him, and the improvements he had added, like the air-conditioning he had forced on her, and she loved now in the blazing summers. She hadn't thought it necessary, and too expensive, and he had insisted. And now she thanked him.

They cleared away the dishes, and left them on the counter. And he brought out a plum tart he had made himself from the fruit on his property.

"It's a German recipe I found," he explained, and when she tried it, it was delicate and delicious.

"You should be a chef," she complimented him.

"I'm better with houses." He smiled at her.

"Me too. Better than with people, in my case," she said. "I used to envy my sister for how extroverted she was, and at ease with people. She could talk to a stone before she went into the convent. She's more subdued now. But she still has a gregarious nature. I was always the shy, serious one, which is probably why I became a writer. It's an easy way to communicate, instead of talking."

"Not for me," he said with a smile. "It still kills me to write a letter. I'd rather talk to people than send emails, which I hate. They're so dehumanizing."

"I suppose so, but it's easier." They finished the tart and he poured them each a small glass of Sauterne that he had brought with him. It had been an exquisite dinner. "It was fantastic," she complimented him. She felt relaxed and sated and had stopped worrying about meeting Michaela while she talked to him. He had a way of making everything seem peaceful. "I'm nervous about meeting my daughter," she confessed to him over the Sauterne, when they went to sit in the living room. The evening was chilly and he lit a fire in the fireplace he had built for her that was even prettier than the original. He had found an antique marble mantelpiece at an auction in Newport, Rhode Island, from one of the Vanderbilt estates.

"She's going to love you," he said confidently.

"How can I compete with Marla Moore, she's a brilliant actress, and very glamorous."

"That doesn't make her a great mother. And there's room for both of you in her life. You have a lot to offer her. And you're younger and have a different point of view." She hadn't thought of that before. "Most actresses are narcissists, that's not easy either."

What he said reassured her a little, and she thought of the things he had told her about himself at dinner, about his marriage, his career, and his family. He was an interesting person, and deeper than she had realized. She was touched that he had read her books, and was very perceptive about them. She wasn't sure that even Carson had understood them as well as Norm had, and seen the suffering in them. Carson focused on the violence and plot twists that made them sell, so he could hit her publishers for more money. Norm had seen beyond that, he had seen her.

They were both looking into the fire, as Norm turned and put a gentle arm around her. He was a big man, and she felt small next to him. Everything about him promised safety and protection. She hadn't felt that way in a long time, if ever. She and Carson had a very different relationship, based on business, which was appropriate at the time. But she was in a different place in her life now. And Carson was six years older, always with an eye on the future, and a bigger deal. She was fine with it then, but wouldn't have been now. He had tried to do the same with Jane, his new wife, but her work had never taken off the way Melissa's had. She had a small following of faithful readers, but he had never been able to make a big deal of her. Melissa had been his star, and the star had closed up shop and gone out of business.

Norm didn't say anything, and then he kissed her. Their silences were comfortable. She felt no need to fill them with empty words or clever repartee, nor did he. He kissed her for a long time, and she was breathless when they stopped. She liked the feel of his soft beard on her face. He kept it neatly trimmed, and never looked unkempt, just manly and rugged. There was something irresistibly masculine about him, as though it was the way men were supposed to look, and she was surprised by how attracted she was to him. She had thought of him as a friend before, but doors were opening and revealing vistas she hadn't let herself consider until now.

"Do we know what we're doing?" she asked in a whisper, as she searched his eyes and he nodded with a smile.

"I think so. I do," he whispered back. "I've been waiting four years for this. This isn't a new idea to me. It just feels like the right time." She nodded, not wanting to disagree, and they kissed again.

"What happens after this?" she asked innocently, and he laughed at the question.

"Let's see where it goes. There's no rush to figure it out. Why don't we just enjoy it?" She nodded. It sounded right to her too.

He tore himself away finally at midnight. He would have liked to stay and spend the night with her, but he didn't want to rush it, and he didn't want her to feel that he had cooked her dinner to seduce her. He had made the meal for her, for them both, for the sheer pleasure of it.

They kissed again as he stood in the doorway, and she thanked him for the delicious dinner. He had taken the garbage out for her, so the kitchen didn't smell of lobster the next day, and she didn't have to do it after he left. He thought of everything.

"I'll call you," he promised.

"I'm going to New York next week to see Ash . . . Michaela." She smiled as she corrected the name.

"I want to hear all about it when you get back," he said with an encouraging look, and she nodded.

"Thank you, Norm . . . for everything."

"Never mind that," he said, kissed her again, walked down the steps, and waved as he drove away a minute later. She stood on the porch for a few minutes, thinking about him, wondering why she had never noticed how handsome he was, and how attracted she was to him. All things in their time, she thought, and went back into the house with a smile.

Chapter 10

Melissa left for New York a week after her dinner with Norm. She drove herself, and had to concentrate on the road. She was so nervous and distracted, she was afraid she'd have an accident. What if she was killed on the way and never met her daughter? She could think of every kind of disaster happening, Michaela's plane crashing on the way from L.A. to New York, taking her family with her. Melissa couldn't believe it was going to be easy, and a happy event. She was sure something bad was going to happen to interfere with the meeting. But nothing had so far.

She checked in to a small, centrally located hotel in Midtown that she liked, which she used to recommend to friends from out of town when she lived there. It had a small elegant lobby, and comfortable rooms. Melissa had given herself two days to shop in New York before the meeting, so she'd have something decent to wear when she saw Michaela.

She had agreed to meet Michaela at the Mark hotel on East Seventy-seventh Street, where she would be staying with her husband and children. Melissa didn't want to crowd her by staying at the same hotel, in case the meeting went badly. But Hattie said there was no reason why it should. Both mother and daughter were excited to see each other, and had waited a long time for this. David was going to join them, at the end, with the children, and they were going to have dinner that night, after a brief intermission.

Hattie was joining them for dinner on their second day together. And on the third day they were all leaving, hoping this was just the beginning. There would be many more occasions to be together after this, if all went well. Michaela wanted Melissa to come to L.A. for Thanksgiving, to meet her adoptive mother, the thought of which terrified Melissa. And she wanted them to come to Massachusetts for Christmas or just afterward. It would be beautiful and snowy and a white Christmas, and there was skiing nearby, on a small mountain suitable for the children.

Melissa walked into Bergdorf, feeling as though she had traveled back in time. She hadn't been to New York in four years, and a thousand memories crowded into her head and assaulted her. Living and working there, their apartment, taking Robbie to the park before he got sick, shopping, seeing friends, life with Carson. She had abandoned an entire life when she left, all the people she'd known, and familiar spaces. She couldn't bear their friends' sympathy, or their look of panic that it could happen to them, and they could lose a child too. They felt sorry for her, but were relieved it wasn't them. She understood, but didn't want to see it. And she had nothing to say to them since her only child was dead and they had nothing in common anymore. She had borne it for two years, while she and Carson were still together after Robbie died, but the moment Carson left her, she fled.

He moved in with Jane almost immediately, and she went to the Berkshires to look for a house. Now suddenly she was back. It was a painful déjà vu for her, and she stood stock-still in the middle of Bergdorf's main floor, unable to move, and then forced herself to head toward the escalator, to find something to wear that Michaela would approve of. She didn't want her daughter to think she was a slob or didn't care how she looked, which she hadn't for four years, in old jeans and T-shirts. But now it mattered.

Melissa spent two hours trying on clothes, feeling even more lost. She felt ridiculous in them, polite little suits and matronly dresses she knew she'd never wear again, and weren't "her." She didn't know what Michaela expected, and didn't want to disappoint her. Hattie called her on her cellphone when she finished her shift, and Melissa was standing in a dressing room piled high with rejects. She was near tears.

"I need to borrow your habit. I've forgotten how to shop. I look awful in everything I've tried on. Can't we say we're both nuns?"

"You'd be struck by lightning immediately, after everything you've said about my being one," Hattie said, and Melissa laughed.

"That's probably true. I can't find anything to wear."

"What about black slacks and a nice sweater? That's what you used to wear most of the time."

"I'd forgotten. Can I wear that to dinner too?"

"You're asking me for advice? My wardrobe comes from the donation boxes people drop off. I have four Mickey Mouse Disneyland sweatshirts, and two from Harvard." They both laughed and Melissa knew it was true. She'd seen them.

"You can lend me one from Harvard if I don't find anything here."

"Buy three black sweaters, and a pair of slacks. She's not going to care what you're wearing, Mel."

"I hope not. I saw Marla Moore at the Oscars on TV last year, in Chanel haute couture. I can't compete with that."

"You don't have to. I think they borrow what they wear, so it probably wasn't hers. All you need to look like is her mom."

"I don't know who I am anymore, Hattie," Melissa

said, near tears. "I'm not a writer, or a mother, or a wife. I live in the country and don't see anyone or go anywhere. I don't have a job, or a life, or anything to impress her."

"Maybe you need to get a life and a new wardrobe, Mel," Hattie said gently, and as she did, it occurred to Melissa that it might be nice to have some new clothes to wear when she saw Norm, if they had dinner again, and she hoped they would. It gave her an idea.

"I'll do pants and sweaters. That works." She went down a floor to where the more casual clothes were, and bought a soft pink cashmere sweater, a pale blue one, a red turtleneck, and two black ones that looked chic. She bought black and gray flannel slacks, and then she saw a lace blouse that looked soft and feminine, and she bought a simple black cashmere coat that looked right for New York, instead of the beaten up gray parka she'd come to town in. She stopped in the shoe department and bought two pairs of black high-heeled pumps, one in suede, a pair of Chanel flats, and a good-looking pair of black boots. She had enough clothes to get her through the next few days, and she thought of Norm when she bought the lace blouse. There was good shopping in Boston too, but she never went.

She reached the sidewalk with her cluster of shopping bags, feeling like herself again. She'd brought a pair of her mother's pearl earrings with her, and a

Chanel handbag she used to love and had found on a shelf in her closet, gathering dust. It was a familiar look when she tried it on at the hotel, and she smiled at the blouse, thinking of the evening she'd spent with Norm, and their kisses in front of the fireplace, drinking the Sauterne. She no longer owned anything to make herself attractive to a man, or to impress a daughter who lived in L.A. and had a glamorous movie star adoptive mother. But the clothes she had bought looked well on her, and showed off her tall, slim figure. The coat was very stylish she realized when she tried it on again.

Just being in the city again was a strange déjà vu for her. It made her think of Carson and how long it had been since they'd spoken and she'd heard his voice. She thought about all they'd been through, and wondered how he was. He was still in the publishing world, and married again, with two teenage stepdaughters. So his life was not so different, but hers bore no resemblance to her earlier life. She spent the winter in rubber boots or snow boots, and sneakers in the summer. Her clothes were functional and not pretty, and she hadn't cared in four years. But now she did.

It was hard to turn the clock back to be someone she no longer was, and she looked older than she had four years before. Hattie said she hadn't changed but Melissa knew she had. She'd been through too much not to.

The next day she went to the hairdresser where she used to get her hair cut. All the stylists were new so they didn't recognize her. She had her long hair trimmed a few inches, so it looked neat when she pulled it back. And she indulged herself with a facial and a manicure, and emerged feeling very sophisticated and almost like a New Yorker again, but not quite. But at least she wouldn't embarrass Michaela now when they met.

She didn't know it, but Michaela had gone through the same thing when she packed her bags for New York. All her clothes were informal and plain, appropriate for her job as a social worker or out with the kids. She and David rarely got dressed up. They led a casual California life. She wore sandals most of the time and flip-flops on the weekends. Marla complained about it and said she was a beautiful girl and should dress like one. She bought her designer clothes, but Michaela had no place to wear them and they sat in her closet until she gave them away or sold them. It frustrated Marla, who was always impeccably and fashionably dressed. Michaela was panicked now about what to wear to look presentable to the birth mother she had never met.

Melissa was a nervous wreck when she got into the cab to go uptown the next day. She was wearing the pale blue sweater, black slacks and black coat, and

Chanel flats, and looked well put together. Traffic was heavy, and she was afraid to be late, but she arrived at the Mark right on time.

The lobby looked like a movie set with a startling black and white floor, a bar, and a restaurant, and Melissa walked cautiously into the restaurant. Michaela had emailed her a photograph so she'd recognize her. Melissa didn't have a recent one but described herself. Melissa glanced around the restaurant and saw her daughter immediately. She was seated at a table, fidgeting with a straw. She looked up and they both knew. Michaela stood up and came toward her as Melissa headed for her in a straight line, and folded her into her arms. They hugged for a long time, and a few people smiled when they saw them. The love between them radiated around them. The years and the circumstances melted away, and they were both crying and smiling when they went back to Michaela's table.

"I never thought this would happen," Michaela said in a choked voice, as they sat down and faced each other, and Melissa took her hand across the table and held it. She hadn't meant to be so affectionate so quickly, but it came naturally to both of them, and it would have been hard not to give in to it. Then Michaela thought of something.

"What do I call you?"

"Whatever you like," Melissa said with a shy smile.

"Marla prefers for me to call her by her first name, so I always have, or at least for a long time. Would Mom be too weird?" She looked hesitant, and Melissa smiled broadly.

"I'd love it, although I haven't earned it and probably don't deserve it," she said. "But I'd be honored."

"What choice did you have at sixteen?" Michaela said gently, and went right to the heart of the matter.

"That's true, but I always wanted to find you later, when I was older. The nuns burning the records changed all that. I almost died when they told me, when I called them to find you, or at least get some information about where you were."

"Yeah, me too. They told me the same thing when I called them, that the records had been destroyed in a fire and were gone forever. I called on my eighteenth birthday. I thought then they'd give me the information, but it was gone. That was fifteen years ago, and now here we are. You're beautiful," she said to Melissa, looking shy again. And Hattie was right. Melissa could see too that Michaela looked like their mother, in a softer version, but didn't act like her. She was warm and affectionate and forgiving. There was no hint of reproach in anything she said to Melissa, and the time flew as they talked. She asked about Robbie, and told Melissa how sorry she was about it. She'd read Melissa's books and told her she loved them. She talked about David and what a good person he was and how much she loved him, and showed her pictures of Andy and Alexandra and told her about them. "Andy loves anything to do with Superman or outer space. Alex loves clothes, as long as they're pink or purple and have sparkles on them." Melissa made a mental note for future presents. She suddenly had grandchildren, and a daughter, someone to talk to and call and worry about. She was sorry they didn't live closer, and Michaela said she wanted her to come for Thanksgiving and meet her other mother, Marla.

"I'd love to, and that scares me to death. Have you told her about me yet?"

"I will now. I wanted to meet you first, and make sure that everything was okay." Melissa was everything Michaela had hoped she would be. She wasn't as outgoing as her sister, whom Michaela already loved, but there was something very touching about her shyness. It made her seem vulnerable and somewhat fragile, in spite of all the hard things she'd been through, which suggested strength. She seemed like a very discreet, kind, intelligent person to Michaela. She wasn't effusive or showy, but there was something very quietly profound and real about her. She was the kind of person one could count on. Melissa told Michaela about the house in the Berkshires and how much she wanted her to see it.

They were still talking intently when David arrived with the children. They had gone to the park. There was a playground in Central Park near the hotel. They were wearing matching red parkas and blue jeans and sneakers. Alexandra's were pink with sparkles and lit up. Andrew's had Superman on them, and Melissa smiled when she saw them.

"This is your grandma," Michaela explained. She had prepared them to meet her before they came, but now she was real.

"Like Gigi Marla?" Andrew asked with interest.

"Yes," Michaela said simply. "Like that."

Melissa chatted with them for a few minutes, feeling awkward at the newness of it, but they were very polite, endearing children, as Hattie had said. Michaela left with her family a few minutes later, and they were meeting up again for dinner at an Italian restaurant in the neighborhood that the Mark had recommended. Melissa took a cab back to her own hotel then, and walked around for a little while, and then went back to her room.

They met up again promptly at six. Melissa had put on another of her new sweaters, the pink one, for Alexandra. They all talked and laughed their way through dinner. She was back at her hotel at eight-thirty, overwhelmed by the abundant blessings of the day. She was going to the park with Michaela and the children the next day, while David went to his meetings.

Melissa had fun running around with them at the playground and was tired at the end of the day. She wasn't used to young children anymore, but she enjoyed it. She brought presents to dinner for them, a pink tutu with silver sparkles for Alexandra, and superhero pajamas for Andy she'd found at a children's store. Hattie joined them for dinner, wearing jeans and one of her Disneyland sweatshirts. They all had a great time together. Michaela and David and the children were flying back to L.A. in the morning, and they talked about Thanksgiving again at dinner. They had so much to look forward to. The meetings in New York had been a great success, and every time Michaela called her "Mom," she and Melissa smiled at each other, savoring the word and all it meant.

Melissa hugged them all before they piled into a cab to go back to the Mark after dinner, and she walked Hattie to the subway to go back to the Bronx.

"I still can't believe this happened." Melissa looked awestruck. "And you did it for me," she said gratefully.

"Neither can I," Hattie said. It had shaken her faith in the Church she had dedicated eighteen years to, and her vocation, but when she saw the look in her sister's eyes, it was worth it. Melissa looked happy again for the first time in years.

"Do you want to come to L.A. for Thanksgiving with me?" Melissa invited her, but Hattie shook her head.

"I need to be at the convent. We throw open our doors and serve free Thanksgiving dinners to the poor, and I'll be working in the kitchen." Melissa didn't criticize her for it, or make a sarcastic comment as she would have in the past. She had deep respect for her sister now, and gratitude for what she had done. They hugged and Hattie hurried down the steps to the subway, and Melissa walked back to her hotel, thinking of the time she had just spent with her daughter and grandchildren, and she liked David too. He seemed reliable and warm, a good husband and father, and it was obvious that Michaela was happy and in love with him. She was only sorry Robbie hadn't met them, and they'd never know him.

Melissa was driving back to the Berkshires in the morning. She had a lot of time to think on the trip home. It reminded her of that saying in the Bible, about returning beauty for ashes. Her life had been so bitter for so long now, her losses so painful, and now she had this sudden, unexpected abundance of love and joy. She didn't feel as though she deserved it, but she loved it.

Norm called her as soon as she got home, and wanted to hear all about it. He hadn't called her in New York because he didn't want to disturb her. He offered to cook her dinner again that night and she accepted. He arrived with hamburgers and French fries from the local restaurant, with onion rings, and she pretended to be surprised.

"What? No lobster?"

"I didn't have time to shop or cook," he said sheepishly. "I came straight from a client meeting. They hate my design for their new pool and patio. Oh God, there are times when I think politics would have been easier. They want a guesthouse too, and they want it to look like Hansel and Gretel's cottage. I won't win any awards for this one." She laughed at his description and the look on his face. Then she told him all about her two days with Michaela. She wore the new red sweater for him. He noticed it right away and said he liked it.

"It sounds like a resounding success." He celebrated with her as they poured ketchup on the French fries.

"She called me Mom. Marla prefers to be called by her first name. She doesn't want people to know she has such a grown-up daughter, and grandchildren. I kind of like it."

"What did they call you?"

"Grandma Mel. It was all I could think of on the spur of the moment. I hadn't thought about it before, I was so focused on Michaela. It bowled me over when she asked to call me Mom. I hope Marla doesn't mind."

"It doesn't sound like she will," Norm said matter-of-factly, as they finished the burgers and he smiled at her.

"I missed you," he said in a soft voice, and then

leaned over and kissed her. "I thought maybe we could pick up where we left off."

"And where was that?" she whispered in a silky tone, teasing him.

"I'll show you," he whispered back, and fondled her breast as he kissed her. He hadn't done that before. They were making rapid progress, but she didn't object.

They adjourned to the living room, and they kissed again, and his hands drifted all over her and under her sweater. Her eyes were closed and she arched her back as he kissed her breasts, took off her sweater and bra, and unzipped her jeans.

"Let's go upstairs," he whispered, and then kissed her neck, and she nodded. He pulled her to her feet, and at the foot of the stairs, he swept her off her feet and carried her easily to her bedroom and deposited her gently on the bed. He was a strong man. She unbuttoned his shirt, and then his jeans, and a moment later, their bodies were intertwined on the bed, their clothes a tangled mass on the floor.

It had been six years since she'd made love to any man, and she'd almost forgotten what it felt like. But it had never been like this with Carson. Their lovemaking had been familiar and predictable. The passion had gone out of it early on. Love had remained, but not excitement. Making love with Norm was like being swept away on a wave into the sky and beyond. He played her body like a finely tuned instrument, and together they reached heights she'd never been to before. She felt totally spent and sated when it was over and she lay blissful in his arms.

"Oh my God, Norm, what did you do to me?" He smiled with pleasure at the look on her face, and kissed her nipples, which hardened at his touch.

"I'll show you again in a little while. I need to rest for a minute," he said, settling down next to her with an arm around her, and he saw that she was smiling broadly. He loved to see it. As she kissed him, all she could think of was that her life had been empty for years, and suddenly she had a daughter, a son-in-law, grandchildren, and a man in her bed. An amazing man, and she was falling in love with him.

He made a fast comeback, and they made love again a few minutes later, and this time she was exhausted when they stopped. He was tireless and an extraordinary lover.

"Your lovemaking is even better than your cooking," she said in a husky voice as she kissed his throat, and he laughed.

"And you haven't even had my soufflés yet!" he said, still laughing, and rolled over and made love to her again.

Chapter 11

After her first few days back after meeting Michaela in New York, Melissa was thinking quietly one morning over coffee, and decided to make a phone call. Norm had stayed with her almost every night, and she already felt as though they had been lovers forever. Their lives seemed in perfect harmony, and she was so comfortable with him, in and out of bed, that she felt totally at peace. She had never expected this to happen to her.

She poured herself another cup of coffee and called Carson on his cellphone. He saw her name come up, as his phone sat on his desk, and he looked startled. He thought something bad must have happened, maybe to Hattie, or to Melissa herself, and answered immediately.

"Mel?" he answered, worried.

"Hi," she said, not sure where to go from there.

"Are you okay?"

"Yes, I am," she said, sounding at ease and grounded. It was odd hearing his voice again. The call was long overdue, and she had decided to reach out. She had been thinking about it for days. "I just wanted to say hello, and tell you I'm sorry." She sounded sincere and he was surprised by what she said.

"About what?" She hadn't done anything to him lately, or even before. They'd had no contact, except her brief emails on Robbie's anniversaries, and at Christmas, and when the fire was threatening.

"I'm sorry I've been so cut off. I just couldn't talk for a while, to anyone. Something wonderful just happened and I wanted to share it with you." He wondered if she'd met a man. She sounded like it. But he knew better than to ask. He wondered if she was getting married.

"Hattie did something crazy this summer. She went to Ireland. The convent there gave her the same runaround they gave me, but she met an ex-nun who had worked there. Hattie found the baby."

"What baby?" He sounded shocked. The baby she'd had at sixteen was the farthest thing from his mind. It was surprising enough to hear from her, let alone figure out what she meant. She was speaking in riddles.

"The baby I gave up." She jogged his memory, and he reacted instantly.

"Oh my God. How'd she do it? I thought they burned all the records."

"They did, but the nun Hattie met knew enough to piece it together. It was a long shot, but she found her."

"In Ireland?"

"No, in L.A. I just spent two days with her last week. She's a lovely girl, with a nice husband, and two very cute kids." Melissa had a family again. It didn't make up for losing Robbie. Nothing could ever replace him, but it was a gift nonetheless, and made an enormous difference. "I think I understand now how you feel about Jane's two daughters. I hated that you were close to them, but it's nice having kids and young people in my life again. I'm not sure how you bridge the gap of thirty-three years in this case, but she has a big heart and we seem to be doing it. I'm going to L.A. to spend Thanksgiving with them."

"I'm glad, Mel," he said, sounding deeply moved to hear from her. "I think about you all the time. I hope you're happy."

"I am. It's better now. It's taken a long time. It's taken all four years I've been here to start to heal." And finding Michaela had made a big difference. Somehow it gave her hope again, and a new outlook on everything. Her life was suddenly about who was in it, not just who was gone. Her sister had given her an immeasurable gift. "I'm sorry I was so hard on you, and so disconnected."

"You weren't hard on me. You were broken. We both were, and we couldn't fix each other." He had needed Jane to help him recover from losing Robbie. Without her, he didn't know how he would have survived it. Melissa had completely shut him out. "Have you gone back to writing yet?"

"No, and I never will. Robbie took that with him."

"No, he didn't. It's still there. I hope you go back to it one day."

"I don't want to."

"I'm sorry to hear it, but I'm glad you found your daughter. Does she look like you?" He was curious about her.

"Somewhat." Melissa laughed. "She looks like my mother. I forgive her for it. She's a very pretty girl."

"It's nice of you to call and tell me."

"I thought it was time to reach out. It's been too long."

"I understand," he said gently.

"Are you happy?" she asked in a soft voice.

"Yes, I am. It's different. It was never going to be the way it was with us. It was so exciting working with you on the books. Jane doesn't have the kind of drive you did. She wants to keep it all small and in control. That works for her. We get along, and I enjoy her daughters." It didn't sound like a grand passion, but it seemed comfortable, and maybe for him that was enough. Melissa had been more fiery with him and he missed that. She was an enormous talent and a brilliant mind. He had never known anyone like her. It would be a real loss to her readers if she never wrote again. She sounded definite about it. "Maybe something will get you writing again."

"I hope not," she said with feeling. "What I have now is enough. I love my house and where I live. I love working with my hands. And now I have Michaela, my daughter." And Norm, but she didn't say it.

"I'm glad you called. Stay in touch, Mel, and congratulations on finding your daughter." He remembered how devastated she had been when she found out the records had been destroyed, and knew she'd never see her again, and now she had. "And give Hattie my love."

"I will," she promised.

"Are you still mad at her?"

"Not anymore. Not after what she did. I was foolish about that too. The convent suits her."

"Yes, it does." They both had a warm feeling after they hung up, and she was glad she'd called him. It was time to stop running away and shutting everyone out, and being angry at them. She had wanted to make peace with him. It wasn't his fault Robbie had died. No one was to blame for that. It had taken six-and-a-half years to begin to heal. Hattie had been a part of it, and Michaela, and now Norm, and Melissa herself. It was a long, painful process.

* * *

The day after she called Carson, she got the results of the DNA test. It was conclusive, which they knew it would be. Michaela was her daughter. It was comforting to know. She'd had the test before she went to New York. She sent a text to Hattie, and emailed the results to Michaela, and signed it "Love, Mom."

Melissa's and Michaela's lives had improved exponentially as a result of Hattie finding Michaela. The one whose life had been negatively impacted was Hattie, Sister Mary Joseph. The unraveling of her religious life had begun when she went to Saint Blaise's, saw the prison where Melissa had been, and her faith in the religious life began to spiral down faster when she met with Fiona Eckles. What she had seen and done there had driven her out of the Church, and Hattie was beginning to think it would have the same effect on her. She could no longer respect a church that had sold babies for profit, no matter how well intended their motives. It had only been a fluke, or a miracle, that she had found Michaela. The others weren't as lucky, and they would never find their mothers. And the mothers who wanted to would never see their children again. It seemed a cruel turn of fate for all concerned. And women like Fiona had been injured too. Hattie couldn't seem to recover from it.

Mother Elizabeth had seen what it was doing to

her, and so far hadn't been able to help her. She had offered to send her on a retreat, or for therapy, and Hattie had refused both.

"What would that change?"

"Even those of us in religious orders are human, Sister Mary Joe," she reminded her. "We make mistakes. They made a big one when they destroyed the records. They thought they were protecting everyone involved."

"They were protecting the Church, not the people in it. And so many people got hurt as a result. My sister was almost one of them."

"You did a wonderful thing for her, and for your niece, but you can't lose your vocation because of it. That's too high a price for you to pay."

"And what if my vocation was motivated by the wrong things from the beginning? Maybe that's what's coming to the surface."

"There's nothing wrong with your vocation, my child." But there was so much she didn't know that Hattie didn't believe her. "You've been here for eighteen years. If there was a flaw in your vocation, you'd have discovered it a long time ago." But Hattie knew that Fiona Eckles had been even older when she asked to be released from her vows. She couldn't forgive herself for her part in what she had done. Hattie had other things on her conscience.

"I'd like to go back to Africa one day," she said

wistfully. "I was happy there, and serving a useful purpose."

"I can sign you up for service there again, but you need to find your footing first. When you feel your vocation is secure, I'll see what I can do to recommend that."

"I'd like that," Hattie said, her eyes brightening. For the first time in months, she felt hopeful. Going to Saint Blaise's had been a dark experience which shook her faith in everything she believed in. It was a cover-up, like others the Church had committed to protect their own. Hattie didn't want to be part of an institution that did that, no matter who was to blame. She saw the Church as an evil force now, which was what Fiona had said to her too. But what would she do if she left? Where would she go? After eighteen years, she had no other life now. She could go to her sister in the Berkshires for a while, but then what? No matter where she looked, she saw no meaningful future for herself. The only thing she wanted to do was return to Africa, but that didn't seem likely either. And it was a form of running away too.

She drove up to see Melissa the week before Thanksgiving, and they spent the day together. There was snow on the ground, and they went for a long walk in the orchards. Melissa could sense that her sister was troubled and her spirits were down, and asked her about it. Hattie hadn't seemed all right to her since she'd come back from Ireland, despite the victory it had been for her.

"It shook my faith," she confessed to Melissa, "in everything I believe and have dedicated my life to. It was so dishonest, and hurt so many people." The cover-up of the rogue priests was a scandal the Church was still reverberating from too. And what if there were other things? "I told Mother Elizabeth I'd love to go back to Africa. She said she could recommend me, but I have to get my feet on firm ground first. I keep thinking of Fiona Eckles leaving the Church because of what happened at Saint Blaise's."

"You wouldn't give up your vows, would you?" Melissa looked startled. She hadn't realized how deeply shaken her sister was.

"I don't know," Hattie answered. "I've thought about it. I'm not sure my vocation was ever for the right reasons."

"Of course it was," Melissa tried to reassure her. "And I don't want you to go back to Africa. I just got you back a few months ago, I don't want to lose you."

"You never will." Hattie smiled at her. "This isn't about us. It's about what I believe in, and why I'm there. It's complicated."

"Life is complicated. People are complicated. And churches are even more so."

"If I'm not sure of my vocation, I don't belong there," Hattie said firmly.

Melissa was worried about her when she left.

Things were going so well for her now, and she could see that her sister was suffering. It was almost as though Saint Blaise's was cursed, and everyone who went there paid a terrible price. It was exactly what Melissa had said about it when she was there. It was hell on Earth. Her own faith had been restored when Hattie had found Michaela, and now it seemed as though Hattie was losing hers. She had never heard her question her vocation before. She was going through a very dark time, her own private hell, just as Fiona Eckles had described. Hattie wrote the ex-nun a long letter when she got back to the convent that night, asking her advice. But she could already guess what it would be.

Norm spent a quiet Sunday with Melissa, the day after her sister's visit. They watched a movie on TV and went to bed early that night. She was making coffee in the morning when he brought the paper in, and the front page on *The Boston Globe* was a photograph of one of the most important movie producers in Hollywood. He was in his sixties, and the headline was that a major actress was bringing criminal charges against him for sexual assault. It was a shocking story and Norm read it as she handed him a mug of coffee. When he finished, he passed the paper to her.

"Wow, that's a shocker," Norm said. He was one of

the most respected producers in the business. The actress, who had two Oscars to her credit and a Golden Globe, claimed that he had raped her five years before, slapped her around afterward, broken her nose, and then sodomized her. She hadn't reported him because she didn't want to lose the starring role in the movie that won her her second Oscar. She had produced photographs, which the producer insisted had been falsified. The victim claimed that he had lured her to his office, and she had been coerced into having sex with him once before, when he promised her another starring role, but only if she let him sodomize her. She said she had finally spoken up because she claimed he had recently tried to coerce her again. He denied all of it, and Melissa finished reading the story and looked at Norm.

"Do you believe her? Maybe she was mad at him about something. Why would she wait five years to report it?"

"Afraid for her career? I think a lot of that must go on in Hollywood. The casting couch, to varying degrees."

"This sounds pretty violent," Melissa commented.

"It's going to have a big impact if someone as big as she is accuses someone as important as him. This is right up at the top of the ladder out there, out in the stratosphere," Norm said.

"It happens in a lot of fields, maybe not as extreme as in this case. There's some of that in publishing, and in business."

"Politics isn't exempt," Norm added. "There's always some old perverted congressman or senator being accused of trying to trade sexual favors for promotions, or chasing some young intern around a desk. It's as old as time."

Melissa turned on the morning news on TV after he left for work, and it was all they talked about, and the morning talk shows were full of it. The producer in question had just come out with a major movie that was expected to be a huge box office hit. And by the end of the day, the latest bulletin was that the film had been pulled from theaters across the country. The actress accusing him had released copies of the photographs of her after he raped her. The producer was not available for comment, the LAPD was pressing felony charges, and his new movie was history. Theater owners were refusing to show it, which was going to represent a colossal loss of money to everyone involved. It had taken enormous courage for the actress to come forward after so long.

Norm and Melissa talked about it over dinner that night. The next morning, two more major actresses had made similar accusations against him. And a famous director had been accused as well. Hollywood was in an uproar, as women were coming forward to accuse other producers of similar acts. All claimed they had been coerced into having sex with producers and directors and studio executives in order to secure important starring roles.

It was mesmerizing watching the entertainment world crumble. Like a soap opera in real life. And some of the actresses involved were so famous, and the producers, that it didn't seem real. It was Hollywood drama. Some other actors were named, and two talk show hosts lost their shows.

"It's an avalanche, isn't it?" Norm said, fascinated by the list of names of men who had been accused, and it all had the ring of truth. Networks were canceling shows left and right, stars were being replaced, sponsors were pulling out. None of the other men accused were denying the claims being made against them. Two famous actors and a producer made tearful apologies on television.

"This is like a bad movie," Melissa said, but it was all too real. She was leaving the next day for L.A., and wondered if Marla Moore would talk about it when she met her at Thanksgiving, or if the subject would be taboo. It was rapidly turning into a witch hunt, but the witches and warlocks were coming out of the bushes in droves, pursued by their irate victims, who felt the safety in numbers and were finally having the courage to speak up. Many minor actresses were making the same claims, and several young gay men. But on the whole, the victims' voices were being heard. Most of them were women.

She was sad to leave Norm over the holiday, so

early in their budding relationship, but he was going to his brother's home in Boston, to spend Thanksgiving with them. She was excited about seeing Michaela again, and sharing the holiday with her family. She had pulled out of her closet an old brown velvet Chanel suit she'd forgotten about to wear to their Thanksgiving meal.

She drove to the Boston airport, and left her car in the lot there, and everyone was reading about the sexual harassment scandal on the plane. Hollywood had been blown wide open, and Melissa guessed that men in the entertainment field all over Hollywood were shaking in their shoes, worrying about who would be accused next. There were dozens of men already implicated after just three days. It was as though someone had pulled a plug, or the dam had broken, and the floodgates were open wide.

When they landed, Melissa took a cab to the Beverly Hills Hotel, and called Michaela after she settled into her room. She was going to their house for dinner that night, and had ordered flowers for them that they could use on the table for Thanksgiving lunch the next day. Michaela said that dinner that night was going to be informal. David was going to barbecue on their patio. Marla would be joining them the next day. She was back from location, but still working on the film, and she didn't like going out when she was shooting. It made her tired the next day. Melissa was planning to be in town until Sunday. She was really looking forward to it. She hadn't even celebrated the holidays for the past four years, and had no one to spend them with. She preferred to read or watch old movies and forget it. But not this year. She had a great deal to celebrate and be thankful for. She was sorry that Hattie wasn't there too, since she had made all their joy possible.

Melissa took a cab to Michaela's address at six o'clock, and the children were running around and excited to see her.

"Grandma Mel!" they squealed as though they had known her all their lives. She had brought Thanksgiving coloring books and a box of crayons for each, a pilgrim doll for Alex, and an Indian headdress for Andy, and a cowboys and Indians board game.

"You don't have to spoil them, Mom," Michaela said, sounding natural as she said it, and Melissa smiled. She loved hearing the word. No one had called her "Mom" in six years.

"I have a lot of years to make up for, especially since I didn't get to spoil you at all," Melissa said gently. "And a couple of coloring books won't spoil them. We'll discuss it when it's time for Andy's first car. That's ten years away, so we have time." Michaela laughed, and Melissa went out to see her son-in-law at the barbecue. He was flipping burgers for the kids, and making ribs and chicken for them, wearing jeans and a dark blue sweatshirt. They had a big backyard, and an attractive single-level house, with a big living room, a dining room, and a play-room, four bedrooms, and a three-car garage. It was in a high-end area of Beverly Hills, and David said they had bought it when Andrew was born. David did very well as an agent.

The meal was delicious, and when they finished eating, the children went to the playroom and took their coloring books with them. They both had iPads to play games on, which Melissa noticed. Robbie had loved his too. It had kept him occupied at the hospi-tal for hours when he had chemo treatments. She still had his tucked away in a drawer with his favorite games on it.

When the children had left the room, Melissa thanked David for a delicious dinner, and asked them both what they thought of the sexual harassment scandal that had everyone riveted. The first story had broken two days before, and the avalanche of claims was gathering momentum.

"I don't think it's news to anyone in the industry, but no one has ever spoken up before, and now ev-erybody is," Michaela answered. "Every day there are new names on the list. A lot of TV shows are being canceled, even some really big ones, and movies are being pulled from the theaters. Marla said they had to replace two people in the cast of the one she's working on, and the director is really pissed. They have to reshoot all of the scenes they're in with new actors. Everyone is taking it very seriously. No one is denying that it's real. Maybe it was time that it happened."

"Two of my clients have been accused," David added. "We referred them to criminal lawyers. We don't handle those cases. And I'll bet there are going to be a lot more."

"It sounds like it," Melissa commented. "It happens in a lot of industries. But maybe not as blatantly as it does in Hollywood." Some of the stories they were hearing were seriously offensive, and tragic in some cases when children and adolescents and very young actors were involved. It had ruined some lives, and was going to destroy a lot of careers. A number of actresses were saying that they had lost parts in important films when they wouldn't agree to play along. "It's all over the news in New England, and the East, and it must be an even bigger deal here."

"It's all anyone is talking about," Michaela confirmed. "Marla says they deserve it. They've gotten away with it for a long time."

Michaela's adoptive mother was much on Melissa's mind, since they were meeting for the first time at lunch the next day, and Melissa was still terrified by the prospect. Norm had done all he could to encourage her before she left. But her mind wouldn't rest until the first encounter was over, if it went well. Michaela was sure it would.

Melissa left early after dinner and went back to

the hotel. She watched the late news and more names had been added to the list, some of Melissa's favorite actors, and she was sorry to see it. More and more victims were feeling empowered to speak up. It was a frenzy, but many of the claims were well founded. Only a few sounded bogus, trying to exploit the current trend. Almost all of them sounded all too real and credible. She turned off the TV and went to bed, and got up early the next morning. She was invited to be at the Fosters' at noon, and lunch was at one. Michaela had said that David was making the turkey and the stuffing, and she was doing everything else, all the vegetables and the pies. They did a traditional Thanksgiving at their house every year, and Christmas at her mother's, which she had catered by a restaurant. According to Michaela, Marla couldn't boil water and never tried. She had a full staff to provide whatever she needed. But Michaela liked cooking with her husband. It reminded Melissa of Norm. It was too late to call him with the three-hour time difference when she got back to the hotel. She knew he'd be asleep, and was driving to his brother's in Boston in the morning.

Melissa had coffee and toast at the hotel. She didn't want to eat much, since she already knew that they were serving a big lunch. She was nervous about meeting the woman who had raised her daughter and stood in as her mother for thirty-three years. She wondered what she would have thought if they had met when Michaela was born, if she would have liked them, and wanted them to raise her daughter. She'd had no say in it, and they'd never met. It was all handled differently then. Birth mothers didn't stay in their children's lives, show up for holidays, or come to birthday parties. In those days, they disappeared out of the baby's life. And they had no voice in who adopted their child. That was all much more recent. Melissa still felt strange about spending Thanksgiving with Marla and having lunch with her. And she was such a huge star.

She put on the brown velvet suit and it looked a little out of date, but not too much so. And she was wearing one of the pairs of high-heeled shoes she'd bought in New York. She had brown and gold earrings that looked like leaves that Carson had given her. They were antique topaz and he'd bought them in London. She was carrying an old brown alligator purse of her mother's that she had saved but never used. She felt a little too proper when she looked in the mirror. She looked like her mother when she went to play bridge with her friends. But she wanted to look respectable and motherly, and didn't want to embarrass Michaela.

She arrived right on time, and the children looked all clean and shined. Alexandra had on a pretty pink smocked dress, and Andy was wearing brown corduroy pants and a white shirt and red sweater, and his Superman sneakers. Michaela said he was supposed to be wearing loafers but he refused, and she went back to the kitchen to keep an eye on the Brussels sprouts. David was basting the turkey, and there was football on the TV.

The doorbell rang and no one answered, so Melissa got up to help. She told Michaela she'd get it, without thinking who it might be. She opened the door and found herself looking into the huge blue eyes of an older blond woman, with perfectly cut hair to her shoulders, diamonds on her ears, in brown velvet slacks and a cream satin blouse, high heels, and a huge gold bracelet on one wrist. She had a flawless figure and a perfect smile, and in an instant Melissa registered who it was. It was Marla Moore, who came in drifting a cloud of Chanel No. 5 behind her. She looked Melissa over appraisingly from head to foot, as Melissa felt her knees begin to shake.

"I am *very* glad to meet you," Marla said in clipped upper class Eastern tones that Melissa recognized immediately, and she sounded as though she meant it. But she was an actress so it was hard to tell. "I've been hearing a lot about you from Michaela. You're even younger than I thought you'd be. You must have been a baby yourself when you had her." She got right to the point as they stood in the front hall and didn't move. Melissa felt frumpy next to her. Everything Marla was wearing was fashionable, flattering, expensive, and chic.

"I was sixteen," Melissa answered, feeling awkward.

"I'm twenty-four years older than you are," Marla said and winced. "I was forty when she was born. My husband was sixty-two. We were old enough to be your parents," she said, as Melissa digested the information. "I've been so nervous about meeting you," she said, and Melissa was stunned to hear it.

"How can *you* be nervous to meet me? I'm just a woman who lives on a farm in New England. You're one of the most famous women in the world, and the most glamorous woman I've ever seen."

"Hardly. But thank you. I've read your books. I bought them when Michaela told me about you. They're brilliant. Do you have any new ones in the pipeline?"

"I retired," Melissa said quietly, touched by the praise.

"That's ridiculous. Not at your age. I'm seventy-three and I have no intention of retiring until they drag me off the set in a body bag. Retiring kills people. Haven't you heard?" They walked slowly into the living room then and sat down.

"I ran out of ideas," Melissa said, feeling lame when she said it. The older woman sitting next to her on the couch was strong and vital and full of energy, and Melissa felt like a loser saying she'd retired.

"I doubt that. Just a hiatus. We all have them. The woman who wrote those books is full of ideas. I'm sure you have another ten or twenty books in you," she said with another smile with her perfect teeth. She looked like a toothpaste ad, or the cover of *Vogue*. She looked like a famous movie star from head to toe, and her hands were perfectly manicured. Melissa hadn't worn nail polish in seven years.

"To be honest, my son got sick and died, so I stopped writing."

"I'm sorry," she said, sounding sympathetic for a brief instant. "My husband died, and I was on set the day after the funeral to start a movie. You can't afford to let your guard down for a minute. None of us can. There's always someone waiting to take our place." It was how she lived, going at full speed in a highly competitive field. She was a force to be reckoned with, and Melissa could see what Michaela meant now. Marla Moore was not a warm, fuzzy person, she was a human cyclone and a strong woman, and she expected those around her to be strong too.

"You're probably right. I've been working on my home in the Berkshires for the last four years. I've done most of the work myself." She sounded proud as she said it.

"That's wonderful and it must be beautiful. But you can do that when you're eighty. The world needs more of your books." She was emphatic about it, and

Melissa smiled as their daughter walked into the room, and smiled at both of them.

"Hi, Marla. So have you told Melissa how to run her life yet?" Michaela teased her. She knew her adoptive mother well, and obviously loved her, from the warm look they exchanged.

"Of course. That's what I was doing when you walked in. She needs to write more books."

"Maybe she doesn't want to," Michaela suggested gently.

"She doesn't have a choice. She has a talent, she has to use it. That's the obligation that comes with talent. You can't put it in a drawer and forget about it." Which Melissa had for the last seven years, since Robbie got sick.

"Not everyone wants to work as hard as you do," Michaela reminded her.

"That's for sure. Well, how does it feel to live in Gomorrah?" she asked her daughter. "Most of my friends are on those lists. The women accusing them are right, of course, and some of them should have been caught and punished years ago. But they got away with it, and now all hell is breaking loose, and they're getting fired left and right. We haven't seen the end of it yet." She turned to Melissa then. "I'm sure you came across it in publishing too. We all do. A lot of women have been badly used. In many cases in Hollywood, if they wanted the good parts, they gave in. It's a rotten business. Always has been. I came across it a few times, but I've been lucky. Most of the producers I worked with are decent men. But many are as rotten as they say. I'm very glad Michaela never went into the business. There's no question, some of those men ruined a lot of lives, and we all knew about them. Now their victims are coming back with a vengeance to ruin theirs. I have no sympathy for them." She was strong and sure and clear. Melissa realized that she liked her. Marla was still a little bit scary, she was forceful and opinionated, but Melissa had a feeling that she was a good person. She was very much the way her adopted daughter had described her. She looked at Melissa then. "I wasn't around as much as I should have been, but I want you to know that I love her very much, and I would have laid down my life for her. If I had to do it again, I would have done a few less movies and been home with her more. I missed some important moments, but I'm here for her, and I love her. And I think she knows that too."

"Yes, she does," Melissa said quietly, "and she loves you very much too. I couldn't have done as good a job as you did, at the age I was, or maybe even later. You had so much to offer her, your life experience and your husband's, and I had so much to learn."

"We all do," she said generously. "I was worried about meeting you. Michaela has been so excited about finding you, or your sister finding her. And you're so much younger than I am, and probably a lot more fun. I'm old enough to be your mother. But maybe together, we can be there for her now. We complement each other, so she has two mothers now." It was the most generous thing she could have said and Melissa was grateful to her and relaxed as soon as she said it. They all did. Marla turned to Michaela then.

"What's your husband doing with that damn turkey? Chasing it around the backyard? We're all starving." Andrew walked into the room then and she looked with dismay at his feet. "Andrew, sneakers are for tennis or the beach. Please put proper shoes on. Superman can wait." He scampered out of the room without arguing to get his loafers, and Michaela thanked her, and then Marla turned to Melissa. "He can wear those when he's with you. I'm old-fashioned, I like boys in proper shoes." Her son-in-law walked in then, wearing Nikes with his suit, and she pretended to swoon. "What is wrong with you people? An entire generation who don't own shoes." They all laughed then, and David announced that the turkey was ready, and they followed him to the dining room, where the turkey was sitting on a platter on the table and looked splendid. He had already carved it, which was the reason for the delay.

It was a lively meal with Marla in their midst. She kept everyone in order, complimented both chefs on the delicious food, and told them countless funny stories about the antics on the set of the movie she was working on.

"If they're not all in jail for sexual assault by then, we should wrap in two or three weeks," she said, "and then we go into post-production. I'm starting a new picture in January. We'll be shooting here and in England and Scotland, so I'll be out of your hair for a month or two at the beginning of the year." She had more energy than anyone Melissa had ever met.

Marla left shortly after dessert and said she had script changes and new lines to study. Before she left, she stopped and looked at Melissa. "I was worried about it, but I'm not anymore now that I've met you. You're a good woman, and I'm happy to share her with you. But get back to work on those books. No excuses. It won't bring your son back if you stop writing. The world needs what you have to say."

"Thank you," Melissa said, feeling awkward, they hugged each other, and a few minutes later, Marla left.

"Wow, she's amazing," Melissa said, after the door closed behind her. "She has so much energy."

David and Michaela burst out laughing. "She certainly does. She never stops. She works like a Trojan, and she probably always will. She still gets a lot of work. A lot of actresses don't at her age. But she always finds a part she loves, and she's not afraid of the hard ones."

"It must have been interesting growing up with her," Melissa said.

"It was," Michaela confirmed. "She was always fair, but she expected a lot. Good grades, good behavior, good shoes. She can't stand laziness in any form. She sets the bar high, for herself and everyone else. And she has a good heart too. I'm glad you like her. I would have been sad if you two didn't get along." She was a force to be reckoned with, but Melissa had great respect for her.

"I'm in awe of her. I want to be her when I grow up," she said, and David and Michaela laughed. Marla was unique. And Melissa was touched by her saying that she was willing to share Michaela with her. She was generous to a fault. "I was so nervous about meeting her."

"She was nervous about you too," Michaela said. "She told me in the kitchen between courses that she thinks you're terrific. And she doesn't say that easily about anyone." Melissa had been interested too in her comments about the sex offenders. Marla knew all the inside scoop and the men involved.

She stayed to watch a movie with them, after they put the dishes in the kitchen. David had the football game on mute on another TV at the same time, so he could keep track of the scores.

And they did fun things in L.A. over the weekend. They didn't see Marla again. She was busy, but she sent Melissa an email, telling her how much she'd enjoyed meeting her, and reminding her to get back to work on the books.

All in all, it was a perfect Thanksgiving. She told Norm all about it when she got back to the hotel and called him. He'd had a nice day at his brother's too. Melissa was sad to leave, but they were coming to visit her two days after Christmas and planning to stay a week.

Norm took a cab to the airport in Boston, and drove home with her. They didn't stop talking all the way home, and when they got to her house, they raced upstairs and flew onto her bed.

"I've been pining for you for four days," he said fervently, as he pulled off her clothes and she laughed and tugged at his. Minutes later, they were making love. He was wonderful to come home to, and she had had a lovely time with her daughter. She couldn't think of a better Thanksgiving. Her solitude in the Berkshires was over. She was alive again, and had so much to look forward to. She had never been as thankful in her life.

Chapter 12

Hattie called Melissa the day after the Thanksgiving weekend, when she got home from work.

"How was it?" Hattie asked her.

"Fantastic. It was perfect. Marla Moore is amazing. She has more energy than anyone half her age. She's glamorous and beautiful. I think she was as nervous as I was before we met. She was afraid I would take Michaela away from her. No one could. Marla's a good mother in her own way. She has her own life and a busy career, but she loves her, and Michaela knows it. She said she's happy to share her with me. I couldn't hope for more."

Hattie sounded distracted when she spoke. "Can I come up this weekend? I want to talk to you." She sounded very serious, and Melissa was worried about her. She had been so down lately, since the summer and her trip to Ireland. She wasn't sure whether seeing Saint Blaise's had done it or talking to Fiona Eckles, but whatever it was, Hattie hadn't recovered yet, and seemed to be getting even more depressed.

"Sure," she responded. "Do you want to stay Saturday night?"

"I can't. I have to help with Mass on Sunday. I'll just come for the day."

"That's such a long trip for you. I hope it doesn't snow."

"Me too."

"Are you all right?"

"Yeah. I'm okay. See you Saturday." She hung up before Melissa could question her further. Melissa had a busy week herself after that. Norm stayed with her every night, but he stayed away on Saturday, so she could spend the day with her sister. Hattie arrived at eleven, which meant she must have left the city around six, since there was a light snow on the road. She looked somber when Melissa opened the door for her, and followed her into the kitchen.

"They didn't have cinnamon buns. I got you chocolate croissants." Hattie smiled at her, but Melissa could see that something was wrong. "What's up? You look like you flunked math." They both smiled. It brought back memories of their youth.

Hattie sighed and sat back in a kitchen chair and looked at her sister. "I flunked vocation. There's something I've been wanting to tell you for years. I should have told you a long time ago."

"Don't be so hard on yourself. You're a wonderful nun."

"No, I'm not. I never had a vocation. You were right. I ran away. I wanted to run as far away as I could. The convent seemed like the perfect place to do it. I didn't have some kind of religious vision or inspiration. I was just scared. So I ran away and hid, just like you said. I was a coward. I still am.

"Do you remember the producer who asked me to go to Hollywood for the screen test? He was offering me a part in a big movie. A good part. I was so excited. I never asked any questions. I flew out there on the ticket he sent me and showed up for the test. Sam Steinberg. He flew out to L.A. to be at the test himself. He told me to meet him in his office. So I did, like the idiot I was then."

"You weren't an idiot," Melissa corrected her. She was listening closely, frowning. "You were a kid."

"A very dumb kid. I walked into his office on a Saturday morning. There was no one else there. He said he was going to give me the test himself, because I was so talented. I could see a huge film career starting, and an Oscar in my future. He locked the door with a button under his desk. He took his clothes off then, and tore off mine. He ripped them right off my back, slapped me around, threw me on the couch in his office, and raped me. After that, he laid me on his desk, and punched me every time I tried to move, and raped me again. He hit me, kicked me, punched me, masturbated on me, and raped me all day. He kept me there till six o'clock. I could hardly walk by the time he let me go. There was no one in the building except us. He threw me a shirt and some shorts while I crawled across the floor. I couldn't even stand up, while he put on his shirt and tie, and his suit. He stood in the doorway and said, 'Sorry, kid, you flunked the test. You're too young for the part. Better luck next time.'

"He laughed then and walked out. I don't even know how I got out of there. I was too ashamed to go to a hospital. He broke some ribs. I was black and blue all over, and I could hardly sit down for a week. Thank God, I didn't get pregnant. His name was on the list of sex offenders last week. Seventeen women have accused him of rape and assault and battery, and described everything he did to me. He's been doing it to young hopeful actresses for years. The Sam Steinberg Screen Test. It's common knowledge in Hollywood apparently."

Melissa felt sick as she listened, afraid that there was more. "I checked in to a cheap motel and stayed there until I could walk normally again and cover the bruises with makeup. When I got home, I did the only thing I could think of. I went straight to the convent, and told them I felt I had a vocation. I didn't have a vocation, but I never wanted to see another man again, or have one touch me. I met a girl on the plane, going back to New York, who was crying, and said she had been raped twice in L.A., and once in New York when she was trying out for an Off-Broadway show. That did it. I knew I didn't want to be an actress anymore. He beat it out of me. All I wanted to be was protected and safe from guys like him. If that's what acting was about, I didn't want it." Hattie was crying by then, and so was Melissa.

"Why didn't you tell me? You could have called me from L.A. We could have gone to the police. We still can." Melissa wanted to kill him after what she'd heard.

"He said that if I did, he'd find me and beat me to a pulp or kill me, and no one would believe me anyway. And he was right. No one would have then. He was a big producer and I was no one. I never wanted that to happen again. I probably was no good as an actress anyway. I couldn't have lived through that happening again."

"I remember when you went," Melissa said, feeling sick. "I was happy for you. It was a big deal. And I remember when you came back and went straight into the convent. I thought you were crazy. It didn't make any sense. Now it does, eighteen years later. I should have figured it out."

"How could you? I lied to get into the convent. And I lied to you. The only reason I wanted to get into the convent was because that bastard raped me and I was scared it would happen again. I've been in for eighteen years under false pretenses. The only reason I joined the order was because I'd been raped, and was too scared to be out in the world, except as a nun."

"Oh, Hattie," Melissa said, and put her arms around her. "Let's go to the police now. It's not too late. He needs to be held accountable and brought to justice."

"Someone else is doing that. I don't have to. I won't do it. I would be disgraced forever."

"If you tell Mother Elizabeth, I think she'd want you to."

"If I tell her, she'll know I'm a liar and I've been a fraud for all these years. But when I saw his name in the papers last week, I knew I had to tell you at least. You have a right to know how dishonest I am, and why I joined the order."

"You're not at fault here. He is. He raped an innocent young girl. He brutally beat you, and raped you. He has to pay for that. It'll carry even more weight because you're a nun now."

"I'm not a nun, I'm a fraud," she said, furious with herself. "I'm going to ask to be released from my vows. I don't belong there. I want to go back to Africa. I can be a nurse. I don't have to be a nun to work there."

"You can't run away from this again. This man needs to be punished."

"Maybe it wasn't entirely his fault," she said, sobbing. "After the first time, I didn't even try to stop him. I was too scared. You would never have done something like that. You would have stopped him. You wouldn't have let him rape you." Melissa was looking hard at her sister, and she wanted to kill Sam Steinberg with her bare hands.

"Let me tell you something about my career. What happened to you was *not* your fault. After my first book was published, I wanted an even better contract on the next one. Carson had gotten me a good deal, but I was ambitious. My publisher called and invited me to lunch. I was very flattered. He took me to the Four Seasons and I felt like a big deal. I had three drinks at lunch. When we left the restaurant, he put it to me. If I'd sleep with him, he'd sweeten the deal on my next book, that is if I sweetened the deal for him first. He didn't rape me or beat me. He coerced me. He enticed me, and I was greedy and stupid enough to go along with it. Carson and I had just started dating. So I went to his place with him. He had an apartment on East Sixty-second Street for just that purpose. I went there with him, like a total whore. I gave him a blow job, and went to bed with him. We had sex all afternoon. It was consensual. When it was over, he said he'd call my agent in the morning and give us a great contract with a huge advance, but he wanted to meet me again. He suggested we meet once a week. He called Carson in the morning and gave me a slightly better contract, not a great one. I took the contract and signed it. I never went back again. I stayed away from him, and I didn't tell Carson. But I knew exactly what I was and what I'd done. I'd prostituted myself to get ahead. I had felt like a slut and had behaved like one. There are a million guys out there like these, waiting to jump on young women, using sex to make their deals. And some of us are dumb enough to buy into it. I never did it again, but I never forgot what I did. So I'm not so lily pure either. And I did it willingly. You didn't. You were raped.

"The publisher I had sex with was fired a few years later, and went to another publishing house. He's probably still playing the same game if he can get anyone to fall for it twenty years later. There's always Viagra if he can't get it up. He's probably seventy-five or eighty by now. There are guys like that in every line of work, and women who fall for it like I did. But those women are speaking up now. They're blowing the whistle on these creeps. That's the only way it's going to stop. Women have a stake in the game now. Men in Hollywood, big men, are losing their jobs, their careers, their TV shows, their parts in movies. Some of them will probably go to prison. It's going to cost them big-time and it should. I was stupid, and lost my integrity momentarily, but you were a victim, Hattie. I want you to go after the guy and put your name on that list. I'll stand beside you all the way."

"I can't do it," Hattie said, sounding strangled, as

the two sisters fell into each other's arms and cried for each other. "I'm so sorry that guy did that to you," she said to Melissa.

"He didn't do it. I did. I went to his apartment with him, like a cheap trick he picked up on the street. As I said, I never told Carson. I was afraid he'd be disgusted with me. He was the head of a respected publishing house. Guys like him have won for years. But they're not winning now. They're losing everything, just as they should." Hattie looked at her mournfully, and Melissa made her a cup of tea and handed it to her. They'd been talking for hours and it was getting late.

"I should go soon. I was going to talk to Mother Elizabeth tomorrow. I don't want to keep it a secret from her anymore. I don't belong in the convent. My motives were never pure. I was only thinking of myself."

"Your motives were entirely pure. Stop saying that. Steinberg's the sinner here, not you."

It was a wicked world and they'd both been victims of it. It was too late for Melissa to make the publisher accountable, she didn't even know if he was still alive and he had probably retired and it no longer mattered. It was ancient history and she'd given up writing. But it wasn't too late for Hattie, and she wanted her to speak up, and add her name to the list of the victims. He had cost Hattie a promising career and wounded her deeply.

"I'll talk to Mother Elizabeth about it, and see what she thinks," was all she'd agree to. And she didn't want to embarrass the convent. She left a few minutes later, after Melissa hugged her tight again and told her she loved her. She felt drained when Hattie left, and she wanted to think about everything they'd said. She was heartbroken over Hattie's story, but it finally explained why she had gone into the convent so hurriedly. They'd both been religious as children, but Hattie had never wanted to be a nun as a young girl. It had never made sense to Melissa before, but now it did. She was a classic victim in the worst possible way, and still blamed herself eighteen years later. She had carried that burden and her secret for all these years. It had cost her eighteen years of her life as a woman, and changed the course of her life.

For the first time, Melissa didn't want to see Norm that night. She texted him and told him she was sick. She said she had a headache and the flu and would call him in the morning. She thought of her own foolishness too, and how disgusting it had been. She hadn't let herself think of it in years, but Hattie's story brought it all back. In her own way, in her youth and stupidity, she'd been a victim too, of the manipulations of someone older and more clever than she was. She would have gotten the contract anyway, because her books were good, but she didn't know that then, so she had sold her soul to the devil. She remembered perfectly now how dirty she'd felt afterward, and swore she wouldn't do anything like that ever again, and never had. He hadn't contacted her again and had probably moved on to his next victim.

Norm showed up at her door the next morning, looking worried. He had a thermos of freshly squeezed orange juice, blueberry muffins he'd made himself, a jar of homemade soup, and the Sunday paper. He offered to make her scrambled eggs and she didn't have the heart to turn him away. She looked rough enough to be convincing about her illness. She had been awake for most of the night, and cried every time she thought about what her sister had said. How could she ever make it up to her? She remembered too how furious she had been at Hattie wanting to become a nun, so she'd had to deal with Melissa's anger and disapproval on top of everything else. All she wanted now was for Hattie to get even with Sam Steinberg and join his other accusers. The list was long in his case, and the charges would stick. No one was rising to his defense. He was a well-known slime bag among his peers in L.A.

"Did your sister come up yesterday?" Norm asked her. There was something about the look on Melissa's face that seemed wrong to him. She looked sick, but she didn't have the flu. Something else was troubling her, but he didn't want to press her and upset her.

Instead, he tucked her into bed, and made chicken soup for her to eat later. Then he climbed into bed with her, put an arm around her, and held her close. He didn't try to make love to her. He could see she wasn't in the mood. "Is there anything I can do to help?" he asked her after they'd lain there for a long time. Melissa thought about it before she answered.

"I don't think so." She didn't want to violate Hattie's confidence, but she trusted him. "Hattie was the victim of one of the men on the Hollywood list," she confided to him. "It's taken her eighteen years to tell me. It's a terrible story. She was trying to be an actress then, and he was a big producer." He could guess the rest. She didn't have to tell him, and he didn't ask. "I want her to go to the police, and add her story to the others. She doesn't want to."

"It has to be her decision," he said wisely, and Melissa knew he was right. "The others will bring him to justice, if she doesn't."

They lay there quietly for a long time, and he brought her the soup at lunchtime. Afterward, she put on some clothes and they went for a walk, without talking. She felt better when they got home. He left a little while later. He knew she wanted to be alone. He was the right man at the right time, and they understood each other. She wouldn't have appreciated him a few years earlier, but she did now.

*   *   *

Hattie called her that night after she'd talked to Mother Elizabeth. She had listened quietly and explained to Hattie that some people didn't find their vocation until after they entered the convent, which had been the case for her. "You would never have stayed all this time if you didn't have a vocation. What do you want to do about this man?"

"I don't know," Hattie said, feeling lost. "Melissa thinks I should go to the police. I don't want to."

"Do what feels best to you. No one can tell you what to do." Hattie repeated that to Melissa when she spoke to her.

"She thinks I should go on a retreat to clear my head. Maybe I will, over Christmas." Melissa didn't argue with her. The mother superior was right. Hattie had to make her own decision. She had suffered enough and carried the guilt for eighteen years.

"I love you," was all Melissa said to her, and she could hear Hattie crying at the other end.

"I love you too," she said softly, and hung up.

Chapter 13

Day by day the list of victims as accusers and sex offenders in the newspapers continued to grow. Many of them were well known, some less so. The revelations were beginning to spread into the political arena, and politicians were listed now too. Everyone was waiting to see where it would spread to next, like blood on the floor, staining all it touched, and spreading faster than it could be stopped.

Melissa thought of Hattie all the time. She was haunted by Hattie's description of the scene.

A week before Christmas, Hattie called. She said in a dead voice that she had decided it was cowardly not to speak up, since others had. It wasn't fair, she said, to let them carry the full weight. Mother Elizabeth had contacted the police sex detail, and made an appointment for the next day. As was proper, according to convent rules, the mother superior would go with her, but Hattie wanted her sister there too, and the superior had agreed. She was calling to ask Melissa to come, and she said she'd be there.

She drove down to New York that night, in case it snowed and she couldn't get there the next day. She stayed at the hotel where she'd stayed when she met Michaela. Norm offered to come with her, but she declined. Hattie wouldn't want him there, and Melissa was going to leave the city as soon as the meeting with the police was over.

Melissa arrived at the convent at one o'clock, and they left together. The appointment was at two, and they drove one of the convent cars downtown. Hattie drove since Mother Elizabeth didn't like to drive. Hattie was wearing her habit, and looked very serious. There was silence in the car, and Melissa suspected the two nuns were praying, so she didn't speak.

The police station where the sex detail of the New York City Police Department was located was on Centre Street. They parked and walked inside. It was an ugly, brightly lit building, with people hurrying down the halls and disappearing into offices. They went to the right door, entered, and were told to sit down. They waited ten minutes, and a woman in a police uniform came to get them, and led them into a room where two female detectives were waiting at a long conference table. Hattie was relieved to see that they were both women. The younger of the two was a sergeant, African American, somewhere in her thirties. The senior officer was a lieutenant about Melissa's age. The sergeant gave them a warm smile. Both were out of uniform, in street clothes, and they greeted both nuns respectfully. They offered Hattie water and she declined. She just wanted to get the ordeal over with and leave. She reached out and held Melissa's hand. The mother superior remained quiet as they began their questions.

Little by little, Hattie told them the same story she had told Melissa. There were additional details she had remembered, all of them equally upsetting. The violence of the attack and the rape itself made Melissa wince, even hearing it the second time. He had hit her again and again, threatened her, battered her, and raped her many times, on the floor, on the couch, on the desk, over a chair. He had sodomized her repeatedly, and between the rapes were the beatings, and the threats warning her not to tell anyone afterward, or he would find her and kill her. She believed him. She had sought refuge in the convent. To her it was a safe house, although to Melissa, after Saint Blaise's, a convent would have been even more frightening. She said she thought the nuns would protect her and he wouldn't find her.

The two detectives made many notes, and asked as few questions as possible so as not to interrupt her.

When it was over, they told her they would be contacting the LAPD to add her case against Sam Steinberg to the others, rather than opening a separate case in New York. It would be more effective to keep all of the cases in a single jurisdiction. They were going to try to keep her case sealed because she was a nun, but couldn't promise it.

There were so many cases being reported now, in the newspapers and online, that it was becoming commonplace. Hundreds of victims had come forward to accuse dozens of men, nearly a hundred so far, and the majority of them well known. The entertainment industry was being decimated. Hattie's case was one of the worst, but not unusual. They filed it under her name at the time, and kept her religious name confidential, which they said would make it harder for the press to find her.

"The press?" Hattie looked panicked.

"They see all the police reports," the sergeant explained, "but there are too many to follow up on, and they're more interested in famous actresses who have stepped up to accuse the offenders." It made for more lively reading. It had been going on for weeks, nearly a month by then, and the number of cases was still growing. It hadn't slowed down. In fact, the furor was increasing.

"You've helped all the other women who've come forward, and those who haven't yet but want to, by telling your story," the lieutenant told her when she thanked Hattie. She looked dazed after telling it again for the third time. It was like reliving it.

"Will I have to go to court and testify against him?" Hattie asked them.

"It's very unlikely. When all the cases have been reported, I'm sure he'll plead guilty. He's not going to go to court against all of you. No jury will look favorably on him. Some of the others may be able to cut a deal, but he's one of the worst offenders. He'll go to prison. Some of them attacked minors, drugged them and raped them. That doesn't seem to be his M.O."

They typed up Hattie's statement on a computer, printed it, and had her sign it. The three women were silent as they wended their way back through the police station, and back to the parked car. It had been an impressive experience, and Hattie had been very brave.

On the way back to the convent, Hattie told Melissa they were sending her to a retreat house in Vermont for a few weeks until she felt better, and also to make sure the press didn't find her. "I'll be there for Christmas." Melissa nodded. They hadn't spent Christmas together in years anyway. Not since she had entered the convent. "I'll write to you," she promised. They hugged for a long time, and Hattie followed Mother Elizabeth into the convent, as Melissa watched them. Then she went to the hotel, picked up her bag, and headed back to Massachusetts. She cried on and off during the trip, and Norm was waiting for her when she got home. He had dinner in the oven. He had made a French dish, hachis parmentier, which was duck with mashed potatoes and black truffles. She didn't think that she was hungry, but found that she was ravenous when she tasted it. It was a good winter dish, and she marveled at his cooking again.

"How did it go?" he asked her after a little while. She looked exhausted, after the meeting with the police and the long drive.

"It was hard, but she was very composed and coherent. They say he'll go to prison, where he belongs." Norm nodded. He thought the idea of these men preying on women and particularly young girls was heinous. Hattie had given up her dreams of acting, the career she had studied for, and her freedom, to hide in the convent for eighteen years as a result. It was a lot to lose, and Melissa wasn't sure that the life she had chosen had compensated for it. She was almost sure it hadn't, and it was obvious she was having doubts now.

Melissa was grateful to nestle in Norm's arms that night.

The next day, after he left for work, she was at her desk paying bills when the phone rang, and she picked it up absentmindedly.

A cheerful "Hi, Mom!" came through the receiver, and for a minute she assumed the caller had the wrong number. The greeting was unfamiliar, and suddenly she realized who it was. It was Michaela.

She had just called to chat. Melissa smiled broadly once she knew who it was.

"Well, this is a nice surprise. How's everything in L.A.?"

"Crazy busy before Christmas. We can't wait to come see you."

"I can't wait to have you." The normalcy of the conversation almost made up for the past week of Hattie's miseries. Michaela had no particular news, she said she just wanted to hear her mother's voice. It reminded Melissa again of how much Hattie had done for her. And she wished she could do more for her in exchange now. Hattie was on a silent retreat so she couldn't call her, nor could Hattie call out.

Michaela and Melissa talked for ten minutes, and then got off. It raised Melissa's spirits just thinking about her. She had presents wrapped for them, and they were going to rent skis and ice skates for the children when they got there. The best Christmas gift of all was the one Hattie had brought her. She had a daughter.

It had been years since Melissa had spent Christmas with anyone, or New Year's, or any holiday except the recent Thanksgiving. She had spent them all alone, in the silent house, watching a movie on TV, or reading a book, without celebration. But this year was different. Norm usually went to his brother's house in Boston, but he had declined, and had told him that at Thanksgiving. He wanted to spend it with Melissa. They had been together for almost three months, and she had never been as comfortable with any man in her life.

He made a simple lamb roast, French style, with garlic and green beans, on Christmas Eve, with a yule log for dessert. She had tasted his soufflés by then and loved them. After dinner, they sat in front of the fire in her living room, and drank Chateau d'Yquem, another sweet Sauterne, it was the best one, which the French called liquid gold. She hadn't had it in years and was reminded of how much she loved it.

"It's been an incredible year," she said, looking into the fire and thinking about it. "I have two important new people in my life, you and Michaela. And her children," she added, "and David. A year ago I was alone, eating a grilled cheese sandwich, thinking about the past. Now I think about the future."

"And what does that look like?" he asked her, as he watched her. He still couldn't believe his good fortune to be sharing the relationship they had. It felt like a dream to him too.

"I'm not sure." The possibilities were limitless. "Maybe we should take a trip together." She hadn't been to Europe in seven years, or anywhere else, except L.A.

"We could eat our way through France," he suggested, liking the idea.

"Or Italy," she added with a smile.

"Or both. Even better."

"Maybe next summer. Maybe Michaela and her family would join us, or we could rent a house somewhere. I have a family again." It made everything more exciting, and added new dimensions to her life. And Norm did too. She liked sharing their everyday lives, and meeting up at the end of the day. "Let's think about it. Could you get away?" He was always busy building houses for his clients, but he had a good crew and several foremen he could leave in charge.

"I can plan it, if I know ahead of time."

They went upstairs before midnight, and lay in bed talking. She was half asleep and beginning to mumble while he was still talking, and she drifted off to sleep while he watched her. He slipped a long, slim box under her pillow while she slept. He had gone to Boston to shop for her, and found just what he wanted.

She kissed him when she woke up in the morning, and he peeled off her nightgown and admired her.

"Merry Christmas," she said, smiling at him, and then pulled him toward her.

"You missed Santa last night. You were snoring when he came by," he said and kissed her.

"He hasn't been here in ages. I'm not on his list," she said with a grin.

"Well, he was here last night. I think he left something under your pillow," Norm said innocently. She thought he was teasing her, but slipped a hand under it and found the box he had put there. She was smiling broadly as she pulled it out, and he watched with pleasure as she opened it. She gasped when she saw it. It was a heavy bracelet of gold links and on the back of each link there was a word engraved. All together it read "Happy First Christmas. I love you, N." She liked the idea of it being their first Christmas. It suggested that there would be more. She hoped they would be lucky enough for that to be true.

"I love it." He put it on her wrist, and she reached into her night table and handed him a box too. It was a sturdy stainless steel Rolex watch he could wear every day at work, with a chronograph, a stopwatch, and all the extra dials and features she knew he'd love. He put his gift on too, and looked like the proverbial kid at Christmas when he thanked her.

He slept naked and she pressed her body against him as they kissed. She loved feeling his body against her. He was powerfully built with broad shoulders and strong arms, and he loved the silk of her skin next to his. He could never get enough of her. He never wanted their lovemaking to end.

"I love you, Mel," he said in a husky voice.

"I love you too." It was the best Christmas she'd had in years. He started making love to her, and she arched her back as he entered her. Everything about their lovemaking was so sweet, and so sensual. They always seemed to be in tune with each other, as they were now. It lasted as long as they could bear it, and then their insatiable hunger and passion took over. They lay spent afterward and smiled at each other. As she looked at him, Melissa couldn't think of a single thing she wanted. She had it all.

Chapter 14

By Christmas, Marla had finished shooting her most recent film. Post-production was winding down, and she only had to go into the sound studio a few times. She was already studying her next script. She was thoroughly professional, always prepared, and rarely went out or saw people when she was learning lines. She did research for months before every picture, and had set a strong example to Michaela for excellence and perfection. Michaela had developed a powerful work ethic like her adoptive mother, and admired Marla for her discipline.

Marla joined them for dinner on Christmas Eve, and after the children were put to bed, she sat and talked to Michaela and David. The tree was lit, and Andy and Alexandra had opened their grandmother's gifts that night. She gave them books and practical things that they could learn from. She had definite ideas about how children should be raised and what they should be taught. She'd applied them to Michaela. She had taught her to read when she was three, and Marla had taken her on location with her, with a nanny, before she started school. After that, the long separations while she worked on movie after movie had begun. She regretted it now, but her career had come first. Michaela understood it and didn't hold it against her, and she had loved her nannies. Marla had insisted on good manners, and the nannies she hired were British and well trained. Michaela had a more informal style with her own children, and she had less help. She liked taking care of them herself whenever she could. David helped on weekends. Michaela had missed having a father. Marla never introduced her to the men in her life. She kept that separate and never discussed it with her daughter.

"I have to admit," she said, as they relaxed in front of the fire after dinner, "I was shocked when you told me you had met your birth mother. After they told you about the fire at Saint Blaise's, I assumed that would never be possible."

"So did I," Michaela added. "I was shocked when her sister came to see me at the office. At first I thought it was some kind of scam."

"I was afraid of that too," Marla admitted. "But I was even more afraid that it might be real, and worried about why she wanted to meet you. It's been such a long time. She wasn't at all what I expected when I met her at Thanksgiving. I thought I'd be jealous and she'd try to 'steal' you. Instead she turns out to be this very nice, normal woman. She's had a sad life, and I realize that she needs you, maybe more than you needed her. I don't think she's trying to take you away, I think she really just wanted to know you're all right. And it turns out that we all like each other. She's young enough to be my daughter too."

"I thought that when I met her. There's something very dignified about her, and proud, in a nice way. She was so impressed by you. She thought you were real too. She's kind of like a young aunt, or an older sister. They both are. I like Hattie too. You'd like her. She doesn't seem like a nun. She's very practical and down to earth."

"So is your birth mother. I like that about her too. That's an awful story about her son. I know what you mean about her being dignified. She doesn't come across as needy or desperate, but there's a terrible sadness in her eyes. Fate takes strange turns. She loses him, and finds you. And now you have both of us. I didn't feel threatened by her, or jealous. I thought I would," she said honestly, "but I don't."

"I was a little afraid of that," Michaela said softly. "I think I would have. You two were funny together."

"I meant what I told her. She should go back to writing. She has an enormous talent. It's a sin to let that lie dormant and not use it. It's not right." Marla believed that everyone should work, at every age.

She had made that clear to Michaela too, who was very serious about her job as a social worker.

"Maybe she'll go back to it someday. She seems to be busy with her house," Michaela said thoughtfully.

"That's not enough," Marla said firmly, "she's too bright for that. Maybe finding you will inspire her." Marla knew they were going to visit Melissa in three days. She was going to a spa in Palm Springs herself, for a week of intense exercise and diet, cleansing drinks and herbal facials before starting her new film in a few weeks. She had invited Michaela to bring the children over to Europe during ski week, while she was on location in England. Michaela had promised to try. They were going to be shooting in Ireland and Scotland too, in rugged terrain. It was a period piece. She had two weeks of fittings for the wigs and costumes, which were elaborate.

Marla stayed until eleven and then she went home. She got up at six every day to exercise, five when she was working on a picture. She applied rigorous discipline to everything she did.

"I'll talk to you before you leave. And give Melissa a hug from me," she said, and kissed Michaela and David before she left. She drove herself home. She usually had a driver, but didn't want to make him work on Christmas Eve. He had a wife and kids, and she was sensitive to that. She was an admirable woman, and much respected by those who knew her well. Her employees were devoted to her, and many of them had worked for her for over thirty years. Michaela had grown up with them.

Michaela and David and the children relaxed at home on Christmas Day. The weather was warm, so they heated the pool and let the kids swim for a short time. Then they went inside to play with their presents. Andrew had his first two-wheel bike, and he wanted to take it to Massachusetts. His parents said he couldn't. He'd have to leave it at home, but he was going to ski instead.

Michaela was excited to see Melissa again, and David was looking forward to getting some skiing in too, although the mountain wasn't challenging there. His own parents had been killed in a freak accident, mountain climbing in Europe, before the children were born, so he thought having a second grandmother would be nice for them. He was easygoing and adored his wife and children, and had gone along with the plan. Michaela had teased him about having a second mother-in-law. Marla was a force to be reckoned with, and opinionated at times. He could already tell that Melissa's points of view were more moderate, less old-fashioned, and more diplomatically expressed, but he loved Marla too, for her honesty and good heart. She'd always been kind to him since they'd met.

Michaela spent the day after Christmas packing for their trip, and she could hardly get the children to bed that night, they were so excited about going to

the snow, building a snowman, ice skating, and seeing their new grandmother again. Michaela hadn't
told them she had more presents for them. She didn't
want that to be the main event, so they had surprises
in store. Melissa was wide awake in her bed that
night too, thinking about them.

Hattie had been at the retreat house in Vermont for a
week by then. The silence felt peaceful and was a
relief at first. So much had happened, and retelling
the rape had brought back terrible nightmares and
memories. She thought a silent retreat would help
them recede again. But as the days wore on, with no
one to speak to, the voices in her head got louder and
more strident every day, voices about what had
brought her into the convent in the first place, reminding her that she had lied about having a vocation. She kept thinking of Fiona Eckles's words in
Dublin about how disillusioned she was with the
Church. She felt as though she was spinning in cir-
cles with a thousand echoes in her head telling her
that she didn't belong in the Church, that she wasn't
good enough or pure enough. She was a liar, a fraud.
All the good she had done in the past eighteen years
faded away and the only thing left were her doubts,
about the Church, herself, and what direction to take
now. She felt frozen in place, and nothing in her life
made sense anymore. The only thing that did was

having found Melissa's daughter for her. She had no regrets about that, and was thrilled with how it had worked out. She was sorry she wouldn't see them over New Year's at Melissa's house, but she would have had to work anyway.

Hattie suspected that the public revelations about the sex offenders in Hollywood were continuing. They weren't allowed to read the newspapers or watch television during the retreat, so nothing would intrude on them, so Hattie didn't know what was going on, or if the press had said anything about her, which was just as well. In fact, her story had been added to the others, but the police had kept her name out of it, and said only that she had been a young actress raped and brutalized by him twenty years ago. Melissa had been relieved to see that it had been kept anonymous, but she had no contact with Hattie so she couldn't tell her. No one could. The whole purpose of the retreat was for Hattie to clear her mind and come back stronger, more at peace, and feeling whole again. For now, she felt fragmented and broken in a million pieces, pulled in all directions. She had reached no conclusions while there. They had said she could stay as long as she wanted and needed to. She didn't even know what day it was. The nuns who ran the retreat told her it didn't matter, and she suspected they were right. A relief nurse was covering her shifts at the hospital. It made her feel that she was replaceable, which was liberating.

*   *   *

The morning that Michaela and her family were due
to arrive, Melissa had gotten up at six and checked
everything, the room that the children would share
with twin beds and antique quilts handmade by local
women, the large, airy bedroom with floral prints
and matching wallpaper from England for David and
Michaela. It had a big bathroom, with a large antique
tub that Norm had found and installed, and it had a
little sitting room next to it that was bright and sunny,
overlooking the garden and the mountains. They
were far down the hall from Melissa's bedroom so
they didn't have to worry about disturbing her if the
children got up early. The house was well laid out for
family and guests. The family who had built it had
five children, and all the bedrooms were big and airy
with peaceful views, with the parents' quarters separate.

She had rented bicycles for them to use when the
ground wasn't icy. They were going to rent the ski
equipment once the children were there and could
be measured for it. Michaela wanted to ski too. David
had been a downhill racer in college, and was bringing his own equipment. If the weather held up and
they didn't get buried in snow, Melissa had a lot of
activities planned for them. And Norm had promised
to give Andy a ride on one of his tractors and his
forklift, which his mother had promised him. They

were going to ice-skate on a frozen pond, visit a breeder of huskies, and Norm had promised to cook for them. There was plenty to keep them busy, and Melissa was grateful for Norm's help to entertain them. His office was closed until after the New Year, so he had plenty of free time.

Melissa had arranged for a van and driver to pick them up at Logan airport in Boston and drive them to her home. She thought they'd be tired from the trip, so she didn't schedule too much for the first day or evening, although it was hard not to. There was so much she wanted to fit in, and do with them, and show Michaela. David had a college roommate nearby in New Hampshire and was going to make a short daytrip to visit him. There would be enough leisure time to let everyone relax, and enough activities to keep them busy. Michaela had packed games and their iPads so the children could entertain themselves if they woke up early.

Melissa had tended to every detail. Norm had been impressed by how well she organized the week they were going to spend with her. They had discussed it, and had decided that he shouldn't spend the night with her with the children there. They weren't married and she didn't want to explain it to them. And after only three months, who knew if he would still be in her life on their next visit. She hoped he would be, but was realistic about it. He was planning to spend time with them, show David the area, and still give Melissa and her daughter time alone together. She and Norm had carefully planned the meals he was going to cook, with his expert knowledge of French and Italian cooking. He was going to make homemade pizza for the kids, and real spaghetti Bolognese, which took all day to prepare, chopping and adding the ingredients and letting it simmer.

Melissa looked nervous as she waited for them to arrive from the airport, and Norm baked cookies for them while she checked their bedrooms again. She acted as though royalty was going to be visiting, and to her they were.

"Relax, they're going to love it here," he reassured her. She still had her tree up in the living room, and her presents for them were piled high, including two teddy bears she had had made especially for the children.

At last they heard the van come up the driveway and stop in front of the house. Melissa waited for them on the porch, and then ran down the steps to greet them. She hugged the children, and kissed her daughter, as Norm, David, and the driver took their bags inside. One of them was full of gifts Michaela had brought for her. She introduced them to Norm, who was waiting in the house.

Melissa took them to their bedrooms, and the children dove onto their beds with feather comforters and the brightly colored quilts. There was an antique canopy bed in Michaela and David's bedroom. The house shone with all the burnished wood that Melissa had hand-waxed herself, and the doors she had sanded that summer.

"The house is so beautiful!" Michaela exclaimed, and Melissa beamed.

"Norm and I have worked hard on it. I did a lot of the work myself."

"She's become a master carpenter and cabinet-maker in the past four years," he teased her, but it was true. She had taken classes in furniture making. The desk in her office looked like an antique, but she had made it herself. She was proud of every inch of the house and everything in it. It was a labor of love, which David and Michaela appreciated. Before starting dinner, Norm took Andrew and Alexandra outside and built a snowman with them. He'd had plenty of practice with his five nephews over the years.

Michaela sat in the kitchen with her mother after she unpacked, and David went outside to join Norm and the children.

"This place is fantastic." Michaela admired everything around her. They had restored it as closely as they could to the original. It looked like an authentic Victorian home, with the finest pieces of the period, and all the comforts of a modern house.

"It kind of became my obsession," Melissa said sheepishly, but the results were what she had envisioned. "It was part of the healing process for me when I left New York. I learned a lot from Norm about craftsmanship and restoration."

The children were wet and happy, and their snowman was as tall as their father when they came inside when it got dark. It had started snowing, and made the place look like a Christmas card. Melissa had music playing on the stereo, the tree was lit, and Norm poured wine for the adults and started dinner. He had done all the prep work before they came. The meal he cooked for them that night was superb. He had his spaghetti Bolognese for the kids, delicate sole meunière for the adults, with flawless mashed potatoes and tiny Brussels sprouts. They had cold crab to start, and chocolate and caramel soufflés for dessert. David and Michaela were in awe of his cooking, and said that it was better than any restaurant in L.A.

"He's an incredible chef," Melissa said, smiling at him, and leaned over to kiss him, as the children giggled. They had opened their gifts before dinner and loved them all. Melissa had bought a handsome heavy navy blue sweater for David, and a soft, off-white cashmere one for Michaela.

After dinner, they sat by the fire, while the children played quietly with their iPads, and then the visitors went upstairs to bed when they got sleepy, and Melissa helped Norm clean up the kitchen.

"Your dinner was a huge hit," she thanked him. "David's right. You should open a restaurant," she said, as they put the clean pots away.

"I'd rather cook for people I love," he said happily. "I'm trying out a new recipe tomorrow for Southern fried chicken, bouillabaisse to start, and chocolate cake for dessert, Sacher torte from Vienna, with whipped cream."

"I'm going to get fat if you stick around."

"No, you won't. And I plan to stick around," he told her, as they turned out the lights and left the kitchen, and they went back to sit in front of the fire. He didn't want to leave her, but agreed that it was the right thing. He didn't want to shock the kids.

Michaela told her about her job the next day, when they went for a long walk. There was a foot of snow on the ground from the night before, and it looked like the trees were covered in lace. Michaela was dedicated to her work, and enjoyed it, and she liked the contrast to the life she had grown up in, with Marla, and David's clients, whom she met with him occasionally.

They took the children skating that afternoon, and the next day they were planning to go skiing. When they did, Melissa and Michaela stayed with the children, while David and Norm took off, and raced down the slopes together. David was faster, and still an expert skier, but Norm loved the sport and could hold his own.

Melissa thought of Hattie in Vermont, and wished that she could call her. She was worried about how she was after giving her testimony to the police.

More names had been added to the list of sex offenders, and several more shows had been canceled. A number of politicians had recently been accused too. David said he thought it was going to touch every sector of business before it was over. Michaela said that Marla's co-star in the next movie had been replaced at the last minute. It was a major purge. Hattie's story wasn't unusual, and many girls much younger than she had been assaulted. A famous child star had come forward, in her late teens now, and said that she'd been raped when she was twelve by a highly respected director, whose films were blackballed immediately. Two of the films favored currently for Oscars had been taken out of the running, because both the director and the male lead had been accused of rape. The entertainment industry had been hit hardest so far, but it was slowly seeping into other areas, and causing shock waves, in big business too. Men on Wall Street were running scared. Inevitably, there were some false accusations by dishonest women hungry for attention, but for the most part, the stories had the ring of truth, and even more shocking, the perpetrators were making no attempt to deny it. They had all been caught red-handed by angry women who had been assaulted by them in some way.

Their time together went too quickly. Every day was packed with fun outings and adventures. Breakfast was lively and fun for Melissa. It reminded her of

Robbie when he was that age. They ate lunch on the run. At night, Norm cooked memorable gourmet meals for them. Michaela asked him for some of his recipes. She wanted to try them herself when she went home, when she had the time.

On the last night, Melissa brought up the idea of their going on a trip together in the summer, to Italy or France or both. They loved the idea.

"Marla invited us to go on safari with her, but I think the kids are too young," Michaela said thoughtfully. "A trip to Italy and France sounds like fun and would be easier."

"We could rent a house somewhere, maybe at a beach, and go on a driving trip together," David suggested.

"We could even invite Marla to come," Melissa added, although she suspected that Marla would say a driving trip would be a bore. Michaela said she visited friends in Saint-Jean-Cap-Ferrat on the Riviera every summer, and some of her friends owned yachts or chartered them, but that wasn't a safe trip for young children either. Marla's summer plans were always more geared to adults.

"I'll check the Internet for rentals in Europe," David promised.

Melissa would have liked to invite her sister to come with them, but she doubted that the convent would let her.

On the last morning, they all had breakfast together. Their suitcases were packed, and the children were wearing warm clothes for the trip back. They could peel off some of the layers once they took off. It was warm in L.A.

Their snowman was still intact on the front lawn, and Melissa said it would remind her of them after they left.

After breakfast, the van for the airport arrived, and Michaela thanked her warmly for a wonderful time.

"We all had so much fun. And I think I gained ten pounds. Nobody will want to eat my cooking after Norm's."

Melissa hugged her, Norm and David brought the bags down, and a few minutes later, with frantic waves and shouted goodbyes, they took off for Boston to catch their flight.

Melissa looked forlorn when they went back inside. Norm put on a fresh pot of coffee, and she looked at him sadly.

"I wish they didn't live so far away. I loved having them here." There were tears in her eyes. Now that she had Michaela in her life, she wanted to spend more time with her, but living in Los Angeles, she wouldn't see them often. Melissa loved the idea of a vacation together in the summer. She wanted to see her and watch her children grow up. It all went too fast, and she had learned that you never knew what would happen. Sometimes the future was not as long as you hoped. She tried not to think about the fact that Robbie was only two years older than Andrew when he got sick.

"You'll see them again soon," Norm tried to console her. He pulled her onto his lap and kissed her. "I've missed you, alone in my bed at night," he grumbled good-naturedly. "What would we do on a trip? Would we have to have separate rooms?" He didn't like that idea. She hadn't thought about it when she suggested the trip.

"They're used to you now. And Michaela and David are very relaxed. I didn't want to shock anybody, but I think we could share a room when we travel."

"Well, that's good news," he teased her. He didn't suggest doing anything more radical about it. He didn't know how she'd react to it, and it was much too soon. And the summer was a long time away.

He followed her upstairs after breakfast. It was Sunday, and she wanted to go for a walk. He wasn't going back to work after the holiday until the next day, so they had a full day together now that everyone had left. They hadn't been alone for four days.

He waylaid her in her closet, putting on her coat, and stopped her.

"Can I make a suggestion?"

"Sure," she said innocently, not guessing what it was. He unbuttoned her coat after she had buttoned it.

"How about a little nap before we go out?" he said, looking mischievous.

"A nap? I'm not tired. We just got up," she said, saw the look in his eye, and laughed. "Oh, a nap!" He kissed her then, she dropped her coat on the floor, and they walked into her bedroom. He had been very circumspect while her family was there, but they were alone in the house now and he couldn't wait to get her clothes off and make love to her.

They jumped into her bed together, while they laughed and kissed, and dropped their clothes on the floor. He was starving for her, as he demonstrated amply, and their walk in the orchard was forgotten.

Chapter 15

Sister Mary Joseph stayed at the retreat house in
Vermont for two weeks, until she couldn't stand it
any longer. She was longing to talk to someone, and
hear someone else's thoughts instead of the voice in
her own head. Two weeks of silence had been challenging. She sent Mother Elizabeth an email at the
end of two weeks and told her she wanted to come
home. And the mother superior emailed her back
and told her she could come home whenever she
wanted to. She was free to leave. She wasn't incar-
cerated there or being punished, although it had felt
that way.

She emailed Melissa the morning she left, and
told her she was going back to the city, and could
speak again. The silent retreat had ended. The entire
house followed a vow of silence, which Hattie had
found extremely trying. In all her years in the convent she had never done that before, except for a day

or a few hours. Two weeks of it had nearly driven her crazy. She knew that some people liked it and found it restful, but she wasn't one of them. They had people come there from Boston and New York, not in religious orders, to do silent retreats. It made Hattie feel more anxious, but as she packed her small bag to go home, she knew what she wanted to tell Mother Elizabeth. So maybe the retreat had served its purpose to help her know her own mind.

The drive back to the city took six hours on snowy roads. There was a shuttle that traveled between various convents, when people signed up for them. They had sent one for Hattie. The driver was extremely cautious, and Hattie thought it made the trip home even longer than it had to be. She was grateful when she saw the lights of the city. She felt a lot better now than she had when she'd left. She had felt paralyzed by the intense police interrogation, and all she wanted was to disappear for a while. Now that she had, she was ready to return, and couldn't wait to get back to work at the hospital. She longed for normal life again, and the trauma of the rape had receded back into memory, and didn't seem quite so vivid. She felt back in control as she walked up the familiar steps of the convent. The other nuns were happy to see her. She unpacked her bag, and was wearing jeans and a sweatshirt when she went down to dinner. The first person she saw in the refectory was Mother Elizabeth.

"Welcome back." The superior smiled at her. She could see immediately in her eyes that Hattie was feeling better. She wondered if she had come to some kind of decision. "How was it?" Mother Elizabeth asked with a look of interest.

"Long," Hattie answered, and they both laughed. "I would never have made it in a silent order."

"Neither would I," Mother Elizabeth admitted, "but it does one good from time to time." Hattie was just glad it was over. "Why don't you come and see me in the morning and we'll talk about it." She wanted to know how Hattie was feeling now, and what she was thinking. Speaking up about the rape had been a painful revelation. "I'll expect you at seven-thirty, after breakfast." Hattie agreed and went to help herself to dinner, and the other nuns had joined them when she came back with her tray and sat down. She already knew what she was going to tell the superior in the morning. She had made the decision at the retreat house in Vermont.

She dreamt of it that night, woke at four A.M., dressed for Mass, and went to the chapel early so she could pray about it.

She ate half a bowl of oatmeal after Mass, and hurried to the superior's office. Mother Elizabeth was already at her desk, when Hattie knelt and kissed her ring.

"Good morning, Sister Mary Joe." She was in her nursing habit, ready for work, as Mother Elizabeth peered over her glasses at her. "You may sit down." Hattie slid into a chair facing her across the desk, like a schoolgirl. "It's nice to have you back. Is there something you want to tell me?" Hattie nodded, cowed by her for a minute, and quickly told herself she was doing the right thing.

"I prayed about it a lot while I was in Vermont. I want to leave, Mother."

"Under what circumstances, and to where?"

"I want to be released from my vows and go back to Africa." The superior had expected it and wasn't surprised. The relief on the younger nun's face had suggested to her that she was going to ask to be released from her vows.

"What makes you think that's the right answer?" she challenged her.

"I feel better since I made the decision."

Mother Elizabeth nodded, unconvinced. She had heard it all before from others, and in her opinion, leaving the convent was never the right answer. She had thought of it once when she was younger herself, after a disagreement with her own mother superior.

"You don't have to give up your vows to go to Africa. We can send you there again if you want. Giving up one's vows is not about geography, or changing jobs. It's about no longer believing in the principles you promised to uphold. Are you upset with either poverty, chastity, or obedience?" she asked her pointedly, and Hattie shook her head.

"No, Mother, I'm not. I think something happened to my faith in the Church after what I discovered at Saint Blaise's. Their adoption mill was a scheme to make money for the Church."

"And to find good homes for abandoned babies born out of wedlock. What's so wrong about that?"

"They treated it like a business."

"There may have been some unfortunate actions by the Sisters who ran it, but the motives were right. And to be crass about it, those infants were better off in rich homes than poor ones."

"True. But poor people should have been able to adopt them too, not just rich ones."

"Do you know for a fact they weren't?"

"No, I don't," Hattie admitted. "The whole thing seems like such a mess, and burning the records was unforgivable."

"That was wrong, I'll grant you. But none of it is adequate reason for you to break your vows."

"I came here for the wrong reasons, Mother. We both know that now. I lied about my vocation."

"And can you truly say you haven't had a vocation in eighteen years? I doubt that, I've seen you work. I know your heart. You're a good nun, Sister."

"Thank you," Hattie said humbly.

"I have a suggestion for you. Take a year's leave, on a sabbatical, and go to Africa. We'll put you in one of our missions there, or a hospital. See in a year if you still want to be released from your vows. If you're sure of it then, I won't oppose it."

"And will you oppose it now?" Hattie looked worried.

"No. But I won't help you. I don't think you're doing the right thing. You need to take more time to decide. That's a very important decision."

"I know it is. I've been thinking about it for months."

"I think that ex-nun you talked to in Ireland influenced you, and demoralized you."

"I don't agree." But a small part of Hattie thought the superior might be right. Fiona Eckles had been so angry at the Church, and had predicted that in the end it would make Hattie want to break her vows too. Maybe she was right. But for Hattie, the decision was spawned by many things, not just the Church making money from an adoption mill.

"I'd like you to give my suggestion some thought. A year's sabbatical before you make a final decision, and then we'll talk. And you can spend the year in Africa, doing the work you love. You can pick the location."

"I'd like to go back to Kenya, if you agree."

"It's not up to me," Mother Elizabeth reminded her. "The bishop approves the postings."

"I'll think about it," Hattie said, disappointed. She didn't want to be put off. She wanted to make a decision. And she knew she didn't have to be a nun to go to Africa. She had researched it, and there were other organizations that had hospitals and programs there. She could sign up for one, she was a registered nurse. It was easier for her with the Church of course. But she was sure that other humanitarian organizations would accept her.

"Take your time with the decision, Sister. It's important. You've invested eighteen years of your life here. Don't just throw that away. Get the demons out of your head, and their voices." She was making a strong case for Hattie remaining a nun, and even though she felt guilty leaving, she wasn't sure that she wanted to stay. "You've been on a roller-coaster ride for the past few months, finding your sister's daughter, the sexual harassment accusations, and your rape surfacing. That was the catalyst that brought you in here, seeking safety. It's *not* what made you stay."

"I don't know what made me stay," she said, looking miserable again. "I've never wanted children, now I even wonder about that. I'm probably too old. But I suddenly realize that I've spent nearly twenty years as a nun and now I'm not sure I should ever have been one. It's an unnatural life. And the people who make the decisions far above us in the Church are just humans like us. What if their decisions are wrong? I think I want to be an ordinary person, not a nun, but just a nurse."

"We are ordinary people, and yes, the Church

does make mistakes. But they make good decisions too. There will always be some rotten apples in the barrel, in every situation, every group. But don't forget there are good apples too. You're one of them. A *very* good apple. I don't want to see you give that up."

"What if it's wrong for me?" Hattie tried to plead her case, but the superior wasn't swayed.

"Why would it be wrong now?" the superior challenged her, her eyes looking deep into Hattie's. "Who turned you against this life of ours? You need to look at that." They both knew Fiona Eckles had. Mother Elizabeth was fighting for her soul. And suddenly for the first time in eighteen years, Hattie wanted freedom. For more than just a year. She didn't want the equivalent of a trial separation. She wanted a divorce.

"I'll think about it," Hattie said, looking anguished. She kissed the superior's ring, left the office, and hurried off to work. She called her sister that night and told her what had happened.

"Why do you have to go to Africa? Why can't you work with the poor here?" Hattie was exasperated. The mother superior didn't want her to leave the religious order. And her sister didn't want her to leave New York.

"I was happy there," Hattie said, annoyed.

"Can't you be happy here? Africa is dangerous,

you could get sick or injured, or caught in an uprising of some kind. I don't want you killed."

"I'd rather be dead than wasting my life. And I'm beginning to think that's what I'm doing here. I came in under false pretenses. I don't belong here, Mel."

"I've been telling you that for eighteen years. And now you believe me and want to leave. I don't want to lose you, Hattie. You're all I have."

"You have Michaela now," she reminded her.

"That's not the same. You and I have history, our whole lives. Michaela is brand new."

"She won't be new forever. You'll make a history with her. I need to do this. Africa is the only place where I felt I did some good." Melissa didn't know what to say to that. Hattie sounded frustrated.

"Just don't rush into anything. This is a huge decision. You rushed into the convent. Now don't rush out."

"I said I'd think about it some more, and I will." But she didn't like the options. All of a sudden Hattie felt like she was in jail and wanted to be free. And it was ironic that, after years of opposition, now Melissa was encouraging her to stay in the order and remain a nun.

She stayed up late, reading and praying that night, and got nowhere.

Hattie knew she had done a good thing finding Michaela, but everything had changed when she did. Not only for Melissa and for Michaela, but for herself too. And in her case, not for the better. Michaela had been found. But she felt lost now.

Melissa was worried about her, and talked to Norm that night. He could see how upset Melissa was about her sister, although he wasn't sure why. Hattie sounded like an intelligent woman and he trusted her to make the right decision.

"Would it be so terrible if she left the convent? I thought you weren't happy about her being a nun." He was confused by her reaction, after what she'd said when they first met.

"I wasn't happy. Her going into the convent made no sense to me for all those years. Now I know why she went in. She's been protected for all of her adult life. First by me, then by the Church. She's an innocent. Look what happened to her when she got raped."

"She was twenty-five years old then. Now she's forty-three. She's not naïve."

"She's never lived on her own, or had to pay rent or take care of herself. Now she wants to go to Africa. What'll happen to her there? She could be killed."

"She could be killed crossing the street in the Bronx, or mugged leaving the hospital at the end of her shift. She loves it there. Maybe she needs her freedom. Maybe she wants to marry and have kids, it's not too late." Melissa looked shocked at the idea.

"It's taken me eighteen years to get used to the idea of her being a nun. Now she wants to quit."

"Mel, there are chapters in our lives. I've had them, you too. My marriage was right when I did it, and so wrong nine years later, or even five. It ended for you with Carson. You had a huge success as a writer, now you're done. Maybe she's just tired of being a nun."

"You're not supposed to get tired of that," she said, and he smiled.

"She's human. People change. Maybe she's outgrown it. She seems to have had some kind of crisis of faith. She should have the right to leave if she wants to."

"I agree with the mother superior. She should take a year to think about it."

"Maybe she will. But your worrying won't change anything. She's a smart woman. Trust her to make the right decision for herself."

"I never thought so before because I don't like nuns. But I think the convent suits her. She was happy there before." Mel was being stubborn about it. She was frightened for her sister if she stepped out into the world.

"I was happy with my wife when I married her. We would have killed each other if we'd stayed married." She knew that what he said was true, but she didn't want to hear it. She wanted Hattie to stay in the little pigeonhole where she'd been for nearly twenty years, not fly off the branch into open skies. It was too risky.

When she said it to Norm, he shook his head. "Maybe she wants a little risk in her life. Not a lot, but just enough to feel she has a voice in her own fate. Let's see what she does before you panic."

"Maybe it's a good thing I never had to deal with my kids growing up. The stress of it would have killed me."

"Just remember, your sister isn't a teenager. She's forty-three years old, six years younger than you are."

"She's never had to fend for herself. And as soon as she did, she ran straight into the convent to hide. That tells you something."

"All it tells me is that she was severely injured when she got raped, and did the only thing she could think of. She's grown up."

"Africa is *not* safe, even as a nun."

"It's what she loves."

"She's running away again."

"Maybe she is. She has the right to. You hid here for four years, before you opened the door and took a chance on life again. We all have to do it our own way."

"What makes you so wise?" she said, and kissed him with a sigh.

"I'm older than you are," he reminded her wryly.

"Five months."

"I guess it makes a difference. Why don't you let your sister figure this out for herself. She may decide to stay in the convent in the end."

"I hope so," Melissa said fervently.

Hattie spent the days after her meeting with Mother Elizabeth researching organizations that ran hospitals, orphanages, and refugee encampments in Africa where there were children, and where they needed medical assistance and hired nurses. The best ones she found were run by the Catholic Church or the United Nations. She had been stationed in two of the Church-run ones during her two years there. But there was a refugee camp for orphans run by the UN that caught her attention. What she read about it said that many of the children arrived at the camp in such dire condition that they died. It sounded like a hardship post, and was in the bush. Most of the children were orphaned as a result of tribal wars. The young girls were frequently taken as sex slaves by their captors, even as young as ten if they were mature. AIDS was rampant, cholera, typhoid, starvation. There were several photographs of the camp online, and she stared at them with tears in her eyes. She knew those faces, and had seen so many children like them. There was little one could do, but if you managed to save one life, or even a few, it was a victory for the human race. Looking at them, she knew she didn't need children of her own. Working with children in such desperate need was enough for her. This was her vocation. She had known it when she was in Africa. She had hated to leave, and longed to go back ever since.

She called the phone number on the website and got caught in the cyber tangle of voicemails, pressing buttons until she reached a human voice. She managed to get an appointment for later in the week, and the next day got permission to leave work early on the appointed day.

Her whole body felt electrified when she walked into the UN office. There was an African woman at a desk, a tall young man with a Swedish accent, and another man who was older and French. Her appointment was with the woman, and they walked into a glass cubicle, where she questioned Hattie intensely about what she'd done in Africa previously, and her motives to return and for wanting the job. She had brought copies of her nursing certificates with her. And she leveled with her.

"I'm a nun. I have been for almost nineteen years. I am planning to ask to be released from my vows in the near future. It's my choice. I'm not being asked to leave. And I want to go back to Africa to do the kind of work I did there. Your camps for orphans offer what I'd like to do. I'd prefer to work with children. I love the work." Her eyes lit up as she said it, and the woman smiled. She had a face like a tribal sculpture, and was beautiful in her native dress.

"We all love it. That's why we do it."

"I finally realized that I don't have to stay in the convent to do this kind of work. I can do it as a lay-person." She put her CV down in front of her. "I can supply references from my order and the bishop, and the people I worked with in Kenya." The UN worker nodded, and took her seriously.

"Languages?"

"Enough French to get by and conduct an examination. I learned some words in local dialects. We had translators when we needed them."

"So do we. They might need you more in the hospital, as a surgical nurse. We don't get enough trained people from the United States." And her credentials were good.

She brought a man in then. The three of them spoke for a few minutes. He said he was Dutch. He had grown up in Zimbabwe and was in New York on a special project for three months, and then he was going back.

"It's addictive," he said to Hattie. He was about her age. "I'm a doctor, and my family want me back in Holland, or Europe at least, so I'm closer to them. Maybe when I'm old. But for now, this is what I need to do." He had a slightly disheveled look, intelligent eyes, and a kind face.

"Me too," Hattie said simply. She was sure now that she was on the right path.

She spent two hours with them. They told her that they would get in touch after the review board evaluated her CV. They would contact her if they wanted references, which would mean that she had passed to the next phase of the process.

"How often do you send people?"

"Every three or four months we send another team out, of varied nationalities and abilities, nurses, doctors, technicians. A team just left a few weeks ago. The next one will leave in about two months." It wasn't long enough to get released by the order. Final confirmation would come from Rome in a year, or even two, but she could start the process.

"Will it matter if I'm not released yet?"

The Dutch doctor answered her. "That's between you and your order, it's not our concern. All that matters to us is that your medical certificates are in order, and they appear to be. Everything looks up to date. And of course your references matter to us too. We've only just started signing people up for the next team. We'll note your preference for the children's camp, but we can't promise that's where you'll end up. It's all about what they need on the ground." She nodded. That made sense to her. He mentioned salary then. She had been about to ask him. It was low, but enough for her needs in Africa, and about what she expected.

At the end of the interview, she thanked them, and the three of them shook hands. Hattie felt calm, and strong and sure. She felt absolutely certain she was doing the right thing.

She didn't tell anyone she'd been there, and she waited until she heard from them again three weeks later. They were ready for her references. She had passed the first phase. They wanted to know how soon she'd be able to leave after she was approved.

"Very quickly," she said. But it meant that she had to start dealing with the paperwork, and they gave her a list of vaccinations that she'd need.

She hadn't said a word to Mother Elizabeth yet, or to her sister, but she knew she had to now.

She was quiet at dinner that night, and avoided the mother superior's eyes. She asked to speak to her after dinner.

When she walked into her office, looking serious, Mother Elizabeth knew. Sister Mary Joseph was still standing when she spoke to her.

"I've made a decision about the leave of absence you offered me, Mother. It's a generous offer. But I'm sure. I want to be released from my vows."

"Do you know what you want to do now?"

"I'm going back to Africa, with a United Nations medical team. I spoke to them a few weeks ago, and I just passed the first phase of the application process. I'll need references from you and the bishop's office."

"When would you leave?"

"I don't know yet. In about six or eight weeks. I'd like to start the papers for Rome before I go." Mother Elizabeth nodded and had tears in her eyes.

"I'm very sad to see you go, and sadder to see you leave the order. But I have a feeling this is the right thing for you. It's what you love, and they run excellent facilities and teams. Does your sister know?"

"Not yet." Hattie looked equally serious, but there wasn't a tremor of doubt in what she said. "If I may, I'll go to see her this weekend." The superior nodded.

"You can stay here until you take off for Africa. We're going to miss you."

"I'll miss you too, Mother. I hope I do a good job there."

"You will. You did before. You have a gift." There was no reproach in what she said, no bitterness. She came around the desk and hugged her and looked into her eyes. "You're going to do a wonderful job. We'll be praying for you."

Hattie was too moved to speak. When she left the mother superior's office, there were tears rolling down her cheeks. As she gently closed the door behind her, she had no regrets.

Chapter 16

Norm came in from his office later than usual on Friday evening. He was working on plans for three new clients, for houses he was going to build for them in the spring. He liked two of the architects involved very much, and was struggling with the third one, a bossy woman from New York. He looked tired when he sat down at the kitchen table. He was too tired to make dinner and Melissa made a salad and put two steaks on the grill for them. He told her about the progress they'd made that day. They were all going to be handsome houses, showplaces, and each one very different.

It had snowed a lot in the last few weeks, and the remains of the children's snowman were still standing. Melissa had been trapped in the house reading on most days.

"Have you heard from your sister lately?" he asked her when they finished dinner. "Is she okay since the retreat?"

"She's acting weird," Melissa said, looking faintly annoyed. "I haven't heard from her much recently. I hope she hasn't done anything hasty. She's still impulsive, even at her age. She called me yesterday. She's going to come up for the day tomorrow, so I'll catch up on her news."

"She's probably still trying to figure out what to do. It's a big decision."

Melissa nodded. Hattie had been quiet, but Michaela was calling her regularly, once or twice a week, just to chat. Melissa loved it. They both did. She had said that Marla was back on location, in the wilds of Scotland somewhere, freezing, working on her latest film.

They went to bed early that night, and were both in a deep sleep when the phone rang at two A.M. Melissa answered it because the phone was on her side of the bed, but all she could hear was sobbing. There was no other sound at the other end, just jagged crying and sharp intakes of breath. Melissa was afraid it might be Hattie, having some kind of breakdown over the decisions she was making, or with flashbacks from the rape. She had mentioned having nightmares ever since she spoke to the police.

"Who is this?" Melissa said calmly and clearly, as Norm sat up next to her, looking concerned. He couldn't hear the sobbing, but the look on Melissa's face and her voice told him something was wrong. "Who is it? Hattie, is that you?"

A thin voice finally came through the phone. "It's Michaela. It's Marla . . . she . . ."

"All right, sweetheart, take a breath. Try to be calm and tell me what happened." Her voice was instantly gentler, and she was relieved that whatever the problem was, it was Marla, not one of the children. Maybe she was sick.

"It's Marla . . . she's still in Scotland, there was a storm. They were night shooting. There was some kind of explosion in the scene. They finished it, and it was too snowy to drive back, so they took a helicopter to get them back to the town where they're staying. There was a huge gust of wind, and the helicopter flipped over and hit electrical lines. It burst into flame, and crashed . . . they were all killed . . . Marla's dead . . . oh, Mom, I loved her . . . she's dead . . . how can that happen? Why did they take the helicopter in a storm? All three stars, the director, and the pilot were killed. I have to go and get her. David says he'll stay with the kids. They want me to identify the body." She started sobbing again, as Melissa looked at Norm and shook her head and mouthed "Marla." But he still didn't know she was dead. He had never met her, but Melissa had raved about her after meeting her in L.A.

"I'll come with you," Melissa said immediately. "Do you have a ticket yet?"

"No, I called you first." She had reached out to her mother for comfort. But she'd had two mothers recently, and now she only had one, and had lost the one she knew best.

"If you can get a flight to Boston or New York, I'll fly to Scotland with you. We'll do this together, Michaela. I'm so sorry. She was a fantastic person."

"Yes, she was." Michaela had been orphaned twice now, which was more than anyone should have to deal with. Melissa wanted to be there for her. She knew what it felt like to lose the person you loved most. Michaela had David and her children, but Marla had been her mother for thirty-three years.

She barely had time to tell Norm what had happened when Michaela called back ten minutes later and David had called the airline for her. She was on a seven A.M. flight to Kennedy in New York, arriving at three P.M. local time, with the time difference. And they had a five P.M. British Air flight to Edinburgh, landing at six A.M. local time the next day. And he was going to book a car and driver to pick them up and take them to the town outside Edinburgh where Marla was. The producer had been on location with them and was going to meet them. They were going to take care of booking rooms for them at a hotel in Edinburgh. David had booked Melissa's ticket on the flight to Scotland too, so there would be no confusion about the flight. Michaela handed him the phone, and he spoke to Melissa.

"I'll pick Michaela up as she comes off her flight at

JFK, on the way to baggage claim, we'll go to British Air together to check in," Melissa said.

"Thank you, Mel," David said, and she could hear he'd been crying too. He loved his mother-in-law, despite her quirks and Old Hollywood glamour style. She wasn't a typical mother, but had been a good friend to him.

Michaela got back on the phone, crying again. "I'll meet you at JFK," Melissa repeated. "Can you manage with carry-on? It will be faster. We'll be tight to check in for the British flight."

"David asked for VIP service when I get off the flight in New York. They'll take us to the British Air terminal in one of those carts. The press is going to be all over us in Edinburgh, and when I get back." Melissa hadn't thought of that, but they had that burden to carry too. She, David, and her children. "It's going to be on the news this morning." Michaela sounded devastated. And as soon as she hung up, Melissa told Norm the full story, or all she knew. "I'm meeting her in New York, and flying to Scotland with her." She looked at the clock on her bed table. It was two-thirty in the morning. "I have to meet her at three when she lands. I want to be out of here by eight A.M., in case there's snow on the road, or it snows again. I'd rather get there early than late."

"I'll drive you," Norm said. "I don't want you driving down there alone." It was Saturday, and he had the time. "I'll stay at a hotel and come back tomorrow. How long do you think you'll be there?"

"I have no idea. Long enough to go through the formalities, and fly the body back to L.A. I guess the production company will help us. I should be back in a few days."

"Don't forget your sister, she's coming up today."

"Oh my God. I would have forgotten." She texted her that she had to leave for an emergency to help Michaela, so Hattie couldn't come up. It was three in the morning by then, and they turned off the light to try to sleep for a few more hours. Melissa set the alarm for six A.M., and went to shower as soon as it rang.

They turned the TV on at seven, and it was all over the news. There were photographs of Marla on the screen, along with the two male stars who had died with her. They had been hired to replace the two who had been let go because of the recent sexual harassment scandals. A third actor had been hired at the last minute too, but he wasn't working that night. The TV announcer said that the entire world would mourn Marla Moore. He said she had made over a hundred films, had won two Oscars, and was seventy-three years old. Her male co-star had just come back from his honeymoon, and the other had four children. They said that Marla was survived by a daughter, a son-in-law, and two grandchildren, but they didn't mention their names.

Melissa and Norm were on the road in good time. It wasn't snowing, but the wind was strong and she was glad that Norm was at the wheel. They'd been driving for an hour when Hattie called Melissa on her cell.

"What happened? I wanted to come to see you." She hadn't heard the news yet. They didn't watch the morning news on TV at the convent.

"Marla Moore was killed in a helicopter crash in Scotland last night. It's very sad. Michaela called me at two A.M., hysterical. I'm meeting her at JFK and flying to Scotland with her, to identify the body. They want a family member there, if possible. She's in terrible shape, so I volunteered to go with her. David is staying with the kids."

"When are you coming back?"

"As soon as we can. I'll stay for the funeral in L.A. I guess it'll be a huge mess with the press. I should be back here in a week."

"I need to see you," Hattie said, sounding tense.

"Why? Is something wrong?" Melissa didn't like the tone of her sister's voice.

"No. But I've made some decisions." And she knew Melissa wouldn't like them. They talked while Norm drove. "I wanted to tell you in person, but I don't want to wait too long. I'm going to file now to be released from my vows," she said in a calm voice. "And I'm joining a UN team in Africa. I'm leaving in about six weeks. They send over medical personnel.

I don't know where I'll be assigned yet." Melissa looked crestfallen when she heard the news.

"I wish you wouldn't do that, file the papers now, I mean. Why can't you wait and see how you feel?"

"I know how I feel. I want to be free now. I won't be released for a year anyway. Mother Elizabeth says I can change my mind before that, but I know I won't. And the job in Africa is exactly what I want to do."

"Can't you do it as a nun, while you wait to see if you're sure?"

"I will be a nun for the next year." She smiled that Melissa wanted her to stay in the order now, when she had been so vehemently against it nearly nineteen years before. "They won't release me that fast."

"And Africa, Hattie? Really? Can't you do something like it here?"

"No. They have a fantastic program and this is what I want to do."

"At least the UN is respectable, and they'll probably take care of you." Hattie didn't tell her that there were still risks involved, but Melissa knew it anyway.

"I'll come to see you when you get back. It's nice of you to go," Hattie said.

"She's my daughter," Melissa said quietly. "It's the least I can do, and I'm her only mother now. She and Marla really loved each other."

"You're a good mom, Mel. You were to Robbie too."

"Thank you, and just for the record, I hate your

going to Africa again. I wish you wanted to be a hair-dresser or a librarian, or an artist or something instead of risking your life in Africa."

"This is what I want to do. I want to work with the kids."

"Maybe you should have your own."

"I thought about it, but these are the only kids I need. We all have children in our lives in different ways. You have Michaela now, and her children. It's not Robbie, but I guess he wasn't meant to stay, and Michaela's kids will need you too, and so will she."

"I can never measure up to Marla," Melissa said sadly.

"You don't need to. You're you. You're different people. I'm not sure Marla would have run to Kennedy to fly over with her. She had other things to do."

"I have nothing else to do." Melissa smiled at the compliment. "Come and spend a few days with me before you go."

"I will. I promise. I just told Mother Elizabeth. I have to give them notice at the hospital, and do a bunch of other stuff."

"How long are they sending you for?" Melissa was sad about it. Now that they were close again, she was going to miss her.

"A year for now. But I can re-enlist if I like it, and I do a decent job."

"You will," Melissa said confidently.

They hung up a few minutes later, and she and Norm talked about Hattie's decision and her plans.

"I think she's doing the right thing," he said quietly. "It's what she really wants, and she seems to be good at it."

"I guess so. I'm going to miss her."

"She'll be back."

"I hope so," Melissa said sadly, looking out the window at the winter landscape sliding by. "It's funny, I was furious at her for years for becoming a nun, and now I'm kind of sad she's giving it up. I've gotten used to it, or maybe I just don't like change." And this was a big one, particularly for Hattie. She was going to be Hattie Stevens again. Melissa couldn't help thinking that life was strange.

They got to the airport at two o'clock, and had an hour to spare. Norm came into the airport with her, and they had a sandwich and a cup of coffee to pass the time. They saw on the big board at two forty-five that Michaela's plane had landed, and Norm walked her to where they were going to meet on the way to baggage claim. A few minutes later, a VIP golf cart appeared, driven by a ticket agent, and Michaela was on it, in a black skirt and black sweater, with a black coat on the cart next to her. Her face was pale and serious, and she was wearing dark glasses. The cart stopped and Melissa could see that she was crying behind the glasses. She had her carry-on bag next to her. Norm had to leave them then. They were going to be driven to the British Air terminal to check in. He held Melissa tightly for a minute, after telling Michaela how sorry he was.

"Take care of yourself, Mel," he said in a husky voice. "Let me know if I can do anything to help. I'll keep an eye on the house," and then he whispered in her ear, "I love you."

"Me too," she whispered back, got on the golf cart next to Michaela, put an arm around her, and they took off with a wave at Norm, who stood waving at them, and then went back to the garage to get his car and drive into the city for the night. He was going to call a friend to have dinner with him.

"Thank you for coming to meet me," Michaela said as they went outside in the cart and crossed the airport. With the VIP service with the golf cart that David had arranged, they were able to check in for the British Air flight on time. They were escorted to a first-class lounge and given a private room out of sight, and then escorted onto the plane an hour later when it was ready to board. The airline personnel addressed Michaela with seriousness, knowing why she was going to Edinburgh. Marla was all over the news by then and had been all day.

There were four first-class seats on the flight, and they had two of them. The service was excellent, and the food was good, but Michaela hardly touched it, and Melissa wasn't hungry either. She covered her daughter with a blanket as soon as they boarded, and held her hand. When Michaela took her sunglasses off, Melissa could see that her eyes were red and swollen. She'd been crying since she heard the news about her mother.

"She wasn't like other mothers, but she was terrific and I loved her," Michaela said softly, and Melissa nodded and tried to get her to close her eyes and get some sleep. Michaela was exhausted, and shortly after they took off, she was sound asleep with her head on Melissa's shoulder, still holding her hand.

Melissa stayed awake for most of the flight, to keep an eye on her, and dozed intermittently. It was a seven-and-a-half-hour flight, and they landed in Edinburgh right on time. There were two airline executives, a ground agent, most of the production crew, and an airport policeman to meet them, and a representative from the U.S. embassy in Edinburgh to assist them too. They were shepherded quickly out of the airport into a waiting van, to make the two-hour trip to the town where they'd been shooting. It was a small village, and looked surprisingly primitive and antiquated, which was why they had used it. They drove past the site of the crash, with a burned crater in the ground. Michaela gasped and burst into tears again. They were taken to the nearest hospital, where the police had brought Marla's remains to the morgue after the crash. The other victims of the crash were there too. Their relatives were due to arrive later that day. Michaela and Melissa had been the first to arrive.

Melissa had texted Norm as soon as they landed, that they were there safely. It was just after midnight in New York, and he was still out to dinner with his friend, but relieved to hear from her. He was worried about her. Identifying Marla's body after the crash would be a terrible experience, and she wanted to spare Michaela from having to do it.

The producer of the movie was very kind, and the head of the hospital had volunteered his office so they could have some privacy.

Melissa left Michaela there, with her permission, and went with the producer to identify the charred remains. It was more of a formality, since they had gotten dental charts emailed by her dentist, and there was no question that she'd been on the helicopter and there were no survivors. Melissa felt deeply shaken by the experience, and they went back to Michaela quickly in the private office where she was waiting and talking to David on her phone.

"Thank you," she whispered to Melissa with a grateful look.

The producer explained to Melissa then that they were waiting for local authorities to sign the necessary papers to release the body, so they could fly her home. They hoped to have them by that night. The pilot's widow was just entering the hospital when they left. They were driven back to Edinburgh then, where the producer had booked a suite in the best hotel. Photographers took their pictures as they entered, and they were quickly taken to the suite. Michaela was looking dazed, and Melissa was feeling sick from what she'd seen at the hospital. Someone poured her a cup of tea and handed it to her in the suite, which had two bedrooms and a living room.

She put Michaela to bed, and pulled down the shades, and she just lay there, staring at the ceiling, and Melissa went back to the living room of the suite to talk to the producer. He looked as devastated as she felt. He knew Marla well.

"I can't believe this happened," he said to Melissa. "None of us can."

"I've known her for thirty years. I worked on my first movie with her. We're chartering a plane to take her home." The production company was sparing no expense for the most famous actress in America. It was going to be a lot easier than taking two flights to get the casket to L.A. Marla's trusted assistants were already working on the funeral arrangements. She was going to be buried privately with her late husband. And there was going to be a private funeral service, by invitation only, with heavy security, and no press allowed at the Church of the Good Shepherd. The rest hadn't been decided yet, except that

Michaela had told David that she wanted lily of the valley and white orchids, which were Marla's favorite flowers, and her assistants were ordering them. They were doing everything possible to keep it from being a circus, which was no easy feat with the press hounding them. LAPD had put police barriers around Marla's home, and they were keeping fans and gawkers at bay. People had been standing in her street crying since that morning, as soon as the story of her death had hit the news.

Michaela slept for a few hours and then wandered around the suite like a ghost, but she didn't want to leave the hotel. Fans were already gathering outside. Someone had leaked to the press that Marla's daughter was there.

The Scottish authorities signed the death certificate by six o'clock that night, and the paperwork to allow them to remove the body and leave the country with it. There had been no foul play, so they released it. And at nine o'clock, a chartered Boeing 737 was waiting at the Edinburgh Airport, ready to take her home. Michaela left the hotel by a back door with Melissa. The producer was staying in Edinburgh to deal with the families of the two male stars. They were sending their bodies home on commercial flights, which was more complicated. They had bent all the rules and cut through all the red tape to release Marla's remains as fast as possible, but they weren't able to do it for all three.

The plane took off at ten o'clock as soon as their flight plan was approved. It was going to be a twelve-hour flight, due to land at LAX at two A.M. local time. A police escort was waiting to accompany Marla's body in the casket to the funeral home, where she was to be cremated. A separate motorcade was waiting to take Michaela to her home with Melissa. Crowds were already gathering in the street and at the airport, to get a glimpse of Michaela, or the casket. The street where Marla lived had been closed since that morning, with thousands of people laying flowers in the street outside her home, and just standing there crying. There was a candlelight vigil that night, which the police made no attempt to stop, although it tied up the whole neighborhood for blocks, and residents who drove in had to leave their cars blocks from their homes. In her death she was being treated like royalty, and Melissa wondered what Marla would have thought of it, since she seemed like a sensible person. But she was a Hollywood legend, the last of the great, glamorous stars. Other movie stars had been interviewed all day, paying tribute to her, which they did lavishly.

Michaela was so overwrought that she slept for most of the flight, and only woke up for the last hour. She washed her face and brushed her hair, changed to a black blouse and a blazer, and her looks made

Melissa think of Jackie Kennedy's return from Dallas after JFK was shot. Michaela looked a little like her, minus the pink bloodstained suit.

When they landed, police were standing on the runway, and escorted Michaela into a waiting black van, and spirited her away with Melissa beside her. The casket was removed separately into another unmarked van, and it proved to be complicated to get it to the funeral home, but they managed it with the help of the Los Angeles police.

David was waiting for them at home, and Michaela nearly collapsed in his arms, and then they sat in the living room and talked for a while. Michaela thanked Melissa for everything she'd done in the last twenty-four hours.

"The city has gone insane," David told Michaela. "Streets are closed, people are crying in the street, they estimate a hundred thousand at the vigil tonight. You can't get within five blocks of her house. To tell you the truth, I think she would have loved it," he said, and Michaela laughed and thought about it.

"I think she would have too."

"This is like mourning royalty. The queen of England or something. The funeral is going to be complicated," he said. "We had three hundred people on the list. Her assistants called and sent emails and texts, requesting an immediate response. They all accepted. We can accommodate them in the church, and they're closing the highway to the cemetery so the paparazzi can't get to us." David put Michaela to bed then. The kids were sound asleep and hadn't been able to go out all day. He took Melissa to the guest room after she said good night to her daughter. Michaela was still looking dazed but a little better than before.

In the morning when Melissa woke up, feeling like someone had battered her body with a lead pipe, after all the stress and travel of the day before, Andrew was standing next to her bed in the guest room, staring down at her, and Alexandra was next to him.

"Our Gigi Marla died," he told her solemnly. "She was our grandma, but we weren't supposed to say it. She didn't like that word. Now we have you," Andy said practically, summing up the situation, to explain it to Melissa. "You're our grandma too," Alexandra informed her. "She fell down in an airplane. It fell down in a storm. It was a helipopter. And God took her out of the helipopter and took her straight up to Heaven. She's there now," she said. "I miss her. Can we play Barbies now on my iPad?"

"Sure," Melissa said, and Alexandra climbed into bed with her in her nightgown. Andrew was wearing his Superman pajamas. Alexandra had brought the iPad with her and turned it on. They were supposed to dress Barbie dolls on the screen in a multitude of costumes. Being a grandmother, especially to a little girl, was new to Melissa, but she'd had fun with them when they'd visited her in the Berkshires.

"You know, your snowman was still there yesterday. He's a little lopsided, but he's still there," Melissa told them.

"I want to visit you again," Andrew said, climbing onto the bed too, and he made a face when he saw the Barbies. Michaela found the three of them there, intent over the iPad, when she came to look for the children a few minutes later. She looked much better, and more human.

"Did they wake you up?" she asked Melissa.

"No, I was awake," Melissa said, grinning.

"We're dressing Barbie," Alexandra told her mother.

"Barbie is stupid," Andrew said.

"So is Superman," Alexandra shot back at him.

"That's enough. Go eat your breakfast," Michaela told them, and they scampered off.

"Sorry if they woke you," Michaela apologized.

"They're adorable."

Michaela had explained about her mother, but she didn't want them at the funeral. They were too young and it would be too upsetting.

There was supposed to be a rosary that night, but the police said it would be too difficult to contain, so they were having Marla's closest friends to Michaela and David's house instead, about fifty of them, for champagne. She would have liked that better. And the number had grown to a hundred by noon.

The funeral was going to be the next day, and the burial immediately following, with a reception for Marla's friends and colleagues at her home afterward. It was a major production. Her three assistants were handling it. They were camped out in Michaela's dining room, and checked with her every five minutes about some detail, wanting her approval.

"I didn't think it would be like this," Michaela said as they sat in the kitchen, and David joined them.

"Of course it was going to be like this. She was the biggest, most glamorous star in the world. She was a legend. This is Old Hollywood, and she would have loved every minute of it. I'm sure she's watching and beaming from ear to ear," he said, and Michaela laughed.

"If you need to get away, you can come and stay with me," Melissa offered.

"I think it will die down pretty fast," Michaela said.

"It may take a while," David said more realistically.

"Thank you for letting me stay here," Melissa said. She didn't want to be intrusive, or let Michaela down either, but she was looking better, with her kids and David around, which added an element of normalcy and comfort for her. With all the intense media attention, they were trying to keep it under control, as small as possible, and on a tight schedule so it didn't turn into a circus. They wanted it to be as quiet and dignified as possible in the circumstances.

Melissa wore a somber black dress that night for the reception of Marla's hundred closest friends. Every famous face in Hollywood was there, and Melissa recognized every one of them. Michaela introduced her to the first arrivals, and after that their living room was jammed. They arrived at seven and left at midnight, and drank rivers of champagne.

The next day looked like a Cecil B. DeMille production, with three hundred invited guests at the funeral, and thousands of fans outside behind police lines, with a police officer every few feet to keep them behind the barricades.

The ceremony was touching, but Melissa felt like she was in a movie, not at the funeral of anyone's mother. It was pure Marla with the flowers Michaela had wanted. Michaela wore a black Chanel suit, and a small black hat, and looked like Jackie Kennedy again. Marla would have approved. Melissa stood behind Michaela and no one had any idea who she was. She thought she looked like a nanny, and Norm laughed when she said it to him later on the phone.

There were thousands of people outside the church. And the highway was closed for them so the funeral procession could get to the cemetery, and back again. Marla got as much fanfare and respect as any president.

And then finally, it was over. Melissa had cold chicken in the kitchen that night with David, Michaela, and the children, and she sent them back to school the next day.

It was so different from Robbie's funeral, and her parents', that it was hard to relate to it, and yet it had seemed so perfect for the huge star Melissa had met only once. It made Melissa realize again how different Michaela's life had been with Marla than it would have been as the illegitimate child of a sixteen-year-old girl from a much simpler background. In the end, maybe the nuns at Saint Blaise's hadn't been so wrong.

"She would have loved it," Michaela said again after the children left for school. David had gone to his office, and life seemed almost normal, although Marla's assistants and housekeeper had reported that there were still about a thousand people standing outside Marla's house. The crowd had dispersed outside Michaela's.

"It must have been exciting growing up with all that," Melissa said, still overwhelmed by it.

"Sometimes. But I didn't really like it. I dreamed of having someone like you as my mother. It's not easy being a star or the daughter of one, and Marla loved to feed the frenzy. She said it was good for the box office. She never lost sight of that. But she had a good heart."

"I really liked her when I met her," Melissa said, smiling at the memory.

"She liked you too."

They sat there quietly, thinking about her for a few minutes. Melissa had said goodbye to the children at breakfast. She was flying back to Boston that afternoon, and Norm had offered to pick her up. She had tried to describe the whole scene to him, and he had watched some of it on TV, the crowds in the streets, and outside the church, many of them crying.

When she left, she promised to come and visit again soon. She hadn't planned to intrude on them too often, but with Marla gone, Michaela was hungry to see more of Melissa, and might need her for a while. She was going back to work herself that afternoon.

Melissa hugged her tight when she left her, and told her she loved her. Then she got into the Uber, and waved as they drove away. It had been an extraordinary experience being there. It was an odd feeling knowing that she had handed her baby over to this woman moments after she was born, and Marla had taken care of her for thirty-three years. And now, when the helicopter crashed in Scotland, Marla had handed their daughter back to her. It was Melissa's turn now. She had waited years for this, and Melissa smiled as they drove away. She had the odd feeling that Marla was smiling at her, and wished her well. She could imagine her saying "Take good care of our girl." And Melissa promised her silently she would.

Chapter 17

Norm picked Melissa up at the Boston airport and drove her home. She tried to describe all of the past few days to him in the car on the way back. It sounded more like a movie now than real life. Marla had been larger than life, and she had left behind a daughter who loved her, and had all the right values and was a good mother herself. It was the only legacy that mattered in Melissa's eyes. More than all her movies and the fact that she was a star. Michaela was her best legacy. And it was Melissa who had given her the gift in the beginning. And now Marla had given her back.

She said something to Norm about it the next day when he got home from work. She'd been thinking about it all day.

"It's funny how people come and go, isn't it? Michaela disappeared out of my life. Then Robbie came, and he left, and now Michaela is back again. Marla left, and now I'm here for Michaela and her kids. Carson walked out, and now here you are. Your wife left, and I came along. One person leaves and another one shows up. It's as though we always have what we need, in different forms, at the right time, and not the way we expected.

"Life takes people away, so cruelly at times, and then gives someone else back. And nothing happens the way we plan it. Robbie should have lived a long life, but he didn't. My marriage to Carson seemed so solid, but it wasn't. It collapsed like a house of cards. And then Jane came along, and seemed like such a bore, but she's perfect for him. And you were completely unexpected in my life. You thought you were married forever, but you weren't. I finally accepted that Hattie would be a nun forever, and now she's not. Michaela was gone forever, and now she's back. We actually have no idea what's going to happen, or how it's going to turn out." He thought about it and agreed with her, and he liked the way she put it.

"We're not supposed to know," he said, thinking about it. "It would take all the fun out of living. Which reminds me, I've been meaning to ask you something," he said, looking nervous. "Now that you're a respectable grandmother and a mother again, and they'll come to visit, do we need to get married?" He was hoping she'd say yes, but didn't know how else to put it without scaring her off.

"'Need to'? No, I don't think so. It's not a guarantee of anything, and we've both learned that it won't protect us. If one of us goes rogue, the whole thing falls apart."

"I'm not planning to go rogue, are you?" he asked her, and she shook her head.

"I kind of like it like this," she admitted. "A little naughty, a lot of fun. It's very sexy. I don't want more kids. I'm almost too old anyway, and you don't want them either. I kind of love it the way it is." He was a little disappointed, but didn't want to sound weak, or "wet," and admit it to her. "You could move in though. That would be nice." She smiled and moved closer to him, and he liked the sound of that.

"I like that idea. It sounds manly, 'she's the woman I live with,'" he said, deepening his voice, and she laughed.

"Just sinful enough, but not too much so," she teased him, and got the desired result. He couldn't keep his hands off her, and didn't want to.

"And if we live together, we can make love anytime we want," he said happily.

"Sounds like a plan," she said, and followed him up to bed.

He moved in that weekend. Hattie drove up for the day to tell Melissa about her plans for Africa, working with the UN team. They were sending her reams of information, and she was leaving in five weeks.

She had just signed her papers for the Vatican and the archdiocese, requesting to be released from her vows. Her hand shook as she signed them, but she still knew it was right.

Hattie and Norm finally met, and had lunch in the kitchen. And afterward Hattie noticed Norm carrying his boxes up the stairs, and she whispered to Melissa. "Is he moving in?"

"Looks like it," Melissa said, with a gleam in her eye.

"Are you two getting married?"

"Not that I know of. Not right now anyway."

"Do you think you would, if he asked you?" She was curious about them. They seemed to get along so well. Hattie liked him a lot. He was someone you could count on. She had always liked Carson, but Norm and Melissa seemed like the perfect match.

"I've learned not to predict the future," Melissa said wisely. "I'd be wrong every time. Like you. I never thought you'd leave the convent."

"Neither did I," Hattie said, looking pensive. She smiled at Norm as he headed up the stairs with a suitcase.

He had finished moving in by the time she left. She was driving back to New York. And she was going to come and spend a few days with them before she left for Africa.

Melissa and Norm talked about it over dinner that night. He made her one of his perfect cheese soufflés.

"I realized today that everyone ends up in their right place," Melissa said. "Michaela with David and her children, with me in the background. You and I. Carson with Jane and her daughters. Hattie in Africa. It's like a kaleidoscope, all the bright pieces get shaken up and form a new design periodically. I like the way things are now. It all happens the way it's meant to, even if we don't like it at times. But there's always a new chapter," she said, looking thoughtful.

"Is there?" he asked her, raising an eyebrow, intrigued by what she said.

"I think there is. It'll give me something to write about." She had never said that to him before.

"Will it?"

"I think so. I have an idea for a book," she announced. She hadn't said that in years. But so much had happened. She looked excited when she said it, and he leaned over and kissed her. She smiled, thinking of Marla and her advice to keep writing. Maybe she was right. Her old books had been fueled by anger. But all of that had changed. Finding Michaela had changed everything. She wasn't angry anymore. The next book would be different. About the mysteries of life.

They finished the soufflé. And Melissa was still smiling when he followed her upstairs, and she started telling him about the book.

About the Author

DANIELLE STEEL has been hailed as one of the world's bestselling authors, with almost a billion copies of her novels sold. Her many international bestsellers include *Invisible, Flying Angels, The Butler, Complications, Nine Lives, Finding Ashley, The Affair,* and other highly acclaimed novels. She is also the author of *His Bright Light,* the story of her son Nick Traina's life and death; *A Gift of Hope,* a memoir of her work with the homeless; *Expect a Miracle,* a book of her favorite quotations for inspiration and comfort; *Pure Joy,* about the dogs she and her family have loved; and the children's books *Pretty Minnie in Paris* and *Pretty Minnie in Hollywood.*

daniellesteel.com
Facebook.com/DanielleSteelOfficial
Twitter: @daniellesteel
Instagram: @officialdaniellesteel

Look for *High Stakes,*
coming soon in hardcover

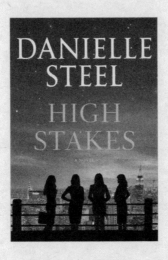

In this captivating novel from
#1 *New York Times* bestselling author
Danielle Steel, five successful women play for
high stakes in their careers at a boutique
literary and talent agency.

Chapter 1

Jane Addison was rushing around her bright, modern new West Village apartment, getting ready for her first day at a new job. She had gotten her undergraduate degree from UCLA, worked for two years at *San Francisco Magazine,* and then gone back for her MBA at UC Berkeley, in their entrepreneurial program. She was twenty-eight years old, born and raised in San Francisco. Her father was one of the most successful venture capitalists in Silicon Valley. Her older sister, Margaret, was thirty-five, climbing the ladder at a rival venture capital firm. Margaret was married, with two children. Her husband was the CEO of a successful tech start-up, which was about to go public. Jane's life was very different from Margaret's, and so were her goals. For the moment Jane wasn't interested in marriage, and didn't know if she ever would be. Having babies held no particular lure for her. Margaret and her husband had met in business school at Stanford, and they liked their stable, married life and their demanding careers. They seemed comfortable and efficient managing both. It looked like a hard juggling act to Jane, a lot of responsibility and too much work.

Jane's dream was to own a small magazine one day or, even better, a small publishing house, but she was a long way from achieving her goals. She was just beginning her work life. She had flown to New York to interview for jobs at the major publishing houses in New York, Penguin Random House, Simon & Schuster, Little, Brown, but nothing that interested her and paid decently had turned up. The magazines she had sent her résumé to hadn't leapt at the chance to hire her. They told her she was overqualified for the openings they had, and figured she probably wouldn't stay long enough to make hiring her worthwhile.

In the end, the only offer she'd had that excited her came from a friend of her father's, an old classmate of his at Princeton. Bob Benson owned a literary and entertainment agency, Fletcher and Benson, in New York. They represented actors, producers, directors, and screenwriters on the dramatic side, and writers on the literary side. The position she'd been offered was as an assistant to the executive assistant of the number two agent on the literary side, a woman named Hailey West. Jane had met her when she was applying for jobs in New York, and she seemed like an intelligent, pleasant, busy woman, committed to the writers she represented. The agency had some very important clients, and it seemed to Jane like a good interim job until the right opportunity turned up, closer to her goals for the future. She still wanted to work at a major publishing house to learn the ropes, but an entry-level job in publishing didn't appeal to her much, and at least a job in a literary and talent agency sounded like fun. Meeting important writers and movie stars would be exciting. The agency was very successful. She'd interviewed with her father's old friend, Bob Benson, and the heads of both sides of the agency, Francine Rivers on the literary side and Allie Moore, head of talent. They were both interesting women, and Bob Benson said that if she did well, she could be a literary agent one day.

Jane's mother came from San Francisco to help her find the apartment in a big, modern, efficient building in the West Village, with a view of the Hudson, in what seemed like a friendly neighborhood. The building had a gym, a pool, and a roof garden for the tenants' use. There was good security and plenty of staff, and her parents liked the fact that she'd be safe there. Her mother had been an interior decorator until Margaret was born, and she still enjoyed decorating their homes and doing whatever she could for her girls.

She helped Jane get her apartment organized and

furnished in record time. Jane was thoroughly enjoying it and grateful to her parents for the comforts they provided. She was well aware that she and her sister had enjoyed benefits all their lives that many of their friends hadn't. They were discreet about it, but Jane realized how lucky she was that she could take whatever job she wanted without worrying about whether or not she could pay her rent. Thanks to her mother, she had a comfortable home all set up for her a month after she arrived.

An old boyfriend of hers from UCLA, Benjie Strong, was working for a start-up in New York. He'd been there since grad school. They had reconnected as soon as she got there. They had been dating for a month and had busy, separate lives. He had slept at her apartment the night before, and had his own place with a roommate in SoHo. It had made the transition to New York easier and a lot more agreeable for Jane.

He was making toast in her kitchen when she helped herself to a yogurt from the fridge. She made coffee for both of them with the espresso machine and handed him a cup. He'd been reading *The Wall Street Journal* on his phone and looked up with a smile when she set the coffee down next to him. Benjie Strong was a year older than she was. He was twenty-nine, and looked like he was going to a picnic in cutoff jeans, a T-shirt, and running shoes without socks. He had gotten his MBA at Wharton, and was a bright guy. There was no dress code where he worked. Jane had already seen that the dress code was casual at Fletcher and Benson, but not to that degree. The men wore collared shirts and jeans, loafers or running shoes. The women mainly wore skirts and tops of some kind, and looked put together even if they were wearing jeans, which some did. They wore makeup and their hair was neat. Benjie looked like someone who had the day off. He smiled broadly when he glanced at her.

"Going to a party?" he asked her, and she laughed.

"Compared to you, I look like I'm going to dinner at a fancy restaurant. Going to the beach?" she teased him back.

"I'm a lot more dressed up than most of the guys I work with. Some of them come to work in shorts and flip-flops, if the weather is decent. No one cares what we wear to work." It was the nature of start-ups, they both knew, and most of the employees were younger than Jane and Benjie, fresh out of college, looking like they had just rolled out of bed. No one shaved, or not frequently, and they barely brushed their hair. Games were provided in common areas, vintage pinball machines or video games, a candy bar, and board games to play on their breaks. The whole atmosphere was keyed to the very young. Many of them worked from home several days a week. And in start-ups or companies like Amazon, they often brought their dogs to work. Amazon, Facebook, and others like them had set the trend years before, and made the work environment highly desirable to the "millennials," mostly in their twenties, who worked there. The surroundings at Fletcher and Benson were more polished, since their clients were adults, and the employees were older than those at most start-ups.

The women she had seen there dressed well and she noticed that most of them wore heels to work. She was wearing a short black denim skirt, a striped Chanel T-shirt she had "borrowed" from her mother to bring to New York, and a pair of high-heeled black Manolo Blahnik pumps. Her long blond hair was pulled back in a neat ponytail, and she was going to wear a white Levi's jacket and carry a black-and-white tote. She looked fashionable, but not too much so. She was slim and had a good figure and long legs. There was nothing suggestive about what she was wearing. The skirt wasn't too short, and the heels weren't too high. Her perfume was a light fresh scent one barely noticed. She looked clean and young and pretty, and she was eager to do a good day's work and learn about her new job and coworkers at the agency.

She and Benjie left the apartment together. Benjie was taking the subway to work in Brooklyn, and Jane had called an Uber to take her to Midtown, where the agency was, on Fifty-seventh Street between Madison and Park Avenues in the heart of the luxury shopping district. It would be hell getting there in bad winter weather, with all the traffic, but it was warm now and a nice area to walk around in during her lunch hour. There were plenty of places to eat or to order food nearby. And there was a kitchen and dining room for employees who brought their own lunch. Many of the employees ate at their desks while they continued to work. The working conditions were extremely pleasant at Fletcher and Benson, even if they didn't provide all the games and snacks provided by start-ups. None of that mattered to Jane.

"Have a good day," Benjie called out to her as she got into her Uber and he headed for the subway. She wasn't madly in love with him, but they had a good time together and shared some of the same interests. They didn't want to live together but saw each other a few times a week on an exclusive basis, which meant that neither of them was dating anyone else. It suited both of them. They had dated briefly in college at UCLA and were enjoying a replay of it now. It made being in New York more enjoyable, having someone to share it with. Benjie had had a serious relationship in business school, but they broke up when he graduated and moved to New York. Jane had never been seriously in love, and she didn't regret it. She wanted to get her career off the ground first and stay focused on that. Her work was important to her, more so than romance at the moment.

It took her half an hour to get uptown in morning traffic, while she read *The New York Times* online in the backseat of the Uber. They arrived right on time, and she followed a mass of people into the building where Fletcher and Benson occupied two floors. She went straight to the executive floor, gave her name to the receptionist, as she'd been told to do, and was about to head for a seating area, when a tall, heavy-set man with white hair nearly collided with her, and then looked her over appreciatively. She didn't know who he was but felt instantly uncomfortable at the way he stared at her. His eyes went straight to her chest, and then took in the moderately short skirt, and glanced past her legs and then back to her face again. He stood in her path like a boulder in a stream, and she had to walk around him to get away from him. He didn't step aside and continued staring at her.

"Are you here for an interview?" he asked her in a deep, gravelly voice. "You can come and work for me if you like." As he said it, the receptionist met Jane's eyes with a knowing look and shook her head almost imperceptibly.

"I'm starting a job today," Jane said in a subdued voice. She didn't want to be rude, not knowing who he was, although she thought his behavior was crass and unacceptable.

"Receptionist?" he asked, making a very broad assumption that if she was a woman, she must have a low-level job. He was out of step with the times.

"In Ms. West's office," she said quietly.

"That's good news," he said. "Well, welcome aboard." And with that, he headed down a long hallway, and Jane took a seat to wait for Hailey West's executive assistant, who appeared a moment later. Julia Benning smiled at her warmly in welcome. She was a pleasant-looking woman in her late forties or early fifties. She took Jane first to the office of Francine Rivers, the head of the literary department. She explained on the way that the heads of both the literary and dramatic departments wanted to see Jane again to welcome her. Julia said that it was customary for them to see the new hires who were going to be working in the executive offices. She left Jane outside Francine's door, and told her she'd come and get her after Jane met with Francine and Allie Moore, the head of talent. Jane had met both women previously during her interview.

Standing there alone a minute later, Jane felt a rising wave of panic seize her as she knocked on Francine Rivers's door. Jane could see her through a wide glass panel: a stern-faced woman in black slacks, a black blazer, and running shoes, with her dark hair pulled back in a messy bun. She was frowning as she concentrated on her computer. She turned when she heard Jane knock and signaled for her to come in, then waved her to a chair. Jane realized then that Francine was speaking to someone on speakerphone and looking at a book cover on her screen.

"It looks all right to me, Elliott. If they make your name any bigger, there won't be room for the title on the cover. And I think the red foil makes your name really pop. I like it."

"The whole thing looks off-balance to me," a disembodied voice came from the speakerphone. "The British cover was much better."

Francine Rivers looked irritated but tried not to sound it when she responded. "Do you want them to make the title smaller?" she asked, only half in jest, and the male voice at the other end answered immediately.

"Yes, I do. Tell them to try that."

"I'll take care of it right away," she assured him, and ended the call and then turned her full attention to Jane.

"I'm sorry. One of my badly behaved 'children.'" She smiled a wintry smile at her. "Hell hath no ego like a narcissistic author. He won't be happy till his name fills the whole cover." She looked closely at Jane then, as Jane noticed that Francine had dark, serious eyes and a slightly sour, jaded expression when she wasn't smiling. "I get all the problem ones. Some of our big authors are challenging. They can be very insecure, like children, and jealous of their competitors. Don't worry. Hailey gets all the nice ones. But she's friendlier than I am, and has more patience," she said, almost smiling. "So welcome to the mothership. We're delighted to have you join us."

She had seen Jane's grades from business school and was duly impressed. Bob Benson had already told her that Jane was the daughter of an old friend of his from Princeton. And he had told Francine who Jane's father was. She recognized the name, of course. Jane was obviously bright and had a good education, so there was justification for hiring her, and not just because of a college friendship between her father and the head of the agency. She had gotten the job on her own merits. Her contacts had merely gotten the door open, not landed her the job. "What made you want to work for a literary agency? Do you write?" Francine asked her. That was frequently the reason bright young people applied for jobs at the agency. They somehow thought that if they worked for an agent, their own work would be discovered, which wasn't how it worked. And most aspiring writers never made a career of it anyway. They didn't have the persistence or the talent. Even after all these years as an agent, it still amazed Francine how hard it was to find a good new writer, especially one who had more than one book in them.

"No, I don't write," Jane answered her. "I want to learn more about publishing," she said naïvely, still feeling nervous and sensing the tension around her. Francine was her big boss and seemed very serious to her. She was the head of the literary department at the agency. "And being an agent is part of it," Jane said as an afterthought.

"We're problem solvers," Francine explained. "Most writers want a mother or a nanny, and need one. That's basically what we do—we nurture them, in addition to getting them book contracts and negotiating for them. We're their advocates and translators and go-betweens between the writers and their publishers. Some of the problems are ridiculously small, and others are enormous and harder to solve. You'll see it all firsthand in Hailey's office. She's gentler with her writers than I am. Occasionally I lose my temper and scare the hell out of them. It whips them into shape, though." She smiled a wintry smile. "I do that with the publishers too. Being an agent is like being a referee at times. At other times, you need a gentle touch to close a deal, or so I'm told. I prefer threats, leverage, and force, myself. It always works for me," she said, and laughed. She looked as strict as she said she was, and as dedicated to her job. Jane readily believed her. "This is not a playground. It's hard work," Francine added for emphasis. She seemed like a take-no-prisoners kind of person. Jane wouldn't have called her bitter, but there was something cold and unhappy about her.

As they were talking, the heavyset white-haired man whom she had seen earlier in the reception area appeared in the doorway. He opened the door without knocking, ignored Jane this time, and looked straight at Francine.

"Seven? The usual?" he asked, and Francine nodded, looking irritated. Jane noticed that her new boss's eyes went dead after he spoke. Francine nodded assent again and he left her office, leaving the door half open. He didn't bother to close it, although it had been closed when he arrived.

"That's Dan Fletcher, one of the two heads of the agency," she explained to Jane without further comment.

Jane nodded. "I saw him this morning when I arrived." She didn't comment either.

"I hope he behaved. He doesn't always when attractive young women are involved. No one has explained the Me Too movement to him. I hope he didn't say anything inappropriate," she said, still looking annoyed.

"No, not really. He just looked me over and assumed I was here to interview for a receptionist's job."

"He thinks that's what I do too." Francine smiled. And then she told Jane how to find Alabama Moore's office, the head of the talent side of the agency. Francine said she had work to do. Jane stood up and thanked her for her time.

They shook hands and Jane left Francine's office and made her way down the long hallway, with countless offices on each side, and people busy at desks inside them, looking at computer screens or talking on the phone.

Jane's only worry was that Dan Fletcher would

appear again and harass her, or invite her into his office, an invitation she had no intention of accepting.

She found Alabama Moore's office after a few wrong turns. She had to double back once, but she finally found her in an enormous corner office with her name on the door. She was the head of the dramatic department. Allie Moore was on an exercise bike when Jane knocked and walked in. She was wearing a white Chanel jogging suit and listening to something on headphones. She smiled and stopped pedaling as soon as Jane entered the room feeling awkward.

Alabama Moore had a dazzling smile, and Jane thought she was very beautiful. She had met Allie in her initial interview and was impressed by her then. She had a mane of blond hair and big blue eyes. She was wearing no makeup and her face looked young and smooth. Jane wasn't experienced enough to recognize the work of a great dermatologist combined with an expert plastic surgeon or to recognize that Allie Moore had had "work" done, along with Botox shots and fillers. She looked as if she were around Jane's age. Jane would have guessed her to be about thirty, when in fact she was forty-three. Her figure was slim and lithe in the white velour jogging suit that molded her flawless body. She got up at four on weekdays so she could be at the gym religiously at five A.M. She owned a loft apartment in Tribeca. She hopped off the bike and invited Jane to join her in the seating area in her office, which consisted of a comfortable couch, two big easy chairs, and an oval coffee table. There was expensive contemporary art on the walls, and her smile was warm as Jane observed her and the effect she created in the outfit she was wearing. It had been a good choice.

"It's great to have you here," Allie said enthusiastically. "You'll like Hailey a lot. She works incredibly hard and is the consummate professional. I'm the official renegade, the rebellious child of the Fletcher and Benson family. I have to be, to deal with the actors, writers, and producers I represent. Some of them are barely more than kids, and they act it. Others should have grown up years ago and never will. They all get spoiled working on movies where people cater to their every whim. But some of them really deserve praise and attention because they have such huge talent. The badly behaved ones get away with it, and will never realize how spoiled they are, until it's all over for them.

"I grew up with Hollywood parents, so I'm used to it. My mother is a well-known actress, you'd know the movies she's been in, and my father produces hit TV shows. My parents' lives were enough to convince me that I never wanted to be on stage myself. I went to USC film school, but I decided I wanted to be an agent.

"My mother trained me to deal with divas from the time I was two. I worked for CAA, Creative Artists, in L.A. for a few years after I graduated, and then I came to New York to work at William Morris Endeavor. Then I met Bob Benson and he made me an offer I couldn't refuse, so now here I am, thirteen years later, and we represent some wonderful talent.

"I'm proud to be here, and I love what I do." She beamed at Jane and was all innocence. "Are you interested in the dramatic side? Maybe you can do some projects for me sometime before they lock you away forever in the literary world. The talent side is much more fun," she said mischievously as Jane thought about it for an instant. She had never considered being an actor's agent or even a writer's agent. This was kind of a sidetrack for her, to learn more about the business, and had been her father's idea when she didn't find a job in publishing at first. She was in love with books, much more than film. But Allie made the dramatic side sound appealing too.

Jane also suspected that there was a lot more to Alabama Moore than she was admitting. She was obviously very bright, her face was smooth and guileless, but her eyes said something different. She was a keen observer and noticed everything, and her welcome was much warmer than Francine Rivers's. Francine seemed tougher. There was something bitter about Francine that came through her pores. Allie seemed to love her job and Jane had the feeling that she lived and breathed for her career and would have killed anyone who interfered with it in any way. They were both highly successful professional women, who seemed competitive while trying to appear as though they weren't. She had a sense that either woman would attack if she felt threatened. This was the big leagues, and they were playing for high stakes, for their clients and themselves. The women who worked at the agency were pros in every way. They had fought hard to get where they were, and it showed in an intensity about their jobs.

Julia Benning, Hailey West's executive assistant, appeared while they were still in the seating area in Allie's office, and a moment later, she whisked Jane away to Hailey's office, which immediately felt like a safe haven to Jane when she got there. The atmosphere was different in Hailey's office than in Allie's or Francine's, and Julia was a gentle guide. There was a desk for Jane near Julia's, which she could consider home base, and an office just messy enough to feel human but not chaotic. Julia showed Jane the closet where she could leave her things, and then showed her the espresso machine. They had their own. Julia felt like a fellow student and upperclassman, showing Jane around her new school.

Hailey was in a meeting in the conference room with a major author when Jane got there, and she returned to her office an hour later. She was smooth and professional and slightly younger than the two department heads Jane had seen that morning.

Hailey was thirty-eight years old, and had an extremely responsible position as the number two agent in the literary department. She was wearing a white blouse, a well-cut, straight navy blue skirt, and high-heeled sandals. She had dark hair and wore it loosely pinned up on top of her head. It gave her a softer, more feminine look than the other two. Jane had noticed photographs of three young children on her desk, but Hailey made no mention of them when they spoke. She was entirely professional and all about business. It was obvious that Julia liked her and respected her, and when Hailey went into her own office and closed the door, Julia filled Jane in on the rest.

"She has three kids," Julia said as they each had a cup of coffee during a brief break.

"Divorced?" Jane asked her, curious, and Julia shook her head.

"Widowed. And her kids are young, a girl, eleven, and two boys, six and nine. The little one was just a baby when her husband died five years ago, at forty-three. He had an aneurysm and died while he was jogging. He was a publisher. She was an editor and used to work for him, and she quit when she had her kids. I think she stopped working for about six or seven years after she got married, and then he died, with no money and no insurance, so she had to go back to work. She couldn't get a job that paid enough as an editor, so she came to work here. Bob Benson knew her husband, so he gave her a job, and now she's number two on the literary side. She needs the job to support her kids. She's totally professional and never misses a day, even when they get sick. A lot of people who work here don't have kids. Employers are always afraid that people with young children won't be reliable, but she is totally committed to her work. She never talks about her kids. It's all about the writers she represents. Francine Rivers has two teenagers and works hard anyway. Allie Moore doesn't have kids. You have to be dedicated to your job here, and willing to work long hours and drop everything when one of our clients has a problem or a crisis. People with kids can't do that, especially single mothers. Hailey is as dedicated to her writers as she is to her kids. She's all about business when she's here. She doesn't stay home with sitter problems. I don't know how she manages, but she shows up no matter what goes on at home. She's good to work for, you'll see. She's very fair." Julia showed Jane around the rest of the office then, and pointed to a project she was working on, and a slew of foreign book covers she had to send to Phillip White to approve. He was Hailey's biggest author, a huge bestselling success. "He hits one out of the park every time," Julia said, describing him. Jane knew who he was and liked his books.

By the time Hailey came back from her next meeting in the conference room, which Julia had set up for her the way she liked it, Jane had been shown where everything was in the office. Julia was neat, efficient, and organized, and anticipated Hailey's every need, after having worked for her for several years.

"I have to be a mind reader sometimes, and hope I guess right. I try to anticipate what she'll want so she never has to ask for anything. If she does, I've failed."

"She's lucky to have you," Jane said with genuine admiration for her. "I don't know how you keep it all straight."

"You'll get used to it. I've been doing this for a long time, it seems like a lot at first, but you'll get into a routine once you know her. She's very clear and straightforward in her requests. You don't often have to be a mind reader. She'll tell you. Just do what she says. Don't put a spin on it or try to improve it. Listen, and follow her directions. That's what matters most. Don't decide you know a better way or a better system. You'll guess wrong and screw it up that way. And if you don't hear or don't remember something, ask her. That's what she wants. Don't be afraid to ask her questions. Better that than to guess wrong. Your asking her questions just saves time in the end." It made sense. Hailey sounded like a practical person from everything Julia said. "You're the first assistant I've had," Julia said with a smile. Bob Benson had created a job for Jane after Hailey had told him that her assistant could use some help. She was swamped.

"What about you?" Jane asked her. "Are you married? Do you have kids?"

Julia laughed in answer.

"Hell, no. Being an assistant is like being married. I'm married to her life and my job. I love it. I don't have time for a husband and kids. That boat sailed without me years ago. I'm fifty-one. I used to want to be an agent, but decided I'd rather be an assistant. Fewer headaches. And Hailey deals with the really crazy writers herself, so I don't have to. It's a perfect job, and there's a lot of satisfaction in it, if you do it right." Jane knew she wanted more than that in the long run. She didn't want to be an assistant forever. She either wanted to be an important agent one day, like Francine and Allie, or Hailey, or own a magazine or a small publishing house. That was still her dream. She wanted to run her own business and be her own boss, not work for someone else. "No guts, no glory," her favorite business school professor had said, and she liked the concept. She saw this job as a stepping-stone to bigger things, and she intended to learn all she could while she was here. She had big dreams. This was just the beginning to her. If she was going to make sacrifices in a job, like long hours, hard work, and a lot of stress, she wanted to do it for herself. She didn't want to still be an assistant at fifty-one. Ten years from now, she wanted to own her own business, with her father's help to get her started, once they agreed that she was ready. That was why she had gone to business school. She wanted to be Bob Benson or Dan Fletcher, not just a member of someone's staff. But this was fine for now, and it sounded like fun, even if stressful at times. They were all busy.

Hailey kept Julia occupied until lunchtime, and Julia gave Jane several projects she could handle on her own. At lunchtime, Jane ordered a salad from one of the restaurants they used to have lunches sent in. She went to the kitchen to get a fork and a soda out of the fridge, and was about to go back to her office to eat while she worked, when Dan Fletcher appeared. He caught her when she had the refrigerator door open, and scraped past her so he could rub up against her. She wanted to turn around and slap him but resisted the urge. Instead she turned around and looked him in the eye. For a second, he looked like he was going to grab her. There was no one else around.

"Is there a problem?" she asked him, momentarily oblivious to the fact that he was her boss and one of the two owners of the agency.

"Not for me. I understand Bob and your father were classmates at Princeton. We'll have lunch and you can tell me about it sometime." He pretended not to see the look of fury in her eyes, and his hand brushed her bottom as she walked past him. He was bold to a shocking degree, and apparently got away with it. No one dared call him on his behavior because of who he was. She went back to her office, shaking with rage. Julia saw the look on her face and was worried.

"Something wrong?"

"How the hell does that letch get away with it? First he squeezed by me, so he could rub up against me, and then he put his hand on my ass."

"Oh. Dan. He does it to everyone. Just ignore him," Julia said with a shrug.

"I'm not going to ignore him," Jane warned her. "I'm going to call him on it if he does it again."

"He's harmless. He's married with kids," Julia said, as though that made a difference.

"I don't care. That's sexual harassment," Jane reminded her.

"He's the boss." She said it as though that absolved him of everything.

"That's my point," Jane said, and dug into her salad. "I'll call a lawyer about it if I have to," she said, still seething, remembering his rubbing past her in the kitchen, his body pressed against hers. He was disgusting.

"You'll never get another job if you call a lawyer," Julia said practically.

"I'm not going to put up with it," Jane said, and ate her salad in silence after that. She wondered how many women in the office he'd done that to, who kept their mouths shut to keep their jobs. She couldn't imagine him doing something like that to Francine

Rivers. She was tougher than that, and looked like she wouldn't tolerate it for a minute. There was an undercurrent of anger in Francine, which Jane suspected would cause her to erupt with very little provocation. Jane couldn't guess if Francine's anger came from her job or her personal life, but she didn't seem like a happy woman. She had a fabulous career and was highly respected, but Jane could sense that something was amiss somewhere in her life.

Jane had no way of knowing that Francine's husband had walked out on her with the nanny, divorced Francine, and married the nanny as soon as their divorce was final. Fortunately, she had never given up her job as an editor at a major publisher. But she could no longer afford to keep it after the divorce. She had taken the job at the agency and was promoted with astounding speed. She was a very talented editor and had a real ability to discover promising young writers who blossomed with her direction and guidance. Several of them were writing bestsellers now. The pay as an agent was better, but the child support her ex-husband gave her was meager. He'd had two more children, so she got nothing from him anymore. She made a very healthy salary, but supporting two children on her own ate up what she made very quickly. At forty-five now, she had dealt with ten years of financial struggles, trying to provide the best she could for her kids and save for college, without taking loans. It took a heavy toll on her. She hadn't cared about her looks for years. Her daughter, Thalia, was seventeen, and next year Francine would have college to pay for. She wanted her to go to an Ivy League college if she could get in, which cost a fortune. Her son, Tommy, was thirteen, and would be entering high school the same year that his sister started college, and they were applying to the best private prep schools. Francine lay awake every night, trying to figure out how to pay for everything. She always found a way, but she had nightmares about what would happen if she ever lost her job. And even with it, and a highly respected position, she spent everything on her kids. There was never anything left for her.

She had moved out of the city to a respectable area of Queens after the divorce, to save money. She missed living in the city, but sent both her kids to private schools, and wished she could do more for them and put aside money for their future. She made too much to qualify for a scholarship for Thalia in college. Bitterness over not having anyone to help her and having a deadbeat ex-husband had been a way of life for Francine for so long that she no longer remembered what it was like to live without it. Constant struggles and financial problems after the divorce had toughened her, and she set the bar high for anyone who worked for her. She tried to be gentle with her authors at the agency, but she found it hard to be sympathetic at times.

Her children complained that she was never home, stayed at the office too late, and never got back early enough to make a decent dinner. She rushed home as soon as she could, put a frozen pizza in the oven, and helped with homework, but most of the time she was too tired to spend much quality time with them. She wanted to be outstanding at her job so she would never lose it. It was her greatest fear, that she'd get fired and wouldn't be able to support her kids in their fancy schools. She made a healthy salary, but her ex-husband had proven to her how uncertain the future could be. Her work was draining, and her life a constant vicious circle of too much work, a lot of stress and pressure, and supporting her kids. It tainted the way she saw the world around her. She knew only too well how competitive the agency was. If you slipped for a minute, someone else would have your job. And she was willing to fight anyone to the death to make sure that didn't happen to her. Worrying about it didn't make her pleasant to be around, and she hadn't had a man in her life in years.

Later that afternoon, Jane met Merriwether Jones, the CFO at the agency. Her life, as Julia described it, was a perfect example of total success and having it all. She was beautiful, a Harvard MBA, nice to everyone, friendly and charming. She was married to a writer, who stayed home to take care of their five-year-old daughter, Annabelle, while Merriwether made a huge salary at the agency. According to Julia, her husband Jeff was a handsome hunk, and they were crazy about each other. She was warm and encouraging to Jane when Bob Benson introduced them. She was one of those women who proved that you could have it all, a family, a happy marriage, and a great career. She reminded Jane of her sister, who was a high achiever who had it all too. Merriwether lived in a townhouse she had bought in the East Eighties. She had grown up in Boston, and her family expected her to get a great education and use it to become successful and make a lot of money, and she had.

Jane's father's old friend, Bob Benson, seemed to have it all too. He was married to a famous entertainment lawyer, had three sons, two in college and one still in high school. They lived in Greenwich, Connecticut, in a beautiful house, and he and his wife both had successful careers. He seemed like an all-around nice person, and everyone said he was a pleasure to work for.

By the time Jane got home that night, after a long Uber ride back to the West Village, her head was swimming with all the people she had met and the information Julia and Hailey had shared with her. Every one of the women who had important jobs, including Julia, was fully focused on her career. And Jane had the feeling that all of them would have been willing to kill to protect their jobs, if anyone tried to interfere with them. Their work ethic appeared to be excellent, and they set the bar high for themselves and everyone around them. The one who appeared to be having the most fun was Alabama, with all the actors she represented. Francine was the toughest and hardest. Hailey seemed to be on an even keel, and Merriwether appeared to be the happiest, with the most well-rounded life. Meeting their expectations was going to be a lot to live up to, and Jane just hoped she didn't disappoint them.

"So how was it?" Benjie asked when he showed up with dinner for them that night. She was grateful to see him. She was too tired to cook and would have gone to bed without dinner.

"Interesting. Action-packed. And my head is exploding with all the information," she told him over couscous and fragrant Moroccan chicken ordered from a favorite restaurant of theirs. He was thoughtful that way, and he had brought a half bottle of champagne so they could celebrate. He was on a tight budget, but always generous with her. "I've never met so many smart, interesting, successful women all in one place. They're all focused on their careers, and are a lot to live up to."

"You don't know them that well yet, who they really are. All you saw today is what they wanted to show you."

"They're divorced, widowed, single, and one is happily married. They're juggling kids, their jobs, and their clients. I don't know how anyone can do all that and get it right, but they seem to. All I want to focus on is my job. The head of the literary department is very tough and seems angry. I guess they're all tough in one way or another, or they wouldn't have their jobs."

"Just make sure you don't end up like that. There's more to life than work," he reminded her, then kissed her and cleared the remains of dinner away, while she went to take a shower.

It didn't sound like fun to him, but he also knew that Jane was more ambitious than he was, and her family expected a lot from her. It was a vast difference between them. Her father had driven both of his daughters hard to become high achievers, and her sister Margaret's success in finance was a lot to compete with. He didn't envy Jane, despite everything her parents had provided for her. They expected a lot in exchange, and she didn't want to disappoint them. His parents just said they wanted him to be happy, whatever route he followed. He wasn't sure the Addisons ever thought that was important. Neither did Jane. All she thought about was what she was going to accomplish in the coming years.

It was a race she was going to run every single day. And the race had started in earnest now with her first serious job. He didn't envy her at all. In fact, when he thought about it, he felt sorry for her. She was going to miss out on a lot in life if she continued on the path she was on. She was driven by a force he didn't really understand. It was a white-hot fire within her. She had to meet her parents' high expectations and her own. It was a tall order for anyone.